Books by Keely Brooke Keith

THE UNCHARTED SERIES

The Land Uncharted

Uncharted Redemption

Uncharted Inheritance

Christmas with the Colburns

Uncharted Hope

Uncharted Journey

Uncharted Destiny

Uncharted Promises

Uncharted Freedom

THE UNCHARTED BEGINNINGS SERIES

Aboard Providence

Above Rubies

All Things Beautiful

The Land Uncharted

Keely Brooke Keith

Edenbrooke
Press

Edenbrooke Press

Nashville, Tennessee

The Land Uncharted

Printed in the United States of America

ISBN: 9781692976200

Cover designed by Najla Qamber Designs

Edited by Dena Pruitt

Interior design by Edenbrooke Press

Author photo courtesy of Frank Auer

The Land Uncharted

Keely Brooke Keith

Edenbrooke
Press

Edenbrooke Press

Nashville, Tennessee

The Land Uncharted

Copyright 2014 Keely Brooke Keith

Printed in the United States of America

ISBN: 9781692976200

Cover designed by Najla Qamber Designs

Edited by Dena Pruitt

Interior design by Edenbrooke Press

Author photo courtesy of Frank Auer

For Marty

Challenge accepted

Chapter One

Lydia Colburn refused to allow a child to bleed to death. Pulling a sprig from a gray leaf tree out of her wind-whipped hair, she rushed inside the farmhouse and found the injured boy sprawled across the bed exactly as Mr. McIntosh had said she would. She dropped her medical bag on the floor beside Mrs. McIntosh, who was holding a blood-soaked rag against young Matthew's lower leg.

The globe of an oil lamp provided the only light in the dim bedroom. Matthew's breath came in rapid spurts. Lydia touched his clammy skin. "He's still losing blood. Get the pillows out from under his head." She slid her hands beneath his fractured limb and gently lifted it away from the mattress. "Put them here under his leg."

Mrs. McIntosh's thin hands shook as she moved the pillows. "I gave him tea from the gray leaf tree as soon as his father brought him in the house." Her voice cracked. "I know he isn't in pain now, but it hurts me just to look at all this blood."

"You did the right thing." Lydia opened her medical bag and selected several instruments. She peeled back the bloody rag, revealing the fractured bone. Its crisp, white edges protruded through his torn skin. "You will be all right, Matthew. Do you feel any pain?"

"No, but it feels weird." His chin quivered as he stared at his mother with swollen eyes. "Am I going to die?"

Mrs. McIntosh drew her lips into her mouth and stroked his head. "You'll be fine. Miss Colburn will fix it."

When Lydia touched his leg, he recoiled and screamed. It wasn't from pain since he'd taken the gray leaf medicine, but even the most miraculous medicine couldn't stop terror.

With his fractured leg tucked close to his body, he buried his face into the pleats of his mother's dress. Instead of mustering her courage and making her son cooperate, Mrs. McIntosh coddled him.

Lydia couldn't reach his wound with him curled up on his mother. Though every physician appreciated a nurturing parent, this was no time to help a child hide. She had to separate them. "Matthew, your mother is right. You will be just fine." She reached for his leg again. "You don't have to look at me, but you must put your leg on the pillow. Matthew? Let me straighten your leg."

Mrs. McIntosh glared at the bloody wound and began to weep. "Oh, Matt, I'm so sorry. My baby!"

"Mrs. McIntosh?" Lydia raised her voice over the woman's sobs. "Rebecca! I know it's hard, but please be strong for your son's sake. I need you to help me. Can you do that?"

Mrs. McIntosh sniffled and squared her shoulders. "I'll try."

It was a start. Lydia lowered her volume. "Good. Thank you. First, I need more light. Do you have another lamp in the house?"

"Yes, of course." She wiped her nose on her sleeve and scurried out of the room.

Relieved that Mrs. McIntosh was gone, Lydia caught the boy's eye. She touched his foot with both hands. "Matthew, you must lie still while I treat your injury. You won't feel any pain since you were a good boy and drank the gray leaf tea your mother made, but now you have to be brave for me. All right?" She was prepared to hold him down while she worked but loathed the thought.

He allowed her to move his broken leg back onto the pillow. She worked quickly and methodically until the bleeding was under control, the instruction of her mentor, Dr. Ashton, playing audibly in her mind. If only she'd known how to treat traumatic injuries a decade ago, maybe then she could have saved her mother.

Mrs. McIntosh's footsteps clicked down the hallway. Lydia wasn't ready for the anxious woman's return, so she called out, "Please, bring cold water and a few clean rags first. I need them more than I need the extra light."

The footsteps receded.

She cleansed the torn flesh with gray leaf oil then looked into the open wound and aligned the bone, trying to complete the job before Mrs. McIntosh returned. Matthew's eyes were squeezed shut. Her heart ached for the pallid and broken boy. "I heard you had a birthday recently, Matthew. How old are you now? Fifteen? Sixteen?"

He opened his eyes but stared at the ceiling. "I'm seven," he slurred through missing teeth. His respiration had settled; the gray leaf's healing power was taking effect.

"Ah, I see you've lost another baby tooth." She cut a piece of silk thread for suture and kept the needle out of his sight while she threaded it. "Soon you will have handsome new adult teeth."

He closed his eyes again and lay still.

Mrs. McIntosh walked back into the room with a pitcher of water in her hands and a wad of kitchen towels tucked under her elbow. She set the water jug on the floor beside Lydia's feet and bundled the rags on the bed. "Is that enough?"

"Yes, thank you."

"I'll be right back with the lamp," she said as she vanished from the room again.

Lydia covered the stitches with a thick layer of gray leaf salve. While she wrapped his leg loosely with clean muslin, the front door slammed and a man's worried voice drifted through the hallway.

Mrs. McIntosh spoke to her husband in a hushed tone and then returned to the bedroom holding a lamp. She sighed. "Oh, thank heavens you're done." She lit the lamp and placed it on a cluttered table by the bed. As she sat on the edge of the mattress beside Matthew, she whispered, "He's asleep."

Lydia slathered her hands with the disinfecting gray leaf oil and wiped them on a clean rag. A mud stain from the hasty ride here had spotted the hem of her favorite day dress. It would come out if she washed it as soon as she got home. At least it was dark enough out that if she passed someone in the village, they wouldn't notice the imperfection.

As she gathered her medical instruments, Mr. McIntosh stepped into the bedroom, holding his wide-brimmed hat in his hands. "Is there anything I can do?"

She stretched her tense neck muscles. "I need two thin pieces of wood to splint his leg."

Mr. McIntosh nodded and left. While he was gone, Lydia cleaned and packed her instruments, arranging them neatly just as Dr. Ashton had taught her. Surely her work here tonight would convince the village elders to award her the title of *Doctor*.

Soon, the boy's father returned with two flat wooden shingles. She used them to splint the boy's leg, then gave the McIntoshes instructions for bandaging and cleaning their son's wound. She offered Mrs. McIntosh a jar of gray leaf salve—her own special blend that was more potent than what Dr. Ashton used when he could still work. "Use this twice a day on the wound. With rest and proper care, your son should heal completely in a few days."

After one last check on Matthew, she followed the McIntoshes out to the porch. Stars crowded the clear sky, and crickets' intermittent chirps pierced the cool night air. Her spotted gray mare snorted as Mr. McIntosh gathered the reins and walked toward her.

Mrs. McIntosh fanned her face with both hands. "Thank you, Lydia."

"Send for me if you have concerns with his wound. I'm always available to help, anytime day or night."

Mr. McIntosh wiped his brow with a cotton handkerchief. "It seems too dangerous of a job for a woman—taking the forest path alone at night like you did to get here." He slapped his hat back on his head and dabbed at the sweat on his neck. "I'm grateful you got here in time to save my boy, no doubt about it, but the way you rushed down the forest path instead of taking the main road worried me. Granted you beat me back here by twenty minutes, but still it's too dangerous at night to—"

"I haven't seen a night dark enough to keep me from my duty." She stepped around him and strapped her medical bag to the saddle, then paused to give her favorite horse a slow stroke down her blond mane. "Good girl, Dapple."

He nodded. "That'll be the last time Matthew climbs to the roof of the barn."

"Yes. Please see to it." She tugged on her riding gloves, ready to be back in her warm, safe cottage on her family's property.

Mr. McIntosh handed her the reins. "I heard your family will gather tomorrow to celebrate Isabella's seventy-fifth birthday. How about I deliver a lamb roast as your payment?"

"That would be excellent, thank you. I'll tell my father to expect you." She mounted Dapple and settled into the saddle. "Aunt Isabella will be glad to have roast lamb at her party."

"A lamb it is. Thank you, Miss Colburn. Oh, and do take the road back to the village. I'd never forgive myself if something happened to you on your way home."

Lydia arranged the dishes on the buffet in the kitchen to make room for the lamb roast. Her father nestled it into place at the center of the bountiful spread. John Colburn's grin was as bright as sunrise at the shore. "I heard you well and truly earned this last night. Good work. And it looks delicious."

She inhaled the savory aroma rising with the roast's steam. "It smells delicious too."

The lamb fit perfectly between the dishes of scalloped corn and buttery mashed potatoes. She carefully aligned the dishes on the buffet and laid a silver server next to each platter. Once everything looked flawless, she squeezed around her sisters and their children and the ladies from church who were all here to celebrate Aunt Isabella's birthday.

After untying her apron, she left the warm room that buzzed with familiar voices and soft laughter. A thrill of excitement tingled her insides. This was going to be perfect.

As she walked through the parlor, she sent a secretive smile to Mandy Foster who was tuning her violin. The music would make the party everything Isabella had asked for. So why hadn't the elderly woman come out of her room yet?

Lydia straightened the turtle-shaped brooch pinned to her dress as she passed the staircase and knocked on her great-aunt's bedroom door.

"Come in," Isabella answered with a gravelly voice.

Lydia turned the glass doorknob and stepped inside. The dark room and the unmade bed struck a chord of sadness in her heart. She left the door open and the late afternoon sunlight that filled the rest of the house seeped into the room.

Isabella sat in her rocking chair by the window, its thick curtains tightly drawn. Her knitting needles clicked in rhythm. "What is it, dear?"

"We're ready for you, Aunt Isabella." Lydia smiled as she spoke, but her blind aunt's face remained impassive. She wanted to run to her aunt's chair like she would have as a child and tug on her hands, begging her to come into the kitchen.

Isabella continued knitting for a moment then lowered the yarn and needles into the basket beside her chair. She reached for her cane. "I do hate a fuss. I hope you didn't waste time on decorations. They are a frivolity."

Lydia stepped closer. "No, there aren't any decorations, but the food looks wonderful. Mr. McIntosh delivered a roast lamb, and it smells exquisite. Everything is ready for you. Won't you come to the kitchen?"

"It does smell good." Isabella's fingers traced the cane's curve. "Seventy-five. Isn't that old?" She sounded surprised by her own age.

Lydia put aside her childish eagerness and knelt beside her aunt, touching her arm. "I think seventy-five is lovely."

"Sweet girl." Isabella patted the top of Lydia's hand. "I'm blind and even I can see that seventy-five is old." She leaned on her cane and stayed in her chair. Her lips twitched before she spoke. "I mostly thought of my mother today. I always do on my birthdays. I suppose that's odd after all these years."

"Not at all."

"Yes, you understand. You miss your mother as much as I miss mine. You always will, dear. I assure you." Isabella stood with stiff movements. "Have your father and Levi come in from their chores yet?"

"Yes, they're washed up and waiting in the kitchen. Maggie and Adeline made all your favorite dishes, and Bethany came straight home after school to help too. You should have stayed in the kitchen with us while we cooked. We had an enjoyable afternoon together."

"The four of you girls together in the kitchen all afternoon and with the little ones whining at your feet—" Isabella guffawed. "My years of finding that enjoyable have passed. Besides, I don't like a crowd—not for long anyway."

"Maggie and Adeline and their families so rarely visit. I like it when we're all together."

Isabella smoothed the front of her dress. "Is Mandy here? I want her to play her violin in the parlor while we eat so I can hear the music— but not too loud. Tell her not too loud."

"Yes, she knows. And several of your friends from church just arrived. They're all waiting for you."

Isabella held her cane in one hand and found Lydia's elbow with the other. "Which dress are you wearing?"

"The maroon one with the white lace at the bottom."

"Your blue dress is softer."

"It isn't cold enough to wear the blue dress."

"It will be cold soon; the equinox is coming. I can feel it. The atmosphere changes somehow on the autumn equinox. It always has. Do you have on your mother's brooch?"

"Of course." Lydia touched the silver turtle pinned to her dress over her heart.

Isabella took one step and stopped. She waved her cane in front of her. "I was born in this house, just as you were. After your grandfather and I were born, our father added this room onto the house. Then when your grandfather married your grandmother, they made this my private room. They added a new nursery onto the house when your father was born. Oh, how they hoped for many children, but neither of your father's siblings lived past infancy." Isabella sighed then smiled, causing Lydia to wonder if the nostalgic interlude was authentic sentiment or a stall tactic. "But when your father married your mother and they had the five of you children, well, that's when the house finally felt full to me."

They inched out of the bedroom then Isabella stopped in the hallway. She faced Lydia, but her unseeing eyes didn't settle. "I've lived seventy-five years in this house, and none of my time was wasted so long as I'm not a burden."

She hated it when her aunt talked like that. "You aren't a burden to anyone. We all love you, and that's why we are honoring you. Come now, everyone's waiting."

Isabella straightened her posture as if readying herself for the crowd. "I can face another seventy-five years, so long as I make myself useful."

Lydia helped her aunt into the kitchen, even though she didn't really need help. After everyone showered Isabella with birthday wishes, John said the blessing. Then, Lydia filled a plate at the buffet table and scanned the room for a place to sit. Unable to find a seat in the crowded kitchen, she took her plate to the staircase in the parlor. From there she could see into the nearby kitchen where her family and their guests crammed around the table with Isabella.

One of Lydia's brothers-in-law sat between his two small children at the table, and the other brother-in-law sat nearby on the edge of the stone hearth with his plate balanced on his open palm. Her two-year-old niece couldn't reach the bread basket and began to cry. The men strained to keep their conversation going over the top of the other voices. The flurry of sound flowed into the parlor.

Levi walked out of the loud kitchen and sat beside her on the staircase. Her brother handed her a napkin. She took it and offered him an olive. He popped the olive into his mouth and followed it with a forkful of potatoes from his plate. Then his expression changed as his gaze settled on Mandy who stood near the front door playing slow and soft music on her heirloom violin. Her eyes were closed as the notes flowed from the instrument. A blanket of auburn curls covered her back and danced along her trim waistline.

Lydia glanced at her brother as he watched Mandy. "She's beautiful, isn't she?"

"Yes, and she knows it." He looked down at his food.

Lydia let it go. She took the bread roll from her plate and picked off one bite at a time as she listened to Mandy's music. One tune ended, and another began. "This is the song she composed for the dance last year. I like it."

"It would sound even better if she played it on one of the new wood violins."

Lydia nudged his knee. "That might be true, but don't let Aunt Isabella hear you say it. She has strong opinions about the new wood instruments."

Levi nodded then continued eating, watching Mandy all the while.

When they finished their dinner, Lydia relaxed into Levi's thick shoulder. Though ten months her junior, he had been bigger than she was since they were toddlers. People who didn't know their family usually assumed he was older.

"Come with me tomorrow and see the land I selected." His voice held a secretive tone. She shifted and looked at him. His light brown eyes matched hers. His hair was the same light brown as hers, but his included lighter strands from days spent working in the sun. "I'm done with the land survey, and I started drawing plans to build."

"Does Father know?"

"He knows, but he doesn't understand." He tapped one foot rapidly on the stair riser. "I'm a grown man. If I want to build my own house, that should be my business."

"People just don't understand why you need to build a new house. They expect you to inherit this house one day, so it seems odd for the overseer's son to break from tradition—especially since you don't have a family of your own yet."

He groaned. "Father says the same things. But I don't live my life worrying about what other people might think. You are like Father—you both take comfort in the founders' traditions. I thought you understood me."

"I do. And I'm sure you'll build yourself a fine house someday, but try to find a way to do it that doesn't cause strife."

"It's not the fact that I want to build my own house that offends Father. It's that I want to build my own life."

"I understand both sides. Father followed Grandfather's footsteps gladly. He's always had the same expectations for you. But you're right—you should be able to decide how to spend your life and where to live."

Levi raked his fingers through his hair. "Then why does he condemn me for not being exactly like him?"

"He doesn't question your character—only your choice of profession."

"They have told me all my life I should be a preacher just as my father is and his father was before him. But I've never felt called to that profession. If I were, I would gladly obey. But I'm not. Just thinking of it fills me with anxiety." He shook his head. "No. Give me a hammer instead. I'd rather build all day long."

There was nothing she could do to make her brother feel better or her father understand, but it wouldn't stop her from trying. "You're an excellent carpenter, and the village needs your work. Be proud that you have the strength for building. Many men don't."

"Father has the strength for anything."

"But he prefers preaching. Try to remember, he is peace loving above all. This friction between you two won't last forever. I truly believe that."

Mandy finished her song, and Lydia and Levi clapped. The sound caused a brief silence in the kitchen, followed by a short applause. Mandy gently placed the violin in its case like an infant in a bassinet. She used both hands to corral her curls into a loose bun at her nape then lifted her violin to play again.

A visit from Levi interrupted Lydia's morning office routine. She didn't have a patient in the cottage, so it seemed like a good time to go look at the land where her brother hoped to build. Levi sat beside her desk as she straightened her papers and prepared to leave with him. Startled by a shrill voice yelling outside, she hurried to the door. Levi beat her to it and yanked it open.

She stood on her tiptoes and craned her neck, trying to see what the commotion was. Auburn curls bounced as a flustered Mandy stomped toward the cottage.

Levi held the door open for Mandy, but he didn't leave the doorway. He furrowed his brow at her. "What were you yelling about, woman?"

Mandy brushed his shoulder as she passed him and looked at Lydia. "I could see that little rat from the road! He had his head at your window, peeping in, you know?"

Lydia's stomach knotted tightly. She lowered herself into the chair at her desk, wishing she could crawl under it. "No, I did not know."

Levi rushed outside, turned his head in both directions, and then stepped back into the cottage. "Who was at her window?"

"Who do you think?" Mandy spat the question at him.

"Frank Roberts?" Levi held up his fists. "I'd like to teach that degenerate a lesson."

"Levi!" Lydia scolded. "You will do no such thing."

"I should. It would serve him right!"

Her temples started to throb. Frank Roberts often followed her around the village. The thought of anyone knowing he liked her made her knotted stomach ache. And now Mandy had seen him peeping in the window. Scandalous gossip would not help her chance of receiving her title from the village elders, not to mention what everyone might think.

The wooden floorboards creaked as Mandy paced them. "It would put Frank right here inside Lydia's home because she would have to stitch his battered face. Oh, he'd love that. Go ahead, Levi, give Frank exactly what he's after—Lydia's attention!"

Mandy and Levi exchanged a fiery glance. At least they were angry at the same person and not at each other for a change. Levi marched to Lydia's desk and dropped into the chair beside it. He drummed one finger on the desktop with rapid thumps.

She had to diffuse their anger and make them forget the incident. Dr. Ashton taught her to keep a calm demeanor around patients to help them stay calm too. It was worth a try with her brother and best friend. She forced her voice to stay steady. "I have dealt with Frank for years," she said, hoping no one suspected she had accidentally caused Frank's fixation. "He's harmless."

"Harmless?" Levi snapped his face toward her. "Lydia, the man was just looking in your window. He's a pervert and has become bolder since you moved out here by yourself last year. You should move back into the house."

Heat stung Lydia's cheeks. She shouldn't have confided in Frank all those years ago; it must have ignited his affection and made her responsible for his advances. "Please, stop it, Levi. I feel terrible when anyone speaks of him. And I won't move back into the house. Since Doctor Ashton can no longer care for himself— let alone others—I'm now the village's only physician. Of course, the elders could bring in a doctor from another village. That's why it's important that I'm accessible to the people. I want the elders to make my position permanent."

Mandy halted her pacing. "Levi is right. You need protection since you live out here by yourself." She turned to sit, but when she only saw the patient cot behind her, she remained standing. "As long as you're unmarried you're open to harassment from a man like that."

Mandy's suggestion of marriage was ironic. It almost made Lydia laugh. "You sound like Aunt Isabella."

Levi snickered, so she sent him a big sister look then returned her attention to Mandy. "I have yet to encounter a danger great enough to give up my medical practice and get married. And even if I found a man to marry, I doubt it would deter a man like Frank Roberts. I'll put curtains over all the windows." She stood and brushed her hands together. "Yes, more curtains. Problem solved. That should ease your minds."

Mandy reached for a long strand of curl and twirled it in her fingertips. "Still, I think every woman should at least consider a husband." Her green eyes gazed at Levi.

Lydia looked at Levi too, but he continued staring out the window. She thought he wasn't listening. Then slowly he turned his face toward Mandy. "This from the woman who prefers to forgo the deep affections of one man in favor of the distant admiration of many men."

Mandy grinned and lowered her pretty chin. It was amazing how Mandy's mood could change from aggressively angry to playfully offended without a breath in between. At least they were no longer talking about Frank Roberts.

Her secret was safe for now.

Levi blew out a breath and stepped to the door. "Lydia, come and get me when you're ready to go look at that land we spoke of yesterday. I'll be in the barn."

After the door closed, she grinned at Mandy. "Sometimes you torment him on purpose."

"Whatever do you mean?" Mandy smiled wickedly as she moved to the chair left vacant by Levi. She crossed her legs high above the knee.

"Any time you suggest marriage as the solution to a woman's problem, I detect insincerity."

"All right, so I felt like aggravating Levi a bit. He can handle it. Would you rather I had pointed out that it isn't your singleness that causes your trouble—it's your fear?"

"Fear?" A short laugh bubbled up. "I'm not afraid of Frank Roberts."

"Maybe not. But you're afraid of what people think of you because of him." Mandy nodded once as if confirming her statement. "See, it's fear. You are afraid others will think if someone as wretched as Frank loves you, you must be wretched too."

Lydia cringed at the truth in her friend's assessment. "That would make me rather snobbish, wouldn't it?"

Mandy traced her finger along the desktop's wood grain, and her face became solemn. "After your mother died, you went to great lengths to prove to everyone that you were all right. You still strive to present yourself as perfect as possible."

"I'd hardly consider that a fault. Father says it's important for someone in my position to have a good reputation."

"Your position as the overseer's daughter?"

"Well, yes, the village has certain expectations of me in that regard, but I meant as a physician. People won't feel they can come to me for help if they think I need help, which I don't. Besides, I'm still awaiting the elder council's decision. I want nothing to jeopardize getting that title. If they knew a man like Frank Roberts follows me around, they might question my aptitude… my morality. I studied and trained for years for this work. I intend to see it through."

"And so you will. I'm sure of that." Mandy's fingers left the desk and found a curl to play with. She glanced at the door then back at Lydia. "I have to teach the music class for the primary students today. Come with me to the school. It will do you good to get out of here for a while."

She rose from her desk. "Thanks, but Levi is waiting for me."

Mandy winked. "Ah yes, his land."

The rhythmic thumps of a horse's gallop vibrated the floorboards. Lydia dashed to the door and opened it just as Mark Cotter halted his stallion in front of the cottage. "Come quickly, Lydia! Doris has gone into labor!"

"I'm on my way." She grabbed her medical bag and smiled at Mandy. "Duty calls."

Chapter Two

A stiff wind blowing in from the sea gripped the hair that framed Lydia's face. She tucked it behind her ear as she sat near her mother's grave. Though Hannah Colburn died when Lydia was only thirteen, she could easily conjure memories of her mother's laugh and touch and scent.

One speckled stone marked the spot, its cold surface interrupted by letters etched in two rows. Thick grass grew wild on the bluffs, but here it was kept carefully trimmed. A faint smile tugged at one edge of Lydia's mouth as she considered her father's attention to the gravesite. His faithfulness in marriage extended to the grave.

Looking out over the endless sea, she relaxed for the first time in twenty hours. The warm light of the sun's gentle rays soaked through her long skirt. She stretched her legs straight out along the ground, relieving the weight of her boots, and leaned her back against the cool stone. Though she had a soft feather bed in her cottage, she needed to settle her mind before she could sleep.

She wrapped her folded arms beneath her woolen shawl and let her heavy eyelids fall closed. The excitement of helping a mother bring new life into the world had energized her through the night, but that energy was gone now. In a village of two hundred fifty-six people, delivering a baby was a rare delight. The fascination was purely professional, as she had never felt the desire to have a family of her own. At a young age she knew Doctor Ashton planned to train only one more physician in the Land. That opportunity drove her to focus on her studies and secure the apprenticeship while most of the other girls put their efforts into attracting male attention.

The only man to express romantic interest in Lydia was Frank Roberts, and she didn't find his attention flattering—mortifying and guilt-inducing, but not flattering. Somehow Frank managed to put his face in front of hers nearly every day, no matter how far out of his way it put him. Long ago her father had made it clear to Frank the attention was unwelcome, but he still followed her around.

She could often feel his black eyes trail her whenever she was out-of-doors. She thought of how Mandy had caught Frank looking through her window two days ago and shuddered. She gave the surrounding space a quick scan: cut grass for fifty feet then the well-worn path into the gray leaf tree forest. Not a soul in sight. She surrendered to the warmth of the morning sun and closed her eyes again.

Something hit Lydia's foot, waking her. She opened her eyes to see Bethany's ankle-length leather boot, which was covered in a floral design she'd scratched into the surface herself, nudging her. She lifted her head from the tombstone and shielded her eyes from the sun. "How long have you been kicking me, little sister?"

"I only kicked twice." Bethany held two dripping buckets of wet sand, one in each hand. Her smile dimpled her cheeks, and her cropped brown waves moved over her shoulders. "Must you still call me little sister now that I'm a full inch taller than you?" Bethany swung the buckets as she spoke. Wet sand sloshed to the ground.

"No matter your height, remember I'm a physician responsible for the health of a village. Besides, both of my elder sisters still refer to me that way. So yes, I'll call you *little* no matter how tall you grow."

Lydia took one of the heavy buckets from her sister and carried it for her as they walked together through the cut grass. Bethany turned her head back toward their mother's tombstone then looked at Lydia. "Is everything all right? Did it go well last night?" Her blue eyes calmed for an instant as they settled on her. "It must have been so exciting delivering a baby! Well, exciting for you but dreadful for Mrs. Cotter."

She made a face and then continued rambling. "When Luke came by the pottery yard this morning, he told Mrs. Vestal that Phoebe and Walter said they could hear Mrs. Cotter screaming through the night. They said she wailed so loudly at first they thought it was one of the animals." She giggled. "And Phoebe said that—"

"Doris Cotter has a healthy baby boy," Lydia interrupted. "She's tired but quite content this morning. That's all that should concern you and your friends." News and opinions could quickly spread through the village. She couldn't have her fifteen-year-old sister overheard talking about her patients.

Bethany chattered incessantly about her friends and her work while they walked along the path through the gray leaf forest. Lydia corrected her twice when the chatter turned to gossip. But she gave up correcting—and listening—when it seemed that was the only speech young Bethany could utter.

As they neared the clearing at the edge of Good Springs, Lydia handed the bucket of wet sand back to Bethany. "Has Mrs. Vestal mentioned anything more about the apprenticeship?"

Bethany gripped the bucket's handle and beamed. "Just today, in fact, she said if I continue my efforts at the pottery yard—while I finish my schooling—she'll have no choice but to award me the apprenticeship. I showed her my sketches for designs with the new pigments I found, and she said once I master throwing clay, my work would be traded throughout the Land. Exciting, isn't it?"

The sound of Bethany's voice bubbling with enthusiasm over a profession brought Lydia joy. "I'm proud of you." She kissed Bethany's cheek. "Well, off you go then. Tell Mrs. Vestal hello for me."

"I will." Bethany smiled over her shoulder and hurried in the direction of the pottery yard to spend her Saturday morning working with clay and dyes and glazes to her heart's content.

Lydia walked along the cobblestone street that ran through the center of the village of Good Springs. A white chapel stood proudly along the west side of the street. Its steeple rose high into the clear morning sky. Her father preached there every Sunday, as had his father before him, and his father before him. The building appeared diminutive from the front when she walked past, but its long sides revealed its depth.

On the opposite side of the street, the library's stone facade cast a shadow across her path. Though a humble building, the library was her favorite place in the village, as it contained the few precious books the founders brought with them when they sailed from America and the journals written over the seven generations since then. The allure of the knowledge inside the library made her consider revising her morning plans, but concern for her ailing mentor compelled her on through the village.

The bare, sandy lot next to the library had been transformed into a market, as it was every Saturday morning. Growers were arranging their wooden crates of vegetables, bushels of fresh flowers, and stacks of packets of heirloom seeds. A tanner was laying out piles of leather. Woodworkers were dusting handcrafted furniture, and a spinner was arranging skeins of wool yarn and woven tapestries. Other merchants were setting up displays of items acquired by trade with other villages in the Land.

Lydia enjoyed the busyness of the market and usually lingered to watch the artists, but today she stepped around the crowds that were already gathering in the open lot and crossed the street. After unlatching a wooden gate at the front of the Ashton home, she climbed the shadowy steps to the front door. A strange sensation urged her to look back at the market, and there behind the carpet seller's display stood Frank, peering at her around a hanging rug.

When their eyes met, he lifted a hand and waved weakly. If he weren't regularly accused of stealing from cellars or found rifling through sheds, she might pity him. As it was, she couldn't be seen acknowledging him, so she instantly looked away.

As she lifted her hand to knock, the Ashtons' door opened. Mrs. Ashton wore a lavender cotton dress and had a knitted blanket draped over her shoulders.

"Lydia, dear! I thought I saw you crossing the road." Mrs. Ashton hurried her inside. "Where are your mittens, child? There is a chill in the air."

Bolts of cloth were stacked throughout the front parlor. Mrs. Ashton—once a prolific seamstress—had spent her life making clothes for many of the families in the village. She still sent for cottons from the textile makers in the village of Northcrest, but the material only piled in her parlor. The stacks had grown since Lydia's last visit.

"It isn't cold enough for mittens, Mrs. Ashton." She glanced around the cluttered room. Two logs were burning in the fireplace. One log from the gray leaf tree was sufficient to heat a small home all winter, and it was only the first day of autumn. "It's quite warm in here. Are you well?"

Mrs. Ashton sat in a wicker rocking chair near the front window. She folded her hands in her lap and began to rock. The chair's cane creaked with each pass across the floor. "I am well, dear." She eyed the armchair on the other side of an oval-topped table and pointed to it. "Sit yourself down and tell me about your family."

Lydia sat as she was told and began to speak, but Mrs. Ashton continued talking. "I heard Levi is still planning to build a separate house. Seems to me he should mind tradition and train under his father. It's too cold today to go without mittens. I do wish you had worn mittens." She returned her hands to her lap and twiddled her crooked thumbs. "I missed the Sunday service last week and probably will again tomorrow. It's simply too cold in that chapel. Besides, Doctor Ashton sleeps most mornings clear until noon. Tell me about your family, dear. Is everyone well?"

"Yes, thank you, we're all—"

"I am perfectly well, of course. Never you mind about us." She leaned closer to the window and squinted as she watched the villagers at the market. "It is about time you were married, Lydia. I worry about you so. You are a pretty girl. Smart, too. Doctor Ashton always spoke of your intelligence. Still does. Is that Amanda Foster I see flirting with the traders? Of course it is. I can see her twirling her red curls from here. She is a jezebel, that woman," she mumbled, then she turned to Lydia. "I made a pair of trousers for your brother. Take them to him when you go home today, dear."

"I will."

Mrs. Ashton looked her in the eye. Lydia thought she felt a connection. It would be brief as the older woman's mental acuity escaped her quickly. Doctor Ashton's mind was still sharp, but he slept most of the time.

Her heart ached for them more each time she visited. It didn't seem fair to her that two people who had poured their lives out for others had to spend their final years encumbered with decaying minds and bodies.

Mrs. Ashton peeled the curtain away from the window and returned her focus to the people at the market. "Doctor Ashton is sleeping now, but you may go check on him if you wish."

"Thank you. I'll only be a moment."

The bedroom was barely wider than the overstuffed bed in its center. Doctor Ashton looked small lying there under a quilt. He'd always seemed grand to her when she was a child.

As a barefoot little girl, she had once stepped on a piece of broken glass, and Doctor Ashton removed it with a pair of silver tweezers. Even then he was much older than her father. She remembered looking at his white whiskers as he pulled the glass out of her flesh and the sound the glass had made as he dropped it from the tweezers into a dish. When the glass was out, he rubbed a salve on her skin and explained the medicine was made with the oil of the gray leaf tree. The pain relief was instant, and the skin healed quickly. He said God gave them a forest full of medicine, and it piqued her interest.

As she approached the bed, she cleared her tight throat. "Doctor Ashton? It's Lydia."

When she rubbed the top of his wrinkled hand, his thin skin shifted over bulging veins. He didn't respond. She felt his pulse and listened to his breath just as he had taught her years before. His time was limited. She said a quick prayer and left the room before her tears had a chance to form.

As Lydia approached her family's house, the aroma of baking bread wafted out of the open kitchen door. Her father had taken over the weekly bread baking after her mother died, though everyone in the house had offered to take the chore, even Aunt Isabella. Born blind, Isabella insisted she could find her way around the kitchen like any cook, but John Colburn always demanded his elderly aunt stay away from the oven.

Lydia stepped through the back door and into the kitchen of the Colburn house. Her foot had barely crossed the threshold when she was greeted by an affectionate onslaught of questions about the new Cotter baby. She only offered a smile for a reply as she walked to the sink where she pressed a wooden foot pedal. Out poured pure, cold water.

After scrubbing her hands, she turned to her family. Her brother, father, and great-aunt waited for a report on the work that had kept her out all night.

"Well, Lydia?" John prodded. "Answer the question, please."

"Which question?"

Isabella, seated at the table, continued snapping green beans. "Let her be." She dropped the pieces into a bowl in rapid succession. "She will speak if we quiet down."

"Thank you, Aunt Isabella. Mr. and Mrs. Cotter have a healthy baby boy. He was born before sunrise, and they have yet to name him. You will have to hear the rest from them."

John wrapped one arm around her shoulder—careful not to touch her with his flour-covered hand—and kissed her forehead. "Spoken like an honorable physician. We will call you *Doctor* before long."

She briefly laid her head against John's chest. "During the last council meeting, did the elders mention granting me the title?"

"Actually, they did."

A jolt of energy brought her to life. "They did? So I have proven myself to them?"

He held up a hand, his skin powdery with flour. "Not quite. Several of the elders are not convinced a woman should be appointed to such a demanding task."

"I can do the job as well as any man." She almost told him to ask Dr. Ashton for proof of her abilities, then realized that would be futile with her mentor's current condition.

"I know you can. They have concerns about your seeing patients—especially men—in your cottage at all hours of the night."

"Can't you do something? You are the overseer."

"I am also your father. I do not want to appear biased." He tilted his head like he did when she was a child. "I believe you are capable of taking on the position. And you are ready for it. That is why I told them: no more stalling."

Finally, good news! "You did?"

"I told them to find out for themselves how you work, how high your standards are, how passionate you are for medicine, whatever they need to know. And to be ready to vote by spring."

"Spring?" Her excitement died. "Today is the autumn equinox. I have to wait six more months?"

"Time will pass quickly. But during these next few months, you must be careful in all of your dealings. Make sure your behavior is above reproach. Some of the elders will be looking for any reason to deny you the position."

After years of apprenticing, she was ready, more than ready to meet the challenge. "I will. Thank you, Father."

He gave her arm a gentle rub then returned to the stove. "Levi, pour your sister a glass of fresh milk." He sent a ladle deep into a pot of vegetable stew and filled a bowl. "I will pay a visit to the Cotter family this afternoon." He set the bowl on the table. "Have something to eat, Lydia. Then go lie down. You will be no good to anyone without proper rest."

Lydia ate the stew while Levi told her about his ideas for his house. Though her brother's carpentry skill was in demand throughout the village, he only spoke of his plans to build his own house. John's brow knit together while Levi talked about the modest home he wanted to build on the hilltop in the gray leaf forest.

She ate quickly, hoping to finish her food before an argument erupted. She swallowed her last bite then washed her bowl and walked the short flower-lined path from the Colburn house to her cottage.

Late in the afternoon, Lydia went with her father to visit the Cotter family. After meeting the newest member of his congregation, John said he had to return home to prepare for tomorrow's service. Lydia stayed at the

Cotters' house to check on the health of the new mother and baby. Upon finding them in excellent condition, she left for home.

Lydia had lived in the village along this stretch of shoreline her entire life. She knew it well and stayed on the packed sand far enough from the water's edge to keep her boots dry but close enough to the ocean to hear nothing but the waves—the beautiful but deadly waves spewed by the vicious currents that churned visibly beneath the surface.

She was alone, except for a flock of seabirds and a heron that seemed content to ignore her presence. The ocean grew dark along the horizon to the east, and the sun sank behind the village of Good Springs to the west. The remaining moments of daylight allowed her to linger along the beach. Realizing it was the autumn equinox, she thought of the long cold nights soon to come.

She slowed her pace to breathe the briny air. The seabirds seemed to slow, too. A deer raised his head above the waving grass near the forest. His round eyes reflected the horizon as he stood frozen in his tracks. There was calm on the shore but not peace. At first she thought her presence was the disruption, but the creatures weren't looking at her. They were looking behind her.

She followed their line of sight, and up in the sky a burst of light caught her eye. It was bright and faster than lightning. Then it vanished, leaving only blurred specks in her vision.

A peculiar black dot dropped lower in the sky. The dot grew in size as it descended to the earth. She held her breath as she focused on the object. The black dot quickly grew. It was some type of cloth with a figure dangling from it tethered by ropes. It sailed closer. The figure was a man.

He wore strange clothes—black from head to toe—and floated down from the sky with fluid grace. Every passing second brought him closer to the shore and gave her a clearer image on which to focus. His head, covered in some type of helmet, was hanging limp; his arms and legs drooped with lifeless sway.

She ran to him as his body landed on the beach. The black cloth followed his body onto the sand. It swished with the breeze then deflated and covered him.

Her boots dug into the sand as she raced to him. She pulled the thin cloth away from his body. The fabric itself was as light as air, but thick ropes and metal attachments gave it weight. Even his helmet was made of a strange material. It was black and shiny with letters painted on the side that read: USA.

She pushed a circular button on the side of the helmet, and a portion at the front of it raised and revealed his face. His eyes were closed and he was unresponsive. She reached her hand to his neck. His pulse was strong and steady.

The tide was coming in. The strange man would soon become swallowed by waves and dragged into the current if she didn't move him.

She shoved her hands into the sand under his shoulders and tried to pull him away from the lapping water. He was tall and solid and covered in gear. His boots alone probably weighed thirty pounds.

She grunted and pulled, but she couldn't move him. She glanced in every direction, hoping to see someone who might help her but saw no one. Her heart pounded in her chest. She had to leave him there and go get help.

"I will be right back! Can you hear me? I will be right back and I will help you!" She shouted over the sound of the waves and her heartbeat.

Charging down the path through the tall grass, she sent the nervous deer into flight. She glanced back once at the motionless man, embedded in the sand on the shore, surrounded by the swishing cloth and the ropes and the encroaching waves.

Chapter Three

Lydia's heart hammered in her chest as she ran through the open doorway and into the kitchen. Her father was sitting at the kitchen table with his Bible open in his palm. Levi was standing at the stove, stirring a pot.

"Father, get the cart and come quickly!"

Both men flinched as Lydia panted orders. "You too, Levi! I need you both. I can't carry him. Come now!" She motioned for the men to follow her.

John stood and his abrupt movement sent the chair screeching behind him as he stepped toward his daughter. "Carry whom?"

"A man by the sea." Determined to save the stranger before the tide came in, she rushed out of the house.

Levi caught up to her and grabbed her arm. "What happened?"

"A man fell to the shore from the sky. He is hurt and the tide is coming in. I couldn't lift him by myself. He's unconscious. We must bring him back here." She dashed past her cottage and toward the barn. The muscles in her legs burned. She neglected the urge to rub them and continued her rapid stride.

When they reached the barn, Levi threw the door open. John followed them into the darkened outbuilding and marched to a storage area in the back. While John and Levi dug out the cart, Lydia caught her breath.

"Who fell from the sky?" Levi questioned, as he removed empty wooden barrels from the cart. Lydia shook her head, annoyed by questions she couldn't answer. John sent Levi a look and grabbed the cart's handle.

The sky faded from purple to black while she led them through the gray leaf trees to the shore. The stars' brilliance in the sky seemed to pulse rather than twinkle. Their frantic rhythm matched the beat of her heart as she returned to the strange man sprawled on the beach. The incoming tide lapped at his bare feet.

He no longer wore a helmet. She knelt in the sand beside the stranger and put a hand to his head. The bluish flesh above his thick eyebrows had swelled to his hairline. What happened in the few moments she had been gone?

Levi and John were silent as they moved closer. They knelt in unison around the unconscious man.

Levi raised his voice in demand. "Lydia, who is he?"

"I don't know." Her reply came in a whisper as she felt the stranger's pulse. She scanned the area for the missing items. "He had boots… large, black boots and a helmet and the cloth…"

"What kind of cloth?" John gestured to Levi and they lifted the stranger onto the cart. The man's head rolled limply to one side, and his eyes remained closed.

"A thin, black cloth. He used it to fly. It was above him when he floated down from the sky… and it was attached to ropes." Being unable to explain what happened made her nervous stomach quiver. "I've seen nothing like it. Any of it."

She stood and peered into the forest. Though the oval moon already gave its gentle light, the night was too dark to see past the first few trees. She checked the beach for tracks but couldn't decipher anything unusual.

Levi pulled the cart through the sand as they left the shore. It took both arms, but he was strong. The wooden wheels dug into the sand at first but began to roll smoothly as they approached the forest path.

Lydia took another look around. Where were the man's boots and equipment?

John walked on the other side of the cart, studying the stranger. Levi often glanced back at the man, too, his eyes dark with suspicion. Surely they wouldn't try to stop her from treating the man's injuries. It was her duty to care for the sick and injured in Good Springs, and that duty included travelers, no matter how they arrived.

Levi pulled the cart close to Lydia's cottage. One wheel squeaked as it rolled on the hard ground. She needed to treat the man's wounds urgently, so she hurried Levi and John as they carried him into the medical office in her cottage.

The men stayed close to her while she examined her patient. She was too focused on her work to be agitated when their protective presence got in her way. John remained silent, but Levi frequently aired his concerns. He voiced certainty that at any moment the stranger would open his eyes and violently attack them all. She ignored her brother's words until her father began to agree with the comments.

She completed her examination and then watched Levi and John for a moment. She hadn't seen them act like this before. Both men stood straight and tall with arms crossed over their chests, as if eager to prove their power. Levi was slightly taller than their father, but both men had thick arms and stern jaws.

She glanced at the man lying unconscious on the patient cot and guessed he was maybe an inch taller than Levi. Though a leaner build, the stranger's strength was defined. His hair was clipped shorter than any man she knew. It was almost as if his head had been recently shaved, but the hair was shorter on the sides than the top. His hair and eyebrows were the same black color as his pants.

"Lydia?" Her father's eyes were widened expectantly.

"Yes?"

"I asked what you plan to do?" John planted his hands on his hips more like a parent reprimanding his child than a person speaking with the village physician.

"I plan to treat his injuries."

"We know nothing about this man. Clearly he is from another land." John picked up the black jacket they had removed from the stranger. He pointed to the unfamiliar insignia embroidered beneath a symbol that appeared to be wings. "I believe he is a warrior. Levi is right—he could be dangerous."

"What do you expect me to do?" She lifted her chin when her father didn't answer. "I'm committed to help any person needing medical attention, whether a resident of Good Springs or a traveler. I cannot—I will not—speculate the danger any patient might pose or allow anyone else to interfere with my care. Is that understood?"

John nodded. "Fine. Treat the man's injuries. But please, be cautious when he awakens."

Levi blew out a heavy breath in protest and turned away.

Lydia plunked down in the chair at her desk and took out a piece of blank paper to start a patient chart. She grabbed her pen and drew a line across the top of the page where she would write the man's name once she learned it. Realizing she was gripping the pen with such force her fingertips were turning red, she laid the pen down, closed her eyes, and drew in a breath. Whoever the man was and wherever he came from, he was her patient and she would help him—with or without her family's approval.

Hours passed and the man remained unconscious. Long after midnight, John rubbed his hands over his face. "I am overcome with fatigue and I must give the sermon at church in the morning. Levi, will you stay?"

"Yes." Levi sat in the chair beside Lydia's desk. He still appeared alert, though his usually clean-shaven face was shadowed with whiskers.

John walked to the door. "Until we learn more about this man, do not mention his arrival to anyone. If I am asked, I will simply say Lydia is treating an injured traveler." He pointed at Levi. "Do not provoke the man if he awakens."

Levi glanced up at his father but gave no reply.

John paused for a moment and looked at the man on the cot before he walked out the door.

Lydia understood her father's caution and even her brother's suspicion, but she was determined to treat the man like any other patient. She remained in her office with her patient through the night, and when she checked on him she found little change in his condition.

Her curiosity about him and his circumstance grew with every passing hour. She expected him to regain consciousness, and even though it was beyond her work as a physician, she already had a long mental list of questions to ask him. Who was he? Where was he from? Were there others like him coming to the Land?

Her most pressing question was about the cloth. The memory of him floating to earth with it replayed vividly in her mind. How did he do it?

Levi stayed in the medical office and glowered at the stranger most of the night. He sat with his arms folded and his head leaning against the wall behind his chair. He left the cottage only once, and that was at Lydia's request for food shortly after sunrise.

Lieutenant Connor Bradshaw needed to gather as much information as possible before he opened his eyes. He wasn't aboard the carrier. It was too quiet. The faded scent of burnt firewood hung in the air. An unlit fireplace was nearby. The occasional turn of a page swished faintly a few feet away. Someone nearby breathed with a light and steady rhythm. The guard was female.

This should be easy.

He covertly rubbed the cot beneath him. Wool. Maybe this was a Red Cross facility. One could hope. In war one must keep hope in a delicate balance.

He took a deep breath and winced at the gripping pain in his ribs. His dry lips drew tightly together and prickled with grains of sand. He opened his eyes, but it took a moment for his vision to focus.

As the double images cleared, morning sunlight filtered through frilly curtains on the windows. The woman in the room sat at a desk with her back to him, reading. She was either a naive enemy or an unconcerned ally.

She turned toward him silently. Her young, unpainted face matched the pure and pretty simplicity of the room. She neither spoke nor moved but only stared. He waited for her to make the first move.

"How do you feel?" she asked.

"You're American." Connor cleared his dry throat.

"No." She stood and stepped toward him in cautious increments.

She sounded American, but he guessed again. "Canadian?"

"No." She reached her hand to his head but hesitated to touch him. She pulled her hand back and tilted her head to the side. "What is your name?"

He ignored her question. "Are you with the Red Cross?"

"No. My name is Lydia Colburn. I am a physician. What is your name?" She stared at him, expressionless.

"Have I been captured or rescued?"

"Who are you?"

When he did not respond, she questioned again. "What is your name?"

Connor turned his aching head and glared at the ceiling. "Lieutenant Connor Bradshaw,

Unified States Naval Aviator, nine three zero six—"

The physician hovered above him. She was dressed like an American Civil War nurse. This made no sense.

He wanted answers. "Where am I?"

"You are in the village of Good Springs." She gently pressed her thumb into his eyebrow, lifted his eyelid, and examined his eye. She repeated the process on the other eye and asked again, "Who are you?"

"Lieutenant Connor Bradshaw, Unified States Naval Aviator. Nine three zero—"

"I'm not sure what you mean." She walked back to the desk and wrote something on a piece of grayish paper. "You have a concussion and three cracked ribs."

"Terrific." He groaned and his hand instinctively covered his aching ribs. The memories began to flood back—his mission, his aircraft, his co-pilot. There was a malfunction or they were shot down. The aircraft's computer systems went haywire. Before he could react, the emergency eject was initiated somewhere over the South Atlantic Ocean. Then he woke here.

The physician moved around the room. She reached into a cabinet on the wall and pulled a glass jar from a shelf. Then she took several dry, gray leaves out of the jar and began to grind them in a stone mortar. She eyed him continually as she worked.

He needed clues to his location. The village of Good Springs she'd said. Where on earth was that?

He scanned the room again. It was a medical office of some sort, but in a world war there was no way to tell who controlled it. The room's rustic interior brought to mind American's pioneer era—wood walls painted white, wood furniture, wood floor—and no plastic, wires, or electronics. A door stood between two curtained windows. The cot he lay on was pressed firmly against the wall. There was a high-backed chair across from him and another at the desk. A narrow staircase divided the wall on the other side of the physician's desk. "What is up there?" He started to motion to the stairs but his hand was weak.

"My private rooms. You are in my home." She gave a small smile.

Was that supposed to comfort him? He kept his expression neutral and looked away. There were no decals or signs, no computers and no modern equipment in the room. The silence afforded by a lack of electronic buzz reminded him of his grandmother's home. He pushed aside the comfort brought by sentiment and focused on the door as it opened.

A man walked in holding a tray of food. He looked young but wore trousers held up by suspenders. The man glanced at the physician as he came through the door, then he settled his gaze on Connor. He set the tray on the desk, moved past the physician, and stood firmly between her and the cot.

The only sound came from the stone mortar and pestle she used to grind the gray leaves.

Connor held still with one hand covering his broken ribs. The man turned and picked up a heavy-looking wooden chair. He held it with two fingers and set it within inches of the cot.

Maybe his interrogation was about to begin. Good. Maybe he would finally get some answers.

As the man sat in the chair across from Connor, he folded an open palm over the fist of the other hand. His deep-set eyes held the threat of aggression. He leaned forward, propping his elbows on his knees. While staring at Connor, the man turned his face slightly toward the physician. "Does he have a name?"

She didn't look up. "Lieutenant Connor. I couldn't make sense of the rest."

She set the mortar and pestle down and reached to the food tray, took a small kettle of steaming water, and poured it into a glass. The powdered gray leaves tumbled from the pestle as she tipped it into the glass. She stirred the concoction with a silver spoon and strained the liquid as she poured it into a teacup.

"Lieutenant?" The man's voice was low and stern. "Are you a soldier?"

"No." Connor's head was beginning to throb. "I'm a naval aviator." He dragged out the words. "I am a pilot in the Unified States Navy. I fly aircraft."

He thought he was speaking their language, yet they both stared with brows slightly lifted. "Airplanes." He stretched both arms out to mimic the act of flying. The movement shot pain through the cracked ribs on his left side. He made his next breaths short and shallow.

The physician took the tea she had made and walked to the cot. "Move away, Levi." She waved him back as if shooing a fly. "I can't work with you hovering."

She held the teacup out to Connor.

He looked at it and back at her. "Look, lady—"

"Lydia," the man called Levi corrected.

Connor kept his gaze on the physician. "Lydia, I appreciate the effort you went to by making a cup of tea for me, but if you're the doctor here, can't you give me something for the pain or at least wrap my ribs or something? I'm here for medical attention, right?"

Levi snickered.

Lydia knelt by the cot. With the two of them near each other, the family resemblance was clear.

Great. He'd been captured by civilians.

"This will remove your pain." She offered the cup again. "And I don't wrap broken ribs. It might make you feel better but you'll only take shallow breaths and could end up with pneumonia." He didn't move and she continued offering the tea. "It's still quite hot, but that will only help it work faster. It's tea from the gray leaf tree." She held the teacup closer to him as if trying to lure a frightened animal. "It will remove your pain and help your body heal much faster."

"Leave him in pain, Lydia. If he can't move, he can't hurt you." Levi barely moved his mouth as he spoke. He stood then rubbed his unshaven face and set the chair back against the wall.

Connor lifted his head and looked past Lydia. He leveled his gaze on Levi. "I'm not going to hurt her."

Levi's nostrils flared. He looked at Lydia. "Don't give him the gray leaf. He's dangerous."

She snapped her head toward her brother. "You should go."

"I will not leave."

"Stand outside my door and keep guard if you wish. This man is injured, and it's my duty to help him. You won't keep me from it." Her voice was as tight as the tension in the room.

Levi turned and moved one calculated degree at a time until he was finally outside. He closed the door but didn't step away from it. His silhouette shadowed the gauzy curtain. Lydia was watching Levi. Maybe she regretted sending her protector outside.

Apparently there would be no interrogation after all—at least not conducted by the physician's brother.

Lydia tapped her fingertips on the teacup. "Lieutenant Connor, this tea is our pain medicine and if you drink it—"

"Connor."

"Pardon?"

"My name is Connor." His hands sank into the cot beneath him as he pushed himself up. He grimaced and fought the pain as he sat up for the first time since he was in the cockpit of his fighter jet the day before.

He accepted the cup of medicinal tea Lydia held out to him but sipped it cautiously. It tasted bitter, yet still more palatable than the putrid drinking water on the aircraft carrier. He took another drink and swallowed hard. His dry throat was disappointed when the cup emptied. "Got any more of this?"

"Yes, but you won't need it." She smiled and took the empty cup. "Have you drunk tea from the gray leaf tree before?"

"No, I've never heard of—" He barely got the words out before heat rose from the core of his being. It radiated in pleasurable pulses as if the tea had ignited a painless fire. While the sensation passed through his body, it melted away every other feeling. The warmth removed the pain from his ribs as if they were healed. It spread down his legs to his toes and through his arms to his fingers. He brought his hands up to look at them. He expected to see light beaming from his fingertips, but there was nothing. The pain in his ribs had caught every breath before he drank the tea, so he hadn't realized how badly his head hurt. Within seconds the healing sensation reached the crown of his head. He briefly saw stars and felt light-headed, then nothing. It was all gone—the pain was gone and the warmth. He wasn't numb, but he felt nothing. And it felt wonderful.

Lydia handed him a glass of water. It was cold and pure and he quaffed half of it in one swallow. He hadn't noticed her fill the glass, and he wondered where the water came from. It tasted better than anything since before the war began. "Thank you." He moved his feet to the floor and began to stand.

Lydia put her hand on his shoulder. Her touch was light and pleasant. "Please don't try to stand yet. The tea removed your pain, but your injuries will require time to heal completely. And with a concussion you really must take things slowly."

He drank the rest of the water and raised the empty glass to her. She began to take the glass, but he didn't let go of it. He waited for her eyes to meet his. He didn't want to frighten her, but he needed to show her he was serious. "Where am I?"

She let go of the glass and looked at the door. Levi waited outside, and if Lydia became frightened, she might call for her brother. Connor had to change his approach. If she were as sweet natured as she appeared, she would respond better to warmth than severity. He smiled and gave his voice the most amicable quality he could muster, considering he was a possible captive. "Lydia, where am I?"

"You're in the village of Good Springs. I'm the physician here. This is my medical office." Her voice grew full. "I saw you float on the air. You fell from the sky last night at dusk. I saw you. How did you do it?"

He wrapped his fingers around the empty glass while he considered answering her. She seemed honest and innocent, but the world was full of enemies with vicious tactics. Who controlled this place? Land was scarce in the middle of the South Atlantic Ocean—certainly beneath the aircraft's location when he and his weapons system officer were ejected.

Maybe this was a trick of an enemy, or maybe his head injury was causing a hallucination. The basic room held a primitive quality, as did the physician and her brother. Maybe this was a remote settlement and the people here were secluded from a world at war. With decades of advanced technology, satellite images, and constant monitoring, nothing was hidden from the global powers.

He couldn't trust the physician, but he could test her. "Where is Good Springs? Is this an island?"

Lydia pressed her palm to her stomach. "Father was right. Last night he said he thought you were from another land... I have never left the Land... I don't think anyone has. I know there are other lands, of course, but I have never thought much about it. I suppose that sounds juvenile to you." She knelt in front of him and put a hand on his leg. "Did you mean to come here? Are you lost?"

He wanted to answer her, and that surprised him. If she were a pawn of the enemy, they had found a talented actress. She effused selfless concern. Her choice to send her brother away to help him proved her dedication to patient care. And her brother had been right—a warrior's job was to be dangerous.

Connor rubbed his chin out of habit and felt a day's worth of stubble. He drew a deep, painless breath and chose not to answer Lydia's question.

"What did you call the medicine you gave me?"

"It was tea made from the gray leaf tree." She pointed at the window. "The gray leaf trees grow throughout the Land, but they are most abundant in the forests around Good Springs. We use the leaves for medicine."

"So it numbs pain?"

"In a sense. And it accelerates the healing process."

"How?"

"We don't know for certain. We have used the gray leaf medicinally for generations, and we know that it works, but we have little knowledge as to how it works." She smiled and tucked a strand of hair behind her ear. "That question is the basis of most of my research." She glanced at a microscope on the counter, and Connor followed her line of sight. The microscope looked like it belonged in a museum. "I believe the gray leaf works by restoring cells to their proper function because—" She stopped herself and looked at him.

He wanted to hear more about her research and the gray leaf tree, but instead she asked again about his parachute and where he was from. She had gained his trust with little effort. His humanness had almost suckered him again.

He put his head in his hands and said no more.

Lydia stood over him for a moment before she returned to the tray of food on her desk. She used a silver knife to spread butter on a thick slice of bread and offered the food to him.

He ignored it and reclined on the cot. With the discomfort of his injuries removed, he simply needed to lie still and close his eyes while he processed the situation.

Connor didn't realize he was asleep until the sound of the door opening mixed into his dream and jarred him awake. It was late afternoon and he'd slept hard—much harder than he had in months. He lifted his hand to rub his eye, far too comfortable for a man at war. It must have been a side effect of the medicinal tea.

A middle-aged man walked in the medical office carrying a picnic-type basket. He sat on the chair across from the cot and lowered the basket to the floor. An august man with a calm demeanor, he crossed his legs at the ankle and grinned as he looked at Lydia.

She sat at her desk writing and had not acknowledged the man's entrance until he spoke.

"Lydia?"

"Oh, I'm sorry." She smiled and gave the man her attention. "Hello, Father. How was church?"

"Just fine." He folded his hands in his lap and sent her a paternal look. "I visited the Fosters after the service. Roseanna sent plenty of food home with me." He motioned to the basket on the floor. "I thought I might share some with your patient. Aunt Isabella is waiting for you in the kitchen. She was told you have been treating a wounded traveler and will join her for dinner." He began to take food out of the basket without waiting for Lydia's response.

Connor sat up slowly and expected someone to protest his movement. When they didn't, he felt less like a prisoner. Lydia stood and straightened the papers on her desk then left.

She was her village's physician and this was her home, but her father was clearly in charge.

Once Connor was alone with Lydia's father, he wondered why the man wanted Lydia to leave. Her father looked like an older version of Levi, but with blue eyes, a trimmed beard, and gray at his temples. He also seemed less threatened.

"I am John Colburn, Lydia's father." He unwrapped their dinner. "I am the overseer of Good Springs. What is your name, son?"

"Connor Bradshaw, sir."

"Levi told me you are a warrior." John handed him a large sandwich of meat between slices of artisan-quality bread. "What army?"

"Unified States Navy, sir." Connor took a bite. He was too hungry to pretend otherwise. The bread was fresh and soft; the meat was tender and flavorful but not a taste he immediately recognized. "Am I a prisoner here?"

"No, Connor, you are not a prisoner." John scratched his bearded cheek. "Lydia saw you arrive on the beach last night. She came to her brother and me for help so she could bring you here and treat your injuries. No one else in the village knows about you, and since we have never had an… outsider such as yourself, I prefer to have an explanation before the villagers start asking questions. You are not a prisoner, but I believe it is best for everyone if you stay here for now."

Connor nodded. The room was small and he hated feeling like a shut-in, but the last thing he wanted was to have curious villagers poking sticks at him. He took another bite and studied John while he ate.

He had no reason to doubt the man. John appeared to be forthright. Connor recognized John's authority and appreciated it.

"I assume you are obligated to return to your army." John paused as though he expected Connor to fill him in on the details, but Connor kept silent. He ate without speaking another word. John did not push him for answers, and it increased Connor's respect for him.

Connor decided he would stay in Lydia's cottage until he healed—which Lydia had said would only be a couple of days because of their medicine. And John was correct: Connor was obligated to find a way back. He would use his downtime to plan his return to his squadron.

He took a drink of water, and John refilled his glass from a ceramic pitcher. Connor looked down at the pure, precious water. It was a good place to start. "Where did this water come from?"

John swallowed his last bite then brushed the crumbs from his hands. He looked at the water pitcher then back at Connor. "Our well." He arched one eyebrow. "Is there something wrong with the water?"

"No. It's perfect."

How could people who behaved generously and courteously live as if the biggest problem facing all of humanity had no effect on them? Connor raised the glass. "Most of the world is engaged in a deadly war because there is not enough of this. And somehow I am sitting here drinking glass after glass of it."

"It is water. I cannot imagine a world at war over a lack of water. The wells, springs, and lakes in the Land are full of fresh water. Our largest river flows deep and pure a matter of miles inland from Good Springs." John gazed at the water in his glass. "Which nation is without water?"

These people had no idea what was happening in the rest of the world. Somehow they really were isolated from civilization. But just how isolated? "Which nations are near Good Springs?"

John cleared his throat. "Good Springs is a village in the Land. Our founders brought a few maps and books of world history with them when they settled here, so we are familiar with other nations, but our people have not had contact with an outside nation since the founders left America. That was a long time ago."

"How long ago?"

"The founders arrived here in March of eighteen sixty-one."

Connor found himself caught not only by John's gaze, but also by the intensity of what he said. This man was no enemy and could perhaps even become an ally. Connor considered the possibility of a completely isolated society hidden from the modern world. He pulled his focus away from John and surveyed the room. The beauty of craftsmanship and old-world artistry was evident in everything. Most of the objects in the room looked antiquated, yet they were pristine and still in use.

John Colburn was the leader of his community, and a protective one. If Lydia was any indication of the rest of their village, Connor agreed they had something worth protecting. During the war he had watched every nation react—many with violence—to the water shortage that affected the human race. These people had no idea what was in store if the world learned of their unspoiled resources. The global powers would act here as they had elsewhere—the strong would invade and the weak would sabotage.

Thoughts of his squadron, his weapons system officer, and their mission flooded his mind. Whether or not he agreed with every position of his country's leadership, he had taken an oath of allegiance. And like everyone else in the war, in addition to his duties as an aviator, he had standing orders to report any potential resource.

As an experienced and professional aviator, he trusted his clear head and controlled decisions. He frequently had to squelch his opinions to carry out missions. This situation was different, and a rush of emotion inundated his mind. Overwhelmed with concern for John and Lydia and their village, his vision swayed. He touched his forehead with his fingertips and felt a lump where his head injury swelled.

"It looks better than it did last night," John said while he looked at Connor's head.

"Huh?" Connor grunted. "Oh, yeah. Lydia said I have a concussion."

"You need to rest. The gray leaf provides quick and painless healing, but the body requires rest." John dropped his napkin into the food basket and gathered up what was left of their dinner. He set the water jug on the side table next to the patient cot. "Drink all you want. We have plenty… for now."

The heels of John's boots thumped the floor as he walked to the door. He stopped at the window and peeled back the curtain. "Connor?"

"Yes, sir?"

"I believe it is best that you and I keep these details private for now. My people are not prepared for a world at war… though I suppose no one ever is."

"Yes, sir." He understood and also needed time to think. But Lydia was curious from witnessing his arrival. She wanted an explanation. "Your daughter… she has questions, sir."

John nodded. "When she asks them, tell her to speak to me."

Sweat beaded across Connor's forehead. He panted as he sat straight up, trembling. His eyes shot open and he searched the space around him with frantic dread.

It was dark. He was in the medical office in the physician's house in a village called Good Springs on an unnamed land in an unspecified location in the middle of the South Atlantic Ocean.

The abject feeling from the nightmare saturated Connor's mind. In the dream, the world's end approached, and he was surrounded by chaos and fire. Then a limpid stream in a lush, green forest appeared in the distance. As he walked to the stream, the noise of the battle lessened, as did the stench of burning flesh. He knelt on the stream's bank and watched water run pure and clear across his fingers. Cupping his hands, he brought the fresh water to his lips. As he began to drink it, the sounds and scents of the battle erupted again. The water in his hands turned to ash.

The shift from feeling like the world was ending to feeling like he was at the end of the earth left his mind reeling. He shoved the wool blanket away from his sweaty body and moved his feet to the cool floor. Poised on the edge of the cot, he wiped his face with his hands and felt the smooth flesh where a lump had once protruded from his forehead.

The wound was gone.

He touched his ribs. They too felt normal. The tea Lydia had given him seemed to be more miraculous than medicinal. Now that he was healed, he was tired of sleeping, tired of wondering, and tired of being stuck inside four walls. He had to get some fresh air and hopefully some answers.

He rose and walked to the window. Moonlight illumined the space around the cottage and revealed a quaint country yard. He grabbed his flight jacket from the back of a chair, but his boots were nowhere to be found. After sliding his bare arms inside the jacket's sleeves, he shrugged it over his shoulders and stepped to the door. Before he opened it, he looked up the stairs to make sure Lydia's door was still closed.

Once outside, he shut the door as quietly as he could. Lydia's home was a matter of feet from the back of another house. By the size of the structure—and the fact that her home did not appear to have a kitchen—he assumed it was her father's house. No wonder her family seemed ever-present. They lived next door.

The crisp air carried the scent of the nearby ocean. He zipped his jacket and stood facing the big house. The grass crunched under his bare feet as he followed a path away from Lydia's cottage to an unpaved road. The road's surface was a mixture of smooth gravel, sand, and shells. It was barely wide enough for one car. There were no streetlights over the road or lights anywhere around the house.

As he glanced back at the cottage, the sound of a cow's moo confirmed the rural nature of Good Springs. He wasn't as concerned with the village's topography as he was with its location. He buried his hands in his pockets and leaned his head back to take in the stars. He knew them well and—even though the aircraft he routinely flew navigated by far superior technology—he was confident he could fly from one continent to another by the stars alone. Something wasn't right.

He blinked and rubbed his eyes then he looked up again. At first he thought the concussion was interfering with his vision. Then he scanned the ground, the yard, and the houses. There was nothing wrong with his eyes. Something was wrong with the sky. The stars appeared to be spread farther than they actually were, and the full moon looked oblong rather than round.

Maybe he was still dreaming or maybe in a coma and none of this had ever happened. He walked back to Lydia's cottage and decided her father was right: it was best if he stayed in the medical office until they understood how he had come to this uncharted land.

Chapter Four

As Lydia opened her eyes, her first thought was of Connor. She rolled onto her back and pushed the bedcovers away from her face. The early light glowed through the curtains of her bedroom window. She wanted to snuggle back under the warm quilt, but her concern for Connor impelled her from her languor.

When she had checked on Connor during the night, her presence in the room startled him. She envisioned the mixture of fear and fury that had lit his eyes and made him look dangerous. Though he had quickly calmed himself—and even apologized for his violent reaction—Lydia was worried about him. He was lost in a foreign land, so she expected him to be restless, but she sensed there were complications beyond her imagination.

The cottage was quiet. Connor was probably still asleep downstairs. She dressed and gathered her laundry to take to the main house. Her father had said they would expand her cottage into a home someday, but she was fine with it the way it was. She liked going into the family home throughout the day. She enjoyed sharing meals with her family and spending time with Isabella while her father and Levi were working and Bethany was at school.

She unlatched the lock that Levi had installed on her bedroom door the day before. Levi had marched up her stairs and started hammering without an explanation, and she had been too tired to request one. Levi had always been protective of Lydia and Bethany, especially since they lost their mother. Though only a twelve-year-old boy when their mother died, Levi had immediately armed himself with the notion of manhood. Adeline and Maggie were now both married and lived under the protection of their husbands, but Levi guarded Lydia and Bethany as if they were his charges.

She understood his intentions and had used the lock just as he had shown her.

As she descended the stairs, Connor lay prone on the medical office floor. His arms were spread out to each side and, with his hands firmly planted, he pushed his shirtless body away from the floor. He paused and then lowered himself back down. He repeated the motion over and over.

She slowed her pace when she saw his motions were deliberate. He let out his breath and sprang to his feet with a blast of energy.

She was not sure what to do. The spectacle left her grinning.

"What? Don't you people work out?" Connor quipped, as he rubbed a palm across his bare chest.

"Work out what?" She was still smiling and forced herself to look away.

He didn't seem to notice when she immediately looked back at him. He sat on the floor, put both hands behind his head, and lowered his back to the ground. With his legs bent at the knee, he contracted his abdominal muscles and sat up, and then he lowered his body back down. He repeated the motion dozens of times and gushed out a breath each time he sat up.

She lingered on the stairs with her arms wrapped around the bundle of laundry. When she realized she was staring at the clear definition of his well-trained muscles, she forced her gaze to return to his face. "I take it you are feeling better?"

Connor forcibly exhaled. "Just perfect." He didn't break his rhythm but continued to sit up, lie back, and sit up again. "Thanks, Doc."

She nodded, speechless, then stepped out the cottage door and walked along the dew-covered path to the main house. After brushing a spider's web out of the way, she opened the door.

Her father was walking into the kitchen from the parlor. John wore work clothes and smiled at her as he lifted his suspenders over his shoulders. "Morning, Lydia."

"Good morning, Father."

"How is your patient today?" John walked to the sink, filled a kettle with water, and set it on the stove with a clank.

With the image of Connor exercising still fresh in her mind, Lydia grinned. She walked to the back of the kitchen and dumped the laundry bundle by a washtub. "I believe he has fully recovered."

She picked up a basket for gathering eggs and went to the linen closet to get a clean cloth to line the basket. Along the bottom shelf of the closet were stacks of old clothes and fabric scraps awaiting other uses. Her mother used to call it the rag pile. There in the rag pile she saw the trousers Mrs. Ashton had made for Levi. Lydia ducked her head out of the closet and held the pants up. "Another miscalculation?"

"Too slim and six inches too long for Levi. Mrs. Ashton makes you all clothes as if you were still growing. They could be altered; however, Levi could not bring himself to tell her."

"I'll take them to Connor."

"No, I will take them to him in a moment." John held out his hand.

Lydia tossed the pants across the kitchen to him and he caught them with one hand. He stood at the stove while the coffee brewed, then filled two cups with the steaming beverage. With the trousers tucked under his elbow, he carried a cup of coffee in each hand and walked out the back door toward the cottage.

Connor stood from the floor, satisfied his ribs appeared to be healed and his strength had returned. When Lydia left the cottage, he pulled on his t-shirt and took the opportunity to search the medical office. He hoped to find some clues as to where this land was and how he might return to his squadron.

At Lydia's desk, Connor lifted the grayish papers she had written on the day before. Her neat and uniform handwriting looked more like some old colonial style than modern American penmanship. The paper she used was thick and rough. A pen and ink well, both made of silver, sat next to an oil lantern at the corner of her desk.

He lifted the lantern and smelled the fuel. It had a pungent scent he didn't recognize. He sat in her chair, opened the drawer on the right side of the desk, and found a tidy stack of paper that appeared to be her detailed patient charts.

After closing the drawer, Connor checked the window and opened the drawer on the left side of the desk. Expecting to find it just as logical as the rest of Lydia's office, Connor gulped at the drawer's chaotic contents: broken seashells, a bound braid of horsehair, and seed pods were mixed with crumpled scraps of paper. He promptly closed the drawer.

The back of her desk was pushed against the wall by the staircase. The balusters were painted white and climbed two per stair up to her private rooms. He stood and looked up the stairs but saw only a closed door at the top of the landing. Curiosity tempted him to ascend the steps, but it stemmed from his personal interest and had nothing to do with his mission.

He moved away from the desk and examined the contents of a narrow bookcase. The shelves were filled with neatly arranged knickknacks, but only a few old books. At first he thought the lack of books was peculiar for a doctor's office, but then his hand felt his ribs— completely healed in two days. There were probably more differences in their healthcare methods than similarities.

Walking past the bookcase, he inspected the medical instruments on a long countertop between the bookcase and the patient cot. The cabinet above the countertop was filled with bandage materials and more medical instruments, most of which were made of silver. He picked up a few of the instruments. Medical tools were gory no matter where he was.

He was already familiar with the contents of the doily-covered side table next to the cot, but he had yet to flip through the pocket-sized books that were stacked on top of the table. He felt like he was riffling through a display of antiques as he picked up the first book. Its cover was made of thick leather and read The Gospel According to John. The inside pages were the same grayish paper Lydia had at her desk, and the printing appeared to be the work of an old block press. In small print at the bottom of the first page, it read Printed in Good Springs in the Year of Our Lord 2024. The ancient looking book was only a year old.

Holding the scripture book between his hands, he looked up at a framed picture hanging on the wall over the table. It was a silhouette of a woman's profile. The contours looked similar to Lydia but not exact… probably the silhouette of a relative. The only other picture in the room hung on the wall next to the door. It was a drawing of an ornate tree formed by cursive writing. He studied it for a moment then moved closer to read the words and realized it was Lydia's family tree. The spiraled writing indicated John Colburn as her father and listed a date of death beside her mother's name. Connor glanced back at the silhouette and made the connection.

As he returned to the cot and sat on its edge, he opened the scripture book. The text was small and neatly printed. Though the translation was from a tradition even his grandmother's church would have considered archaic, he found the words to be his first glimpse of familiarity since he had awoken in this place. He read for a moment and then the door opened. He assumed it was Lydia and continued reading.

His senses sharpened the moment he smelled coffee. When he saw it was John, he stood up, almost at attention out of habit.

John slowly closed the door with his back while carefully holding a steaming cup in each hand. He had a folded pair of brown pants tucked under one elbow.

"Connor. I am glad to see you are well. Do you drink coffee?"

Connor accepted the ceramic cup; its handle was large enough to put his whole hand through. As he sipped, the coffee's warmth rushed through his system. It was dark and bold, and endowed with the taste of high quality. Definitely not a military blend. "Thank you, sir."

"My pleasure." John tossed the pair of trousers onto the cot. "Those should fit. You might have to cuff them." He took a sip of his coffee and squinted at the t-shirt Connor wore. Then he looked down at Connor's bare feet. "I will get you a proper shirt later and shoes as well." He sat in the chair across from the cot and motioned for Connor to sit back down. "I apologize if I disturbed your reading."

"Not at all," Connor replied, glad for the company.

"Do you understand what you are reading?"

"Yes, sir, I do."

"Excellent." John took a sip of his coffee. "You are welcome to attend our church while you are here in Good Springs."

Connor rubbed his chin. He was grateful, even comforted by John's graciousness, but he was still in active service. Even though the military's resources were stretched thin, he assumed a search party was looking for him. He intended to find them or be found before he was declared dead. "Thank you, sir. But I can't stay here."

"That is true. Since you have fully recovered, you must come to my house. You may stay as my guest."

"Again, thank you," he said, unsure how to explain the situation. "I meant that I must return to my people. I'm required to return to duty."

"I do not know how you will leave the Land."
John turned his head toward the window. "I still
do not understand how you arrived."

Connor nodded. "I've thought about that a lot
myself. I don't know how I will leave, but I can
tell you how I arrived. I'm a pilot. I fly aircraft for
the Unified States military. Do you have any
type of aircraft here?"

John only shook his head.

"Do you know what an airplane is?"

"No."

"Do you have cars here?"

"No. I am not familiar with anything of the sort."

Connor scratched his head as he thought of an
explanation. "An aircraft is a machine that flies
in the sky. The aircraft I fly have a crew of two:
the naval aviator and the weapon systems
officer." He held out the scripture book and
flew it like an airplane. "Imagine this is the
aircraft. We were flying high in the sky over the

South Atlantic Ocean. That ocean." Connor pointed to the east. "My people have highly sophisticated technology and can make the aircraft fly very high and very fast. But something went wrong and I was ejected." He was concerned his explanation would not make sense, but John appeared to be focused as he listened. "The ejection seat deployed a parachute so I could float safely to the ground. That's what Lydia saw from the beach the evening she found me."

John sat quietly, and his brow creased as he stared into his coffee cup. Then he looked up as if a thought had occurred to him. "You mentioned two people were in the aircraft. Was the other person ejected too?"

Connor widened his eyes, somewhat surprised by John's perception. "I hope so."

"If so, where is that person now?"

"I don't know, sir." The possibility of Lieutenant Mercer's death knotted Connor's stomach with grief. "I was knocked unconscious during the incident. I awoke here. I don't know what happened to my weapons system officer... or to the aircraft... or my boots for that matter." The absence of his gear, especially his boots, was worrisome.

"You will have to ask Lydia about your boots," John said. "I recall her remarking on missing equipment and boots when we went back to the beach with her that night. I have not heard anyone mention anything that would suggest knowledge of the event—aside from my family. Levi and Lydia are aware of your mysterious arrival, of course, but the others in my household only know Lydia is treating an injured traveler, which is common here from time to time. And I often invite travelers to stay in my home. The trouble is: everyone—my family and the people in our village—will ask where you are from. I cannot tell people that you fell from the sky, nor will I lie." John's blue eyes were serious and full of concern. "What shall I tell them?"

"Arizona."

"I beg your pardon?"

"I'm from Arizona. It's a state in America."

"I see. I was hoping for an answer that would not draw more questions, but I appreciate your honesty. And what about your name? Bradshaw, was it?"

"Yes, sir. Bradshaw. Why is my name a problem?"

"Eight families founded our society. There are eight surnames in the Land. Not one of them is Bradshaw." John's matter-of-fact explanation attested to the simplicity of his society.

"Hasn't anyone ever changed his name here? You know, come up with something new?"

"It is forbidden." John's expression remained serious. "Our genealogy is very important to us. Anyone wishing to take a wife must compare his lineage to hers to ensure quality breeding."

"Quality breeding?" Connor wanted to laugh at the concept but could tell this was a serious matter for the isolated society. "As in no cousin marriages, that sort of thing?"

"A man may not marry a woman with whom he shares a great-grandparent." John gave a quick glance out the window as if something outside caught his eye. "We will try not to mention your name… or Arizona." He walked to the door then turned back to Connor. "Come into the house with me. I want you to join my family for breakfast."

"Thank you, sir." He was grateful for the chance to leave the cottage and be around people—no matter how bizarre the situation was. And he was beginning to like John Colburn. He reminded himself of the destitute condition of the rest of the world and pushed aside any notion of enjoying the place.

This was not his real life, and he had to find a way back to his carrier. He had no idea how to do that without an aircraft or a boat, but he had to get out of the cottage before he could begin to plan his departure. At present, he could leave the Colburn property and use his survival skills to live in the wild, or he could accept the invitation to be a welcomed guest in the home of a leader in a peaceful community.

Lydia opened the door to the kitchen pantry and stepped inside the cool, dark room. The morning sunlight that was beginning to brighten the kitchen spilled into the pantry. She filled a bowl with fresh fruit from the bushel baskets that lined the floor. The baskets were heaped with recently picked pears and plums and three varieties of apples. Villagers often brought fresh produce from their gardens and orchards to the overseer's home. She'd never seen the pantry go empty.

Isabella lumbered into the kitchen. With her cane, she felt the floor to detect anything out of place. Isabella grunted as she lowered herself into her usual chair at the end of the table.

Then she reached for the linen napkin on her plate, snapped it open, and smoothed it over her lap.

Lydia washed the fruit and placed it in a bowl on the table between a bowl of boiled eggs and a plate of bread. She greeted her aunt, and Isabella mumbled a response.

Bethany hummed as she came in and sat at the table next to Isabella. She plunked a stack of schoolbooks on the table's edge and reached for a slice of bread. She hummed as she buttered the bread then stopped humming and took a bite. As she curled her long legs beneath her body, Lydia sat beside her and sent her a parental look. It went unnoticed.

Levi shuffled into the kitchen and walked straight to the cupboard near the sink. He yawned as he took a coffee mug from the upper shelf and yawned again as he moved around the table to his chair on the side by the fireplace. As Levi pulled his chair away from the table, its legs smacked into the stone edge of the hearth. Lydia flinched as the motion set off a memory of her mother's death. She pressed her palm against her stomach and immediately removed it when Levi glanced at her.

Lydia looked over her shoulder at the back door and wondered if her father would bring Connor into the house for breakfast. She glanced back at Levi as he reached for the coffee pot. His face changed. Levi glowered at the back door.

John and Connor were chuckling about something as they walked into the house. Their smiles didn't dissipate as they moved to the table. Connor glanced at Lydia and rubbed the top of his head to smooth his extremely short hair.

Lydia had assumed her father would bring the stranger into his house as a guest. He usually invited travelers to stay if they had no place else to go, and she expected he would treat Connor no differently. She also assumed Levi had realized that too, but the way he froze and glared at the two men suggested otherwise.

"Good morning, all," John greeted. "This is Connor. He is a traveler. He will be staying with us for a while." John stepped to his seat at the head of the table and motioned to the empty chair at his right. "Have a seat, Connor."

Lydia left the table to retrieve silverware and a plate for Connor. The first plate she drew from the cabinet had a slight chip, so she put it beneath the stack and took the next plate. As she returned to the table, she noticed how Levi slid his knife through the butter and slathered his bread without taking his eyes off Connor.

"Connor you know Lydia, of course, and you have met my son, Levi." John picked up the bowl of eggs, took one, and passed the bowl to Connor as he continued the introductions. "This is my youngest daughter, Bethany, and my aunt, Miss Isabella Colburn."

"Just call me Aunt Isabella. Everyone does."

Bethany craned her neck to see around Lydia and stared at Connor while chewing with her mouth open. She smiled when Connor glanced at her, then she returned her attention to her food and heaped a spoonful of preserves onto her bread.

"It's good to meet you all," Connor said. His greeting was met with complete silence.

Lydia froze and waited for their reactions. Maybe he didn't realize there was a difference in his dialect. It was slight but noticeable to them. Levi sighed. Bethany looked up from her food; her eyes were wide. Isabella raised her brows and her lips twitched. Lydia braced for her aunt's reaction.

"Goodness, man!" Isabella broke the silence. "What sort of speech is that?"

"Aunt Isabella," John interjected. "Connor has traveled a long way. He was injured a couple of days ago. Lydia has been attending to his medical needs in the cottage."

"Oh, you are the fellow who suffered the head injury!" Isabella said as if she had put it all together. "It has affected the way you speak— made you slack-jawed or something. Poor creature! That happened to my cousin as a child. He never did fully recover." She lifted a porcelain teacup to her mouth; her audible sips echoed in the silent kitchen.

Lydia grinned at Connor. His brows were furrowed and his eyes shifted as if he were confused. John shrugged and took a bite of his breakfast. Bethany snickered. Levi groaned and shook his head.

John gracefully redirected the conversation and asked Bethany about school. She launched into her usual discourse on why she should not be required to attend school at all when many of the other students were away harvesting. She contended her time would be best spent at the pottery yard while the weather was favorable. When her complaints went unendorsed, she raised her voice for more attention.

As Lydia drew a breath to correct her sister's impertinence, Bethany huffed and left the table.

When John finished eating, he left the kitchen and returned with a pair of shoes for Connor. Lydia glanced at her father as she cleared the table. "I will be going to the Cotters' to check on Doris and the baby today. That is," she said as she looked at Connor, "if you are all right."

Connor lifted his chin at the door and mouthed something. Lydia realized he wasn't sure if he should speak again in front of Isabella. She nodded and set the dishes in the sink, then wiped her hands on her dress and walked outside with Connor following her.

Lydia sat in the chair at her desk in the medical office and released a long breath. Connor followed her inside and closed the door. She grinned as she thought of Isabella's reaction to the way Connor spoke. Knowing her aunt, Lydia was relieved Isabella said no more about it than she did.

"I planned to examine your eyes and reflexes once more before I release you from my care. However," she smiled, "considering my aunt's assessment, perhaps I should make you stay in bed a few more days, at least until your speech is more familiar sounding."

"Yeah, I'll work on my enunciation." Connor grinned. "You have an interesting family, Doc." He pulled the other chair closer to her desk and sat down. "Your dad is cool." He held up a pair of leather shoes. Shoving his fist inside, he bent them back and forth then slipped them on his feet. "Not bad."

Lydia picked up her pen and started to write on his medical chart. She looked again at the shoes and remembered the boots he wore when he landed on the beach. She had forgotten about them since that night. "What happened to your shoes? The boots you wore when you fell from the sky?"

Connor's grin vanished and his gaze intensified. His swift expression change frightened her. The momentary comfort she had with him only seconds before was gone.

"Since I was unconscious when my boots were removed, I was hoping you could tell me what happened." His tone was levied with just enough suspicion to put her on the defensive. She tried to not be offended. He was from a different culture and probably had different customs. Still, he could show some gratitude for her saving his life rather than hinting at accusation.

"I don't know what happened." She thought back to when she first saw him—a scene she'd replayed over and over in her mind. Dreams of a motionless man floating to earth had plagued her sleep since his arrival. She didn't know how he flew in the sky, and he hadn't answered her questions when she asked. Now that he had recovered from his injuries, she wanted answers. She looked him directly in the eye. "I was walking home along the shore that night. I was alone. It was dusk. There was a flash of light in the sky, and then you floated down to the earth. It looked as though you were going to land in the ocean, but the wind carried you with that cloth. You fell into the sand. I tried to pull you from the water's edge, but you were too heavy. The tide was coming in, and the currents around the Land are deadly. I was afraid you would be pulled out to sea. You were unconscious and there was nothing I could do." Her words were pouring out with more emotion than her professional training allowed. She tried to steady her voice. A fully qualified physician could handle harrowing situations. She kept her eyes on her desk instead of looking back at Connor. "So I left you there while I ran home to get my father and brother to help. When we returned, your boots were gone and so was the cloth that had carried you."

Connor slid his arm slowly across the desk and took the pen out of her hand. She looked into his eyes, and where she expected to see animosity, she saw compassion.

She had so many questions. He came from a world she couldn't imagine, and that made her afraid of the answers. She just wanted everything to go back to how it was before he arrived.

He laid her pen on the desk. "The cloth you saw is called a parachute. The machine I operate is called an airplane. It flies in the sky. Something went wrong with my aircraft. I floated to the earth using the parachute. That's what happened." His voice softened. "I can see the stress my arrival has caused and I'm sorry. You saved my life, Doc. I am grateful. Yesterday you asked me if I meant to come here. I didn't. I don't even know where this place is. I have flown over this part of the world many times and I've never seen any land here before, nor has anyone else that I know."

As Lydia listened to Connor she remembered the founders' writings and how they had acknowledged God's providence from the moment they ran aground on this uncharted land. Connor hadn't intended to come to the Land either. Maybe his arrival was providential too. Her desire to demand answers lessened. He'd spoken the truth, and that brought her peace. "I'm glad I was there to help you." She thought again of what started their conversation. "However, I can't explain your missing boots." His description of his parachute proved it was a tool and held no power of its own, so another person must have removed it… and his boots. There was no one else at the shore that night. And for a person to steal from an injured man and not move him away from the incoming tide would certainly reveal a level of wickedness that—though innate in every person—was rarely acted upon in the Land. She glanced at the windows and felt cold. "Unless…"

"Unless what?"

She stood and stepped to the window. Frank could be crouching outside even now. The last thing she wanted to do was expose her humiliating problem to a stranger, but if Frank had robbed Connor, he deserved to know. "There is a man in our village… he isn't like most people here." She lifted the edge of the curtain and looked around the yard. "He doesn't behave respectably. I don't like to speculate, but he might have been there when

I found you. I didn't see him that evening, but he often… follows me."

"Follows you?"

"From a distance mostly." She felt foolish for actions that were not her own, but no logic could make the guilt go away. "My father has spoken to him about his behavior, but he still does it. His name is Frank Roberts." She turned to look at Connor but he was already standing behind her.

"Where does he live?" His voice was low and serious.

She moved back to her desk. "In a cabin past the bluffs. I am not accusing him of stealing from you. Please understand it's only a possibility that he was there that night and—"

Her words were interrupted by the slam of the door. He was gone.

Connor rushed out of Lydia's cottage fully charged for a fight. He stopped between the cottage and the back door of the Colburn house and took a deep breath to settle his pulse. The hum of waves floated on the ocean breeze from the east. A man and woman walked along the road to the west. He turned his face away before they looked at him.

He had to find the man Lydia mentioned, Frank Roberts. He put his hands on his hips and looked up at the wood-shingled roof on the Colburn house. His eyes squinted in response to the bright morning sun. It wasn't simply the mention of a creep following Lydia around that got his blood boiling, or even the thought of being robbed while he was unconscious. He blew out a breath and thought about what really upset him: his arrival was haunting Lydia.

It wasn't until he heard her voice crack that he realized how disturbing all this was for her. He had gone from a life of full-intensity, non-stop, life-or-death action to finding himself in a completely peaceful, antiquated society on an uncharted landmass. He was grateful to be here rather than dead or, worse yet, in enemy hands. He was even interested in the way of life here, but he refused to downshift mentally, knowing what he had to go back to. Yet Lydia lived in this place and it was all she knew. He thought of the devastation he had witnessed in his world and the level of mystery and danger his arrival brought into her world. She had not asked for any of this.

Guilt overwhelmed him.

She had saved a man's life; she shouldn't have her life ruined because of it. He would find a way to get back to where he belonged—in the cockpit of a fighter jet—and leave these people in peace.

He shooed a fly away from his face as he stepped into the kitchen. Everyone was gone except John, who stood in front of a cabinet by the pantry. He was gathering tools from a wide drawer and placing them into a leather shoulder bag.

"Connor." John glanced up. "I want you to come with me today. There are several areas of the chapel in need of repair, and I could use an extra pair of hands."

Connor rubbed his whisker-covered chin. He needed a shave, but first he had to find the personal locator beacon that should have been attached to his emergency equipment. "Actually, I was just making my own plans for the day." If he could get the beacon and activate it, the search party would pick up his signal. The man Lydia mentioned might have the gear, and he might have already activated the beacon. If so, Connor wanted to be there when the search party arrived.

John continued packing tools into the bag. "What were your plans?"

"I have some equipment to recover. Tell me how to find Frank Roberts. Lydia said he lives in a cabin past the bluffs. Where are the bluffs?"

"I see." John placed a hammer into the bag and then pulled a cord to close it. "I too have considered the possibility that Frank Roberts might have followed Lydia and witnessed your arrival to the Land. I have also wondered if Frank was the person who took your boots and your equipment. There are not many people in our village who would behave so despicably or that could keep silent about something as extraordinary as your arrival. However, I do not think it is wise to confront Frank at this time. If he did not see you fall from the sky or steal your equipment, you would only be involving someone who cannot be trusted."

The desperate Unified States military was strapped for equipment, so the aircraft had been outfitted with ancient surplus. Still, if the locator beacon worked, Connor could activate it before the search was discontinued. "Is there someone else I should consider? I really need to get that gear back as quickly as possible."

"Not among my people. You said there was another person with you in the aircraft. He might have survived also, or perhaps other warriors followed you here. Have you considered your people? Or even one of your nation's enemies?"

"Yes, sir. It's possible my weapons system officer survived and landed nearby. But I assure you, neither he nor any other American serviceman would have removed my boots and left me there." He considered the possibility of enemy troops. "I can't tell you if other nations are aware of your land. You and your people would know if your land had been invaded. You said no one has mentioned anything out of the ordinary in your village. Are there other villages here?"

John nodded. "There are eight villages in the Land."

"Eight? How big is this place? What is the population? What kind of communication do you have with the other villages?" Connor allowed the questions to roll out of his mouth as quickly as they came to him.

John's hands halted their work. "Traders frequently travel from Northcrest to Southpoint by boat on the river. Most deliveries come to Good Springs from the river by wagon. Often the traders deliver messages, and people frequently travel with them between the villages. If anything is out of the ordinary, we will hear about it. That is why it is important to keep your situation private. We do not want to cause panic." John lifted the bag and pulled its strap over his shoulder. Then he pointed to a bucket of nails on the floor. "Grab that and come with me." John walked past him and out the door.

There might be more to the situation than Connor first thought. He needed to recover his gear and plan his departure, but he had to do it without causing trouble for John Colburn and his family. He clutched the bucket and decided to follow John to the chapel.

He glanced at Lydia's medical cottage as if making a mental note of the one safe place in this strange land. As he and John approached the road and turned right, his eyes followed it to the left. The gravel path inclined a few degrees, cut a trail between the trees, and disappeared over a small hill.

The ocean breeze smelled salty-sweet and bent the tall grass in rippling waves along either side of the road. The trees looked similar to those in other lands he had visited in the Southern Hemisphere, except for one tree that appeared to be the most abundant here. He studied the leaves as they passed under a low-hanging branch with a silvery undertone.

Connor pointed to the unfamiliar tree. "Is that a gray leaf tree?"

John nodded. "The Land is full of them. Gray leaf lumber is easily hewn yet stronger than iron, and it does not rot as quickly other woods. One quartered log from the gray leaf tree heats a house for the entire winter. Its paper lasts for generations. And I believe you have experienced the medicinal value of tea made from its leaves."

Connor grinned as he recalled the sensation. He reached up and snagged a leaf from a branch as they passed and inspected it while walking toward the village. In shape and texture, the leaf reminded him of eucalyptus, but its silver color and distinct scent left little similarity to any tree he knew.

The road changed from gravel to brown cobblestones as they approached the center of the village. Connor dropped the leaf and stepped around a clump of horse manure as he surveyed the town. The village reminded him of something from a childhood storybook. Pretty cottages with high-sloped roofs lined both sides of the street. Flower gardens and trimmed shrubs surrounded each of the modest houses. A white chapel in the center of the village boasted a high steeple that rose into the blue sky. Across the street from the chapel stood a stone building with a tapered, wooden door. The building's windows were shuttered, piquing Connor's interest.

John climbed the steps to the entrance of the chapel and Connor followed. The front of the church seemed narrow, but as they entered the building its depth impressed him.

The high, arched ceiling echoed John's full voice as he told Connor the building's history. "My father was the overseer here before me, and his father before him. It was my grandfather's generation who extended the building as the population of Good Springs flourished and the church needed more space." He lowered the tool bag to a pew. "There are over two hundred fifty people in Good Springs now. Most of the villagers attend service each Sunday, and the chapel still accommodates them all. However, the pews get a bit wobbly over time." He put his hand at the back of a long bench seat and shook it, demonstrating as he spoke. Kneeling, he pointed beneath the wooden pew. "There are two screws here and also here on each side. Also under the support at mid-length."

John stood, opened the tool bag and drew out a few tools, some iron but many of them made from silver.

Connor picked up a silver tool and inspected it. "I've noticed a lot of your common tools are silver."

"There is a mine in Southpoint and silversmiths there. Their work is traded throughout the Land. Silver is the most plentiful metal found in the Land."

If the people here used silver for screwdrivers, what did they considered valuable? "What is the currency in the Land?"

"We barter."

"For everything?"

John nodded. "It is a system that has been equitable for our people for seven generations. We have never known dearth in the Land." He pointed to a closed door at the other end of the long chapel. "I will be in my office if you need me."

Chapter Five

Dark clouds puffed in ominous billows from the south, promising cold autumn rain. Lydia tightened her light-blue shawl around her neck and hid her hands in leather gloves. A burst of wind plucked leaves from the deciduous shrubs along the road and whirled them in the air. Red and gold specks of foliage contrasted against the dull overcast of the late-afternoon sky.

She still had a mile to walk before she was home. She usually enjoyed walking and saved her hurrying for emergencies, but the more the wind howled, the more she rushed. She wanted to be home in the shelter and the warmth near her family. Being the middle of five children gave her a lively upbringing, but once Adeline and Maggie had their own homes in another village, the Colburn house was quieter. Still, someone was always there.

Bethany was full of life and often had a friend around, and Lydia found their conversations entertaining. She enjoyed her brother's company too, but the discord between Levi and her father was proof he needed his own house—and family.

Connor would be there, but she probably would not get to speak with him much. He had gone with her father to the chapel to work every day for two and a half weeks. Her father said Connor was helping him with some of the repairs that were needed around the building. When Connor came home each evening, he sat silently at the dinner table and then retired to the guest room for the night with the door closed. John had said Connor needed time to himself and they should leave him alone. Lydia assumed Connor was trying to avoid Levi's glares, Bethany's incessant chatter, and Isabella's bizarre comments.

She couldn't blame Connor for avoiding everyone, but her curiosity was growing along with a desire to engage him in conversation. They hadn't spoken privately since the last morning he was in her cottage. Her imagination had carried her away many times since then. She wondered about his life and work and the world outside the Land. But no matter how frequently the mystery of Connor's life played across her mind, she had her own work to keep her busy—and for that she was grateful.

As Lydia passed the Fosters' property, a large dog with muddy brown fur scampered down the front steps of the farmhouse. It charged at Lydia and danced around her with its tail wagging and its tongue lapping at her boots.

"Hello, Shep!" She greeted the dog as she stopped to pet it. "Why, you are an absolute mess!" She wrinkled her nose at it.

"Shep! Shep!" Mandy called as she walked out to the road. "Leave Lydia alone, you dirty old mutt!" Mandy wore a long green coat with black buttons down the front and carried a violin in a wooden case. "Hello, Lydia! Have you come to visit me?" She greeted Lydia with a hug.

"Actually, I was just passing by."

"Excellent! I'm on my way into the village. I shall be your company." Mandy wrapped her arm around Lydia's. They walked arm-in-arm along the road just as they did when they were children. The dog followed for a short distance then turned around and lumbered back to its place on the front steps.

Mandy flashed a smile. "Levi has been here most of the week building new cabinetry for Mother. It will be beautiful when it's done, but for now the kitchen is an utter wreck. Mother says anything Levi builds is worth the process."

"I'm sure she's right." The wind whipped a few strands of Lydia's hair into her face. She immediately caught the hair and tucked it behind her ear.

"Who is this traveler your father has taken in? I asked Levi about him and, of course, he won't say a word. Mrs. Ashton told Mother she sees the traveler working at the chapel all the time— painting handrails and washing eaves."

"His name is Connor," she answered, purposefully omitting his surname. "He was injured and I helped him. Father asked him to stay as a guest." She tried to keep her tone nonchalant, but the desire to speak about the situation overwhelmed her.

"Connor? That's a masculine sort of a name." Mandy looked out across the pasture that was part of her family's sheep farm. "What do you think of him?"

"I don't know." Lydia looked too, grateful for the distracting view. The pasture rolled on as far as the eye could see. The green winter grass was beginning to sprout through what remained of the summer blades. It was a brilliant contrast against the darkening sky.

"What sort of man is he?" Mandy prodded.

Lydia didn't know how to respond. She had more questions than answers when it came to Connor. How could she tell Mandy that the man is from another land, flies machines in the air, and speaks of things she has never imagined? "He is… different."

Mandy's eyes sparkled as a smile spread across her face. "I see," she said with her tongue in her cheek. "Is he likable?"

"I'm not sure. I suppose he's cordial."

"Cordial?" Mandy snorted. "I heard he is an inch taller than Levi and has deep brown eyes, full of mystery and passion."

"Indeed? You heard that from Mrs. Ashton?" Lydia scoffed, unable to imagine the elderly woman relating those details.

"No, from Bethany. Is it true?" Mandy batted her eyelashes playfully.

Lydia laughed. "I can confirm his height and the color of his eyes. The mystery and passion are Bethany's assessment, I suppose, though she said nothing of the sort to me."

"Well, you rarely speak of romantic notions. You can't blame the girl for saving her observations for a more willing listener."

"I have no need for romantic intrigue. I'm perfectly content with—"

"Your work," Mandy interjected. "You know, it wouldn't hurt you to be intrigued from time to time."

"Ha! My life is filled with bloody bandages and midnight calls for help. I wouldn't make a normal wife." Lydia fidgeted with her gloves. "Still, that doesn't mean I have nothing to say on the subject. Bethany would do well to hear my opinion also."

Mandy chuckled. "Indeed she would. In fact, I would enjoy your opinion on the matter myself, beginning with the mysterious traveler."

"Why? Are you intrigued by him?" Lydia asked.

"Not for myself."

"Not for me either, I hope." Her cheeks warmed like she was blushing, but she could not imagine why. She turned her face into the cold wind, hoping to relieve the color before it was noticed. "I am concerned for him," she admitted. "Deeply concerned."

Lydia didn't have to look at Mandy to know she understood her seriousness and was ready to listen. "He is in great difficulty. I don't know all of the complications, but I know they are tremendous. I want to help him, but his problem is one that I cannot solve. When I think of his situation, I'm instantly caught between wanting to know more and wishing he'd never come."

Mandy's smile faded. "So this isn't a matter of romantic intrigue then?"

"Certainly not."

"I must admit I'm rather disappointed."

"Why?"

"Oh, I'm not disappointed in you but for you."

"Don't be." Lydia returned her face to the wind.

The road sloped downward as they approached the village. The rooftops of her cottage and the family home peaked above the trees in the distance. She would beat the rainstorm home, but the wind brought a cold mist that gave her a chill.

In the dark of night Connor hurried out of the gray leaf forest and to the side of the Colburns' barn. He took shelter beneath its overhanging roof. The light rain hadn't hindered his covert exploration of the land around Good Springs, but it was coming down hard now and he was officially soaked. If the rain let up soon, he could keep exploring; if not he'd give up and sneak back through the window of the Colburns' guest room.

Even the rain was challenging him and—even though he shivered in the cold wind— surrender was not an option.

He leaned against the side of the barn and pulled a sprig of leaves out of his jacket pocket while he waited on the rain. He rubbed the leaves between his fingers and smelled the oil the leaves left behind. The mysterious gray leaf tree—it provided potent medicine, incomparably efficient fuel, and lumber stronger than metal. He couldn't compare its smell to anything else on earth. Strong—like the tea Lydia made from it—but pleasant.

As he wondered what other capabilities the tree might possess, Connor was struck by his captivation by this place they called the Land. Every night under the cover of darkness, he had climbed out the guest room window and explored down the coast and into the forest, hoping to find answers to his questions. He needed to know the Land's geographic location, how he could alert the Unified States military, and how he could leave.

John had been forthcoming with what he knew: over the past seven generations the people of the Land had spread out in villages along the four hundred miles of coastline and some sixty miles inland, where a mountain range stood impassable. John had said there was no sign of human life ever having lived in the Land before the founders arrived, and to his knowledge no one there had ever encountered a person from another land—at least until Connor's arrival.

After two weeks of spending his days questioning John and his nights exploring, only two of Connor's original questions had been answered. With no communications equipment available, the only possible way for Connor to contact the military was with the locator beacon—if it made it to shore with him and if the thief who had stolen his boots also had the beacon. The ocean current around the Land churned with such fierce riptides the people dared not go near the breakers. Boats were only used on the streams and rivers inland. The only way to leave the Land would be by aircraft.

His last remaining question involved the location of the Land, and to answer that he needed the clouds to dissipate. Though he left the guest room each night with the intention of charting the stars, he usually got sidetracked exploring the forest, the bluffs, and the shore. The more he explored the Land, the less motivated he was to return to battle. His fascination with the Land soon quelled his feelings of disloyalty.

As he breathed in the scent of the wet gray leaf trees, he acknowledged there was simply no way for him to leave the Land. He glanced down at the soft wings woven into the material of his jacket. That symbol once meant everything to him—and it still should—but without a way to return to duty, he had to distance his mind from his first love: flying.

He heard someone inside the barn, so he walked beneath the eave and around to the door. He stepped inside and saw lantern light illuminating one of the horse stalls. "Hello?"

"In here." John's voice called from the back of the barn.

Connor walked through the outbuilding, which was ripe with the mixture of hay and manure. He found John in an empty stall seated on an overturned bucket, prying rivets off a saddle strap. He propped an elbow on the open stall's gate.

John glanced up briefly then continued working. "Did the rain hinder your efforts this evening?"

"For now." He mindlessly swirled the gray leaf twig between his fingers.

John pointed to a tool on a shelf beside Connor.

Connor handed the tool to him and wondered why he was in the barn in the middle of a rainy night mending a saddle. The next stall over was empty also. "Where are the horses?"

"Lydia's horse threw a shoe yesterday and she left him with the farrier. She took my horse tonight."

"Lydia is riding a horse in the rain in the middle of the night—right now?"

"Someone needed medical attention."

"It seems dangerous for her." He was surprised by John's lack of concern. "Does it bother you?"

"She is one of the strongest riders I know." John held the tool closer to the light and scratched something off its surface. "When she is called upon to treat the injured or ill, she can ride her horse through a foot of mud on the forest path at night so fast she always beats the messenger back. She is careful and independent and dedicated to her work. She left to apprentice with Doctor Ashton when she was sixteen, and I learned then the surest way to rile Lydia is to stand in the way of her work." John blew out a breath and looked at Connor. "And yes, it bothers me. But every village needs a good physician. It just happens that in our village the person called to that position is my daughter."

Connor shifted his weight and leaned his shoulder against the rough stable wall. Though he had quickly sized up everyone in the family when he first entered the Colburn household, he assumed he would not be around long enough to get involved personally. But like the Land, he found the Colburn family too fascinating to disregard. The multi-generational mix of personalities fit together in a way that felt both seamless and polarized. There was the blind great-aunt who remained disconnected, yet forcibly involved; the adult son desperate to protect the home he was trying to leave; the baby of the family, awkward in her newly adult body but too energized to sit still long enough to know it; and the smart, independent physician who had been emancipated only to her father's back yard. They all had a place in the family, but their collective significance was empowered by John's leadership.

John was also the village's overseer—not simply by right of birth but by natural inclination. He exuded a fatherly presence that

Connor—having never known his father—craved. Connor found himself absorbing John's wisdom and strength, and he also desired the overseer's approval.

"The rain will not end tonight." John stood from the overturned bucket and snapped the mended saddle strap a few times between his hands, testing the strength of his work. "It will continue at least another day."

Water rhythmically pelted the roof of the barn. Though Connor thrived with a challenge, even he knew when to resign. "Yeah, I guess I'll go back to the house." He stepped away from the stall and tapped his knuckles on the splintered gate. "Good night, John."

Lieutenant Justin Mercer leaned his back against a frigid, steel wall. He had already waited an hour in the dark corridor below the flight deck of the aircraft carrier. His legs begged him to sit on the cold floor, but he was determined to show his superiors he was physically recovered from the crash and fit for duty.

He stood at attention when the conference room door opened. The rear admiral and other officers walked out. They passed without acknowledging him.

"Lieutenant Mercer," a man called from inside the room as an ensign held the door open.

Mercer gave a nod of recognition to the ensign and walked to a laminate conference table. Commander Jenkins and a civilian psychiatrist were sitting at the table.

Mercer's commanding officer looked at him. "Lieutenant, this is Deborah Davis. She is a civilian psychiatrist from Washington who is aboard for research purposes, but she has offered to help you through this situation."

The woman motioned to the chair across from her. "Have a seat, Justin." She wore wire-rimmed glasses and had her hair pulled tightly in a low bun. "I have gone over your medical files and I'm familiar with the crash." She peered over her glasses at him and then swiped her finger across a tablet's touchscreen. "This says you were stranded at sea for thirty-six hours before the rescue. Those are the hours we are going to focus on together."

Mercer wasn't going to let them do this to him again. He ignored the psychiatrist and glared at his superior officer. "Commander, we've been over this several times. I know what I saw. There was land. I was completely alert during the descent. Lieutenant Bradshaw is there on that land. I saw him drift toward it."

"Lieutenant Mercer, we have searched extensively for Lieutenant Bradshaw and for the land you reported seeing. There is nothing out there but ocean for hundreds of miles."

"But Commander, we know the South Atlantic Anomaly disrupted the aircraft's readings and might have caused the malfunction that engaged the ejection system. Maybe the radiation could be interfering with the readings from the platform. There is land out there. I just know it."

Jenkins sighed and leaned back in his seat. "Lieutenant, I understand the trauma you suffered from the crash. I expected you to be confused and frustrated after such an experience, but we are too strapped for resources to placate one grieving officer any further. We have recovered most of the aircraft and even parts of the ejection equipment. There is no way Lieutenant Bradshaw survived. He has been declared dead." Jenkins paused when Mercer dropped his head into his hands. "We left a monitoring unit at the rescue site. We have four stations globally that will continue surveillance in the area via satellite for any atmospheric irregularities. Believe me, the Unified States government wants to find the land you reported. But unless Lieutenant Bradshaw's personal locator beacon is activated in the next few hours, we have to move on. You have to move on."

Jenkins stood and motioned to the psychiatrist. "Ms. Davis is here to help you. We need you back in the cockpit, Lieutenant."

Mercer didn't stand when his commanding officer left the room. The psychiatrist began asking questions about his feelings and his memories after the crash. His thoughts drowned out her voice in his head. All he could think of was the green of the trees and the clear, blue waterways of the land he saw from above. During the two-mile descent under the parachute, he had focused on that land. What he saw was real. Bradshaw was there. He had to do something to get back to that land. He would go to the admiral himself if he had to. He would make sure they found Bradshaw and that beautiful land.

Lydia inhaled the cool air and delighted in the dry atmosphere cleansed by two days of rain. The street's cobblestones gleamed as she walked from her family's home at the edge of the village to the library. The chromatic drama of the changing landscape caught her eye as she shifted a stack of books held in the crook of her arm.

The oranges and reds of the changing leaves seemed to wave to the unflinching evergreens. The gray leaf trees stood thick and silvery, fully equipped to keep their foliage through the coming winter.

The old door to the library was narrow and made of heavy planks salvaged from the ship that brought the founders to the Land. Lydia turned the doorknob and pushed it open. The musty room was dark, save for the light of an oil lamp. Connor was sitting on a wooden stool in front of the tall study table, reading a journal written by one of the founders.

He glanced up at her. "Hi, Doc." He looked back at his book.

"Um, hi," Lydia replied using his vernacular. She walked to the table and placed her books opposite Connor, then she moved around the room, opening the shutters on each window. Sunlight poured into the one-room library. "I did not expect to see you here," she said.

"Your dad suggested it. He said the pressman is away traveling."

"Yes, I know." She wasn't there for the printing press, but she was pleased to hear Connor had gained some knowledge of village life. "Why did my father suggest you come to our library?"

"He told me all the knowledge of the Land is here in these journals." He motioned to the shelves. "This collection of information is absolutely remarkable. To think, only eight families founded this entire society. The founders really seemed to have the perfect blend of profession, artistry, and genius. It blows my mind how each person wrote all the knowledge of each profession or craft or life wisdom for future generations. And each generation has done the same ever since. This is really an extraordinary culture you have here, Doc."

"You have the knowledge to fly machines in the sky and yet you find us fascinating?"

He grinned. "Mind blowing."

"So you said." She chuckled at the image given by his figure of speech. "I'm pleased you are so captivated by our society." She walked back to the table and sat on a stool across from him. "I love the Land, but I have nothing modern to compare it to. What are you reading now?"

He lifted the journal to show her the cover. "I'm currently reading your ancestor's theology notes." It was one of her great-great-grandfather's journals. He had been the overseer of Good Springs over one hundred years ago and had written prolifically on his study of the Bible.

"Once again, you have surprised me, Connor." She opened her journal and flipped through her medical notes, but was thinking about his situation. "What are you hoping to find in all of these volumes?"

He glanced up from his reading and squinted as if his eyes had not yet adjusted to the crisp light that flooded through the clear glass windows behind her. "I'm just looking for some answers."

She walked to the shelf where she would find the medical volumes she intended to study. One was missing. She looked back at Connor, and he was holding it up. "Henry Ashton, Senior, Medical Notations, Nineteen Fifty-four," he read the title aloud.

"Yes, thank you." She took the journal and scanned the other books stacked on the table beside him. He had selected journals covering sundry topics. "You have a wide variety of interests. Do you plan to give a lecture on one of these subjects at the party tonight?"

"What party?"

"The Fosters' barn party. I was only joking about the lecture, of course."

He lifted a palm. "A barn party?"

"Yes, the Foster family owns a large sheep farm, and they have a celebration for the village every autumn. There will be music and dancing and food. Many of the village families have parties in the autumn. It's how we celebrate abundant harvests and productive herds. The Fosters' party is by far the grandest. I'm sure you'll enjoy it."

"Oh, I'm not going."

"You must."

He looked amused. "I appreciate the invitation, but I'm not going."

She tried to reconcile his breach of custom. "Do they not have parties in your land?"

"Yes, we have parties."

"Perhaps you don't understand our ways. Since you are a guest in my father's home, you must attend the events my father attends. So unless you wish to dishonor my father, you will go to the party." She sat again at the study table and tucked her skirt around her legs. It was chilly in the library, which was intentionally without a fireplace.

"I've worked with your dad every day for nearly three weeks. I'm beginning to consider the overseer not just a leader to be respected but also a friend. The last thing I want to do is dishonor your dad." He looked straight at Lydia, and though neither of them had moved an inch, she felt the space between them decrease.

"Then you will go with us," Lydia confirmed.

"Sure." He crossed his arms over his chest. "I would like to be briefed before the mission."

"What do you mean?"

"Tell me what to expect. I don't want to draw any attention to myself or to the fact I am your society's first foreigner. What do I wear? When do we leave? Should I bow to the host?"

"Oh, please don't bow to anyone! You are right: you'd draw attention to yourself if you did such a thing!" Lydia chuckled. "We will leave before sunset. The Fosters' farm is not too far to walk, but Aunt Isabella will be with us, so Father will drive the wagon. Our household is to arrive together. I'm sure Father will lend you clothes, though nothing fancy is required. I suggest you speak as little as possible, since you use some words that are strange to us. However, you should be friendly when you are spoken to." She imagined the many people who would want to meet the overseer's guest. "I'll do my best to deflect any questions regarding your origin so you aren't tempted to lie."

"I'd appreciate that." He leaned forward on his elbows. "You mentioned music and dancing. Is that for our entertainment or our participation?"

"Both. There will be excellent musicians and they will likely play a range of tunes—some are for listening and some are for dancing. No one is expected to dance every dance, but everyone must dance at least once to show a good spirit."

"I'm sure I can handle that." Connor flashed a confident grin. It was the same grin her brother had referred to as infuriating. She was beginning to find his confidence charming.

She returned her eyes to her book even though he was still looking at her. She told herself the cultural curiosity was mutual, but she found it difficult to focus on the words she read until she felt him look away.

Chapter Six

Music drifted on the wind as Connor rode with the Colburns along the road to the Fosters' sheep farm. The moment the horses pulled the wagon onto the Foster property, Bethany leapt from the back, landed on her feet, and raced through the yard. Lydia looked like she was going to scold Bethany, but she didn't have a chance. Bethany ran past picnic tables and into a massive barn.

Levi jumped from the side of the wagon and walked to the front, where he helped Isabella down from the bench seat. He guided the elderly blind woman through the grass and to the tables.

Connor offered his hand to help Lydia down from the wagon. He walked beside her toward the crowd. "What do we do first?" he asked Lydia as he took in the scene. Rows of picnic tables lined the yard between a farmhouse and a barn big enough to park a jumbo jet in.

Levi was helping Isabella to a table where a group of older women sat. He moved gently with his aunt, and she laughed at whatever he said to her. After he made Isabella comfortable, he walked to Lydia and Connor.

"First we greet the hosts," Lydia whispered to Connor between greeting other people. "I will introduce you to Samuel and Roseanna Foster. Then we can go into the barn, or we can stay out here until dinner is announced, but we cannot sit down until all of the elderly have chosen their seats."

"Fair enough."

As they walked closer to the tables, the smell of roasted meat filled the air. It made Connor's stomach growl. Several people waited in a line to greet the hosts. Levi met him and Lydia at the back of the line and positioned himself between them. He pretended not to care and watched the activity inside the massive barn.

The barn's two immense doors were rolled open, and the light from dozens of hanging lanterns streamed out with the music. A drummer, a guitar player, and a violinist played a folk song. Some people were already dancing. Boots stomped the hay-strewn floor, and skirts twirled vibrantly.

When introductions were made, Connor smiled at the women and shook the men's hands. He tried to use only the words they used if the conversation required more than a hello. It was pleasant to be among a crowd, even if it wasn't his crowd.

The last wagon drove up as the light of the sun faded. Connor watched Levi in disbelief. Levi was social, even jovial, with people, moving from one conversation to the next, and people approached him as if he was well liked. It was a stark contrast to the surly, aggressive man Connor had experienced. John wove through the crowd and around the tables, being greeted by everyone, proving the father-son resemblance.

Folk music streamed from the barn. When the song ended, the smiling people emerged from the barn. They gathered around the tables and filled the empty seats.

Connor watched Lydia for his next cue. She was standing with a young couple and admired their baby while the mother appeared to be describing a rash on the child. John walked past him and gave him a hearty pat on the back like they were old pals. "Find a seat, son. We are about to say the blessing."

"Come on," Levi mumbled as he passed. His selective social smile was gone. "Sit over here."

Connor followed Levi to a table on the outskirts of the crowd. A young man seated at the table jumped up when he saw Connor. "You're Connor, the traveler. I'm Everett Foster. Bethany told us about you."

Connor glanced at Levi, wondering what Bethany had told them. Levi looked away, evidencing his desire was to protect the people from Connor and not the other way around.

"Ignore my little brother," a smooth, feminine voice cooed.

A beautiful woman tossed a fistful of red curls over her shoulder. She offered her delicate hand to Connor with her fingertips pointing down. "I'm Mandy Foster. Welcome to our farm."

He hadn't yet witnessed any women shaking men's hands, so he wasn't sure if he would be breaking some primitive rule if he touched her. He didn't have to worry long. Everett bounced between them wanting Connor's attention. "It's my home, too!" he said to his older sister. "Welcome to my home! I'll sit by you while we eat. I have to eat quickly because I have to play guitar again soon. Did you hear me playing? If not, don't worry. You'll be able hear me better on the next song. We always save the new wood instruments for after dinner. Some travelers haven't heard a guitar or violin made of new wood. Have you?"

"No." Connor uttered one syllable and was relieved when Lydia joined their table.

Mandy and Everett flanked Connor on the long bench seat. Levi sat across from them between Lydia and Bethany. While they ate Connor tried to occupy himself with his food, but he had become a novelty to the Foster siblings. He would take a bite and look to Lydia if asked something he should not answer, and she would change the subject politely and swiftly.

Everett and Bethany made a comedic pair and kept the conversation youthful. Levi glared at Connor often, but then his gaze would drift to Mandy. Mandy sent Lydia encrypted facial expressions. Connor would have found it all amusing, but Lydia looked uncomfortable.

Mrs. Foster dashed by. "Amanda! Everett!" she summoned as she passed. "It's time to get back in there. Start by playing something lively, would you? Your father and I will start the dancing, and I feel like a jig!" She picked up her layered skirt to show her polished ankle boots and then scurried into the barn.

Everett jumped up and followed, play-wrestling another teenaged boy on his way. Mandy smiled at Connor and excused herself before she left the table. She sauntered between the other tables, assured many eyes were on her. Connor scanned the crowd and confirmed she was correct.

After a moment, music surged from the barn. The instruments sounded different. It must be the new wood that Everett mentioned. The violin was full and bright, and each note resonated clearer and more robust than any he'd ever heard. It was loud but didn't hurt the ear. The guitars began to play next, and then a drum. The fullness of the sound amazed him, considering there was no electrical amplification.

Connor stood and followed the crowd inside with Lydia and Levi right behind him. The audience encircled the musicians and dancers. Children clambered to the top of haystacks and sat perched above the crowd. Several teenagers were assembled in the hayloft looking down at the party. Some people in the crowd were keeping the beat by shaking little gourds that had been hollowed out and filled with seeds. Lydia smiled and clapped while she watched the dancers. Mr. and Mrs. Foster were especially lively, and dozens of couples had already joined them on the dance floor.

Connor took it all in and didn't attempt to conceal his amusement.

After the jig, the man playing the drum hit it slowly with his hand to count off a beat. Some of the dancers stayed with their partners, and some walked away. A few of them picked new dance partners. Mrs. Foster walked over to John and held out her hand, inviting him to dance. John accepted her hand and danced with her. They looked like comfortable, old friends. Mr. Foster danced with another woman. The dancers embraced but kept distance between their bodies.

Every tune was a different style, and the dancers appeared to know the steps from memory, but nothing Connor recognized. He was obligated to dance once, and he dearly hoped it wouldn't have to be a jig.

"Hello, Miss Colburn," a young girl said as she passed Lydia.

"Hello, Miss McIntosh," Lydia replied and smiled at the girl.

It got Connor's attention. After the girl passed, he turned to Lydia. "With only eight last names in the whole place, doesn't the miss and missus business get a little confusing?"

"We are simply being polite." Then she chuckled. "I suppose it could get confusing for an outsider."

"Right, because you are Miss Colburn and your elderly aunt is also Miss Colburn."

"And the woman over there in the purple dress—" Lydia pointed covertly to a young lady in the crowd, "—is also Miss Colburn."

"A cousin?" Connor asked.

"Fourth or fifth, I think."

"Oh good, then Levi can marry her," he joked, remembering the rule of lineage John told him about when he was still in Lydia's cottage. Lydia laughed and it pleased him. Finally, a woman liked his humor—and such a pretty and smart woman at that. She tried to appear to be all business, but she relaxed when he joked.

"She would probably be thrilled with the notion. However, Levi is unlikely to—" Lydia froze.

Connor followed her line of sight to the door. A man with a thick mustache and beady black eyes walked into the barn. He was a head shorter than most of the other men. He glowered at Connor.

Lydia leaned in. "Have you two met?"

Frank Roberts snapped his eyes away. He climbed the stairs to the loft where a group of teenagers lounged and sat in the shadows.

Connor only took his eyes off him long enough to glance over at Levi, who was also watching Frank. Levi's expression was a raw mixture of disgust and anger. For once they had something in common.

"Connor?"

"Huh?" After a moment he broke his stare and returned his focus to Lydia. "I'm sorry. What did you say?"

She moved closer. "I asked if you and Frank have met."

"Not officially. But you were right about the boots." As soon as he said the words he regretted it.

She pressed a palm to her stomach and drew a short breath.

He wished there was something he could do to divert her attention, and he glanced at the stage. The song ended and all of the musicians—except Mandy—put down their instruments. The dancers fanned their sweaty faces as they dispersed. Many of them went outside to the cooler air; some sat on benches around the outskirts of the barn. Mandy stood with her bow held high above the beautiful new wood violin. The crowd hushed and waited.

When the room was silent, she began to play. Slowly and sweetly the notes filled the air. She played a few measures before anyone went forward to dance, and then only a few dancers began the slow and ancient movements.

Connor recognized the waltz and was thankful that when he was a kid his grandmother taught him to lead the rotating box steps in her living room. He held out his hand to Lydia. She didn't move.

"You said I have to dance once to show a good spirit." He kept his voice quiet. "I know this one." He took her hand and led her onto the dance floor without giving her a chance to protest. Her blank expression revealed neither disdain nor delight.

He took it as a challenge and confidently placed one hand in the middle of her back. She lightly touched his shoulder and kept her elbow up. As he held her hand in his and began the steps, she turned her face away. He was less focused on form and glanced from the awestruck villagers to her father, her brother, the beautiful violinist, the creep in the hayloft. They were all watching him and Lydia.

Lydia moved stiffly and didn't want to be led. She probably wanted to stay focused for both of them in case he didn't know what to do. He was in her world and she'd rescued him, but he no longer needed her help. He was capable of things she couldn't imagine, and he wanted her to know it.

As they continued turning in rhythmic procession across the floor, Lydia's eyes closed. Maybe she would let the full, melodic sound of the music sooth her anxiety. Her hand loosened its grip and he was leading. She was letting him. He was confident she wouldn't regret it.

As Mandy let the last notes ring out, Lydia opened her eyes and gazed at him. He stopped moving but kept their hands in place for a moment longer than the other dancers. He couldn't read her expression. Before he formed a thought, a man burst through the crowd at the door.

"Lydia! Lydia Colburn! Come quick!" the man shouted.

She turned and dashed through the parting crowd to the man at the door. He was panting as he explained some horrific incident. She followed him to his wagon and climbed aboard. Connor rushed to follow. As he passed John and Levi he said, "I'm going with her."

"No!" Levi declared as he stuck his hand into Connor's chest. "You are not!"

Levi was asking for a fight. No matter how good it would feel to release some of his tension, Connor preferred taking a punch from Levi to upsetting Lydia by fighting with her petulant brother.

John stepped between them. Levi removed his hand from Connor's chest and stomped away.

The musicians began to play another song, and John inclined his head toward Connor. "I left something on the bed in the guest room. I thought it might help in your efforts. Isabella will need me to take her home soon. Perhaps this would be a good time for you to leave."

Connor nodded to John and left the barn. He passed the tables outside without making eye contact with anyone and walked through the Fosters' yard to the road. The sandy gravel crunched under his feet as he stepped onto the road and began the mile walk back to the Colburn property.

The cool night air felt good after being in the stuffy barn with all the villagers. He slid his hands into his pockets and breathed in the scent of the gray leaf trees. It mixed with the ocean breeze and had an intoxicating effect he hoped he would never get used to.

As he left the road and walked onto the Colburn property, a wagon in front of Lydia's cottage caught his eye. Light sifted through her gauzy curtains. She was in her office with the patient. He wanted to check on her, but she probably wouldn't appreciate the interruption. She was a professional no matter how rudimentary their society seemed to him.

He opened the back door of the main house and walked into the kitchen. The house was dark and empty; it felt weird to be there alone. He lit the oil lantern on the kitchen table and left it there for John and Isabella. He walked through the living room, around the staircase and down the darkened hallway to the guest room.

The moonlight that came through the sash window was faint but sufficient for him to see a bundle on the bed. Whatever John had left him was wrapped in felt and tied with a leather cord.

He untied the cord and unfurled the felt cover to find an ancient mariner's telescope. Its three brass sections were nestled on a collapsed wooden tripod. It must have come from the ship that brought the founders to the Land. Overwhelmed by John's gracious gesture, Connor knelt by the bed and assembled the telescope.

After midnight, Lydia allowed her patient to go home. Though it only took a few stitches to close up the two wounded fingers the patient had accidentally sliced to the bone with a butcher's knife, Lydia was not sure how much blood had been lost. The way the patient's husband told it, their entire kitchen was splattered red by time he got her to settle down. The patient insisted half of that blood belonged to the chicken she slaughtered for their dinner.

Lydia kicked off her shoes and sighed, finally alone in her cottage. She made the last of her notes in her medical record for the incident and set her pen back in its silver holder. As she began to put out her lamp, Lydia remembered the pile of bloodied rags on the tray beside the patient cot. She had forgotten to take them to the fire pit. Doctor Ashton had taught her that what little they knew about blood assured them anything it touched must be destroyed or sanitized.

She gathered the rags into a paper bag, pulled her shoes back on her feet, and grabbed a match.

The clear night sky allowed the gibbous moon to light her path, but it was still too dark for her comfort as she walked into the shadow cast by the Colburn house. The thought of seeing Frank earlier in the evening made her shudder. Maybe she shouldn't walk alone in the dark, but the chore had to be done. She focused her vision into the distance and hurried her pace.

She turned the corner at the side of her cottage and headed for the fire pit behind the barn. As she stepped around a bush, she was suddenly trapped, her whole body seized by someone. She sucked in a breath to scream, but he put his hand over her mouth. Immobilized by fear, she widened her eyes and tried to think.

"Shhh! Shh! Don't scream! Doc, it's me," he whispered. "It's Connor. Please don't scream. You're okay."

She caught her breath. He still had his hand over her mouth. Her heart raced violently.

"Please, don't scream. Are you going to scream?"

She shook her head, and he slowly removed his hand from her mouth. She spun on her heel. "What has gotten into you?"

"Shh! Keep your voice down!"

She tried to gain her composure, but her pulse had yet to stabilize. "You scared me half to death!"

"Hey, you scared me just as much as I scared you."

"I highly doubt that." Fuming, she picked up the paper bag she'd dropped in the commotion. "What are you doing stalking about in the middle of the night?"

"Looking at the stars. What are you doing out here?"

"I have to burn bloody rags." She held up the bag as she marched to the fire pit.

He followed her across the moonlit yard. "Was your patient a bleeder?"

She didn't have to look at him to know he was smiling. Not amused, she hiked through the wet grass across the yard. "I don't talk about my patients," she whispered as she turned behind the barn.

Connor stayed in the shadow of the barn, but she stepped through the gravel to the fire pit. She struck the match and lit the paper bag before throwing it into the stone basin. Satisfied it was burning, she turned to him. "Why are you really out here?"

"I'm looking at the stars."

The simplicity of his answer was intentional. There was more to it than stargazing. She straightened her shawl and wrapped it around her arms. She was cold and tired but couldn't resist the opportunity to probe. "What are you hoping to find in the stars?"

"Maybe some answers."

"Just as you said in the library." She shook her head in disappointment and started to walk away. Overwhelmed with the urge to become indignant, she stopped and peered at him through the dark. "I know your situation, Connor. I might not know the details of your technology and the abilities it gives you. But it's only because of a lack of information and not a lack of intelligence, I assure you."

His confident half-smile was barely visible in the moonlight, but his eyes shone with delight. "I know you're intelligent, Doc. And you're right: you could easily learn anything I taught you. Do you really want information?"

"Of course."

"Fine. Come with me."

Connor took Lydia's arm and led her to the back of the Colburn property, where a path directed them through the edge of the forest and out to the bluffs. After walking along the path through a patch of forest, they came to the rocky edge of a cliff overlooking the sea. There high above the ocean was the old telescope he'd set up and pointed into the clear night sky.

He pointed at it. "Your dad let me borrow it."

Lydia's jaw dropped and a smile lit her eyes. "This was my great-grandfather's telescope. I haven't seen it in years. May I?" She touched the eyepiece.

"Of course." He waited as she looked through the telescope. She instantly pulled away in surprise. "I've tweaked it," he explained.

She was already looking back through the eyepiece again. "If that means you've made some small adjustments which greatly improved its performance then yes, you have tweaked it." She continued to gaze through the telescope. "This is incredible, Connor. I don't know what all I'm looking at, but it's spectacular."

After a moment, she pulled her face away from the telescope but kept her hand on it. "So all these nights I thought you were locked away in your room being unsociable. Is this what you have really been doing?"

"I only got the telescope tonight."

"And what were you up to all the other nights?" She looked back through the eyepiece once more.

The breeze blew up the bluffs from the ocean below and stirred the chill in the air. He put his hands in his pockets to keep them warm. "At first I was going out at night to get the lay of the land. I wanted to know where I was, and I wanted to look for a way to return to my people."

"Did you find a way?" She didn't sound like she was sure she wanted the answer.

He rocked back on his heels and hoped he was right about her. "Nope. I found my boots, though."

"So you said." She pointed at his feet, which were still cramped into the pair of borrowed shoes. "Where are they?"

"In Frank's cabin."

She stepped back from the telescope and wrapped her arms in her shawl, sending a frightened glance behind them into the forest. "I didn't think of him. Just now, I mean. Coming out here with you, I completely forgot about him."

Though he'd never let on, he was glad to hear her say it. "I know where he is, Doc. You are safe with me." He turned the telescope and pointed it at a cabin further down the bluffs. "Look," he directed.

Lydia stepped to the telescope and looked. She popped her head up as if trying to see without it and then looked again through the eyepiece. "I had no idea you could see his cabin from up here, or that you could use this to peer into someone's window. He has no curtain. His lamp is still lit this late at night. Oh, there he is!" She put her hand over her smiling mouth. "I'm not sure we should be doing this. Can he see us?" She continued to gawk at the man who usually gawked at her.

"No. We're in the shadows and too far away. I've seen him parade around in there wearing my boots. No sign of the other equipment, though."

"Think no more of the boots. I have arranged for a shoemaker to take your measurements at the market tomorrow."

"How many gutters will I have to clean out to pay for that?"

Lydia chuckled. "None. I paid for it in stitches this evening." She pulled away from the telescope. "However, I can't replace your parachute." She looked pensive then asked, "Do you need the parachute to leave?"

"I wouldn't get very far!" He laughed. He loved her innocence. He loved the innocent feel of the whole place.

During his nights of reconnaissance and his days of conversations, he had learned there was no way for him to leave the Land. He didn't want to leave anyway. Enough time had passed that any search for him by the military would have been called off. Alerting anyone to his whereabouts could alert everyone, and that would risk an invasion of the Land. He refused to be the cause of that.

His personal mission had changed from escaping from the Land to trying to protect it. How could he tell Lydia that without telling her what he needed to protect the Land from? Plus, he'd promised her father to keep silent about the condition of the world. He took a step closer to her. "I don't need the parachute, but there were other items that could cause harm to a person if he didn't know how to use them."

He didn't know how much of the ejection seat's gear had made it to the Land. He didn't care if Frank shot off a flare and it burned his cabin to the ground. He didn't care if Frank got a compass or a shiny new knife to play with. Only one item could cause a problem if Frank had unknowingly activated it.

"There was a device attached to the equipment I had when I landed. It's very important I find it."

"What sort of device?" Lydia asked.

"It's a beacon."

"Of light?"

"No, a personal locator beacon. It sends out an electronic signal, which is designed to give rescuers my location." He didn't want to worry her with all of the possibilities he had to consider. "I know you're smart and can understand anything I explain. I also know you would try to solve any problem I present. I have to spare you that burden. Your dad knows the details of the possible dangers. I won't do anything he's against."

She stepped away from the telescope. "I appreciate your desire to spare me the details. I'll do my best to leave the speculation and the worry to you and Father. However, my fascination with your work won't allow me to rest." She pointed to the telescope. "When I look up through this I see the moon and stars and celestial wonders I can't explain. My people have some knowledge of these things, but you have more. Yes, I'm concerned more warriors might fall from the sky and they might not all possess your friendly nature. But I'm more curious as to what you see when you look through this." Her voice was soft and settled when she spoke. "Does the night sky appear the same from here as it does from your land? Do you use the stars to navigate your aircraft like sailors do their ships? Do you see other warriors' flying machines up there? Tell me, Connor, what do you see?"

She'd figured out far more than he gave her credit for. "I see a sky that looks totally different from the way it does from anywhere else on earth. In fact, I believe there is some type of atmospheric phenomenon over the Land. From here the stars appear to be spread wide, but they aren't actually positioned where they appear to be. From here it's like I'm viewing them with a fish-eye lens. Also, when I look up I should see man-made satellites and aircraft." He stopped to choose his words carefully. "There is a lot of activity in the sky all over the world. I see none of that from here. During the daytime, many aircraft leave visible contrails in the sky—long streaks of cloud, depending on atmospheric conditions. I haven't seen a single contrail since I came to the Land. I doubt it's due to a lack of air traffic. And the moon isn't oval—it's round."

"What do you think all this means?"

"The atmosphere over this location is somehow skewing our vision of the sky. If I'm right, the view from above could also be skewed through the phenomenon. The Land would appear minuscule—possibly undetectable. This might be why the Land can't be seen by our technology. On an image taken from outer space it appears there is only ocean here."

"What about ships on the sea? Could they see the Land if they passed by?"

Connor shrugged. "I'm not sure. I don't know how far this atmospheric phenomenon extends. If it's shaped like a bubble, then it's possible that passing vessels wouldn't see the Land. Modern ships navigate with equipment that must frequently adjust readings for magnetic and oceanic currents, so people might have been sailing past the Land for centuries without knowing anything was amiss. From what I read in the founders' journals in your library, they didn't see the Land until they ran aground here."

"That's true," Lydia confirmed. "The founders had been at sea nearly four months and were desperate for land. They believed God provided this place for them. You said yourself you didn't know how you came to our shore. Perhaps it is as simple as Providence."

"Perhaps. The people here have an advantage. See, after the time in history when your founders left America, people there developed ways to generate and send electricity into every home. There have been so many inventions since then that our civilization is now based on the constant use of electricity. Every populated area in the world gives off light that can be seen from space. All the electronic gadgets also emit electric signals. We have computers that store and send information, and our world is buzzing with these signals. We've launched equipment into outer space that monitors everything happening on earth—everything except here in your land. There is electronic silence here. This entire chunk of land is completely off grid. As long as your people don't learn how to generate electricity or produce radio waves or start tinkering with electronics, I think the Land could remain undetected. And… as long as I can get that beacon back from Frank before he activates it."

Lydia was quiet. Connor turned to the telescope and began to disassemble it. He removed it from its tripod stand and wrapped its sections carefully in the felt cloth just as he'd found it. Then he loosened the hinges on the wooden stand and collapsed its legs.

He nestled the bundle in the crook of his arm and offered the other arm to Lydia. She slipped her hand beneath his elbow and glanced back in the direction of Frank's cabin before they walked the path to her family's property.

As they left the forest path and stepped through the short grass behind the barn, Lydia stayed close to him, and he liked it. She hadn't said a word the entire walk. Though he enjoyed her voice, he was also enjoying the silence.

When they got close to the cottage, she whispered, "Connor?"

"Yes?"

"There are experiments."

"What do you mean?"

"With electricity. I've heard of such things. Not in Good Springs, but in other villages."

Connor kept walking. He was focused on leading them through the dark shadow of the Colburn house and back to her door safely. He and John had already discussed electronics and Connor's theory of how to keep the Land undetected. John hadn't mentioned any experiments with electricity in the Land. What would Lydia know that the overseer would not?

When they reached her door, he stopped and looked at her. "Are you sure? Your dad said he knew nothing of electricity in the Land."

"Yes, I am quite sure." She kept her voice quiet. "Three years ago I traveled to every village in the Land. It was during my medical training. There was a man in Northcrest whom I distinctly remember discussing the electric motor he planned to build."

Connor's concern grew as she spoke, but he tried to appear unfazed. "How far away is Northcrest?"

"A week's journey."

"On foot?"

"Horseback. Of course, it's in the opposite direction of Stonehill, and there was an inventor there who also spoke of electricity."

He drew a deep breath and kept his visage neutral despite the possibilities she had mentioned. He opened the cottage door and checked inside the medical office. "We can talk to your dad about it in the morning."

Lydia nodded then walked inside her cottage. "Good night, Connor."

Connor pointed at the door before he closed it. "Does this lock?"

"Yes."

"Lock it."

Chapter Seven

Sleep evaded Lydia while troubled thoughts churned in her mind and prompted an early rise. Though Connor had acted unconcerned about the electrical experiments she mentioned, the notion of anyone producing signals that could jeopardize the safety of the Land worried her. Her life was devoted to healing the individual, but the more she considered the implications of the Land being invaded, the more trivial her work felt. Instead of resting during the night, her anxious mind devised a plan of action, making the new concern a priority. By dawn, she decided she should travel to the other villages and warn the inventors of the hazardous potential of their designs.

She yawned as she stood at the kitchen sink and filled a kettle. Intending to speak to her father about the matter before the rest of the household came to breakfast, she tried not to make any noise that would wake the others. She set the kettle on the stove as quietly as possible, but her tired hand caused the kettle to clank against the stove. She left it there to boil and carried a bread basket to the table as her father walked into the kitchen. Eager to discuss Connor's theory of the Land and her plan to save it from being detected, she drew a breath to speak but promptly closed her mouth when Bethany trotted into the room.

"Good morning, Father. Good morning, Lydia," Bethany chirped. "The party was splendid last night, wasn't it?" She twirled once before she sat in her chair at the table. Then she selected a muffin from the bread basket and picked a berry from its top. "Oh, Lydia! Your waltz was mentioned throughout the evening. All the girls said if they were you they would be fully intrigued by Connor."

"Bethany!" Lydia huffed, her unrested nerves intolerant of her sister's meddling.

"Not to worry, dear sister. I told them you've never been intrigued in your life." Bethany popped a berry in her mouth and smiled in a way that rankled Lydia's already irritated mood.

"You keep that to yourself!" she snapped, surprising even herself.

John cleared his throat with forced volume. Both girls looked at their father and knew what he meant. As John carried the coffeepot to the table, he changed the subject. "Bethany, will you be working at the pottery yard all day?"

"Yes, Father." She ate the last bite of muffin and chased it down with half a glass of milk while walking to the sink. Bethany gave her father a loud kiss on his bearded cheek and flashed Lydia a pouty glare as she headed out the door.

Lydia wanted to speak with her father before anyone else came to the kitchen. As John poured the steaming coffee into his cup, she sat beside him at the table. He took a muffin and offered her the bread basket. She held up her hand. "I must speak with you about something."

"You seem agitated this morning." John tilted his head. "Is this about something that happened last night?"

Her father trusted her, but still she decided to avoid mentioning her evening of stargazing. Preparing to speak, she willed herself to level her voice and demonstrate the control that was expected of the village physician. "Connor said he has discussed the condition of the outside world with you."

John set the bread basket on the table and then leaned back in his chair while brushing his fingertips together. He raised one eyebrow at her. "What did he tell you?"

"He said he believes the Land is undetectable to the technology other nations use partially because we don't have electricity here. If we did invent ways to generate electrical signals, the Land's existence might be detected by other nations. He was kind not to burden me with the details, but it seems we should try to remain hidden from the outside world."

"Yes, it would seem that way. He asked me if I knew anything of electricity, but I knew nothing of the sort." John picked up his coffee cup and sipped once. "Do you know of any such inventions in the Land?"

"I do, Father. Not here in Good Springs, but when I was traveling. There was a man in Stonehill who came into the medical office there. As he was being treated, he spoke of his inventions. He told us about being inspired by the lightning and how he was trying to create electric currents. I looked through my notes last night. The man's name was Jeremiah."

John continued sipping the hot coffee. His eyes narrowed in concentration as he listened to her.

"And in Northcrest after the church service one Sunday, a man told Doctor Ashton and me about his plan to build an electric motor. He said his grandfather had written that his grandfather told him about an electric motor he saw as a boy in America. I don't remember his name, and I can't ask Doctor Ashton. He only wakes long enough to eat. He might not remember even if I asked him." The thought of Doctor Ashton's condition brought a wave of grief. Lydia looked down at her hands. "I should go and warn those men not to continue their experiments."

John reached out and put his hand on top of hers. "I do not like to see you burdened like this. We will let Connor know about these mentions of electric experiments, but this matter is not for you to fret over. You have your own responsibilities. This village needs you to focus on your work." She looked at him then, and his lips curved in a gentle smile when her eyes met his. "It might seem like an accident to him, but I believe Connor landed here for a purpose. Since he understands these matters of technology, we will allow him to do the work."

Lydia turned her head and looked out the kitchen window; her focus blurred as she considered what her father said. She found comfort in the notion that Connor came into their lives for a purpose; still, he would need her help if he went to other villages. He wouldn't know to whom to speak or how to approach them. Her father said the task would be Connor's work. John might not agree, but she should go too.

Levi walked into the kitchen. He shuffled to the coffeepot, poured himself a cup, and then sat at the table across from her. He leaned on his elbows and held the steaming cup of coffee in both hands.

Too mentally preoccupied to eat, Lydia went to the sink to busy herself with dishes.

As Connor left the guest room, he walked as quietly as he could past Isabella's bedroom. She might not be awake yet, and he wanted to talk to John before anyone else went to breakfast. He stepped through the hallway and into the living room without making a sound. As he passed the staircase, murmurs came from the kitchen. He was too late.

He was grateful for the Colburns' hospitality, but it was awkward to be a houseguest. And this situation took awkwardness to a whole new level. Though John was graciously hospitable, Levi seemed to hate him, Bethany had a crush on him, and the old lady thought he had a speech impediment.

And then there was Lydia.

He had spent most of the night lying flat on his back staring at the ceiling thinking about her. He had envisioned the dance they shared, the light in her eyes when she saw the telescope set up on the bluffs, and the feel of her close to him—trusting him—as they walked on the path through the dark forest.

He stopped in the living room to tuck in his shirt. He needed to concentrate on the matter he had to discuss with John—the possibility of electronic signals being produced within the

Land. He walked into the kitchen but slowed his pace when Lydia, Levi, and John all looked at him. The only sound in the room came from the crackle of gray leaf wood chips in the stove's firebox.

Levi wore a scowl and promptly looked at Lydia, who was standing by the kitchen sink cleaning something. John nodded cordially to Connor and began to refill his coffee cup. Lydia came to the table without saying a word and sat in the chair beside Connor. He passed her the bread basket, and she accepted it but set it in the center of the table without taking anything to eat. Something was wrong.

She trapped her bottom lip between her teeth as she tapped one finger on the table's edge with nervous repetition. He watched her for a moment, but looked away when he felt Levi's glare.

As he began to eat, Isabella inched into the kitchen. She whacked the table leg with her cane and put her hand out precisely on the back of her chair. With his plan to speak to

John alone temporarily foiled, Connor reached for the coffeepot and decided to wait until after breakfast to mention Lydia's knowledge of electrical experiments in the Land.

"Good morning," Isabella said, beginning her daily ritual to see who was at the table before she sat down. Each person in turn was to say good morning, Aunt Isabella. Since Levi was seated to her right, he responded first, then John. Lydia responded and nudged Connor for his reluctant greeting.

"Good morning, Isabella." He waited for whatever comment was sure to come.

"Good morning, Connor. You made quite an impression with your waltz last night. From the way the old women spoke, I'm certain you caused many pleasant dreams. They said you were an adept dancer and effortlessly rhythmic." Awkward silence filled the room.

Isabella's eyes roamed and she chuckled. "Am I the only person here with a pulse?"

Lydia poured a glass of juice and put it in Isabella's waiting hand. "The Fosters' party was pleasant, Aunt Isabella. What would you like to eat this morning?"

"Just an egg, darling," she answered.

Though Isabella was capable of getting her own breakfast, she liked Lydia's attention. She set the boiled egg on her aunt's plate and stepped to the sink. Since she wasn't eating, maybe she was also waiting to speak to John.

John pushed his empty plate away and picked up his coffee cup. He leaned back in his chair and gazed at Connor. Levi was also sitting in front of an empty plate. His occasional impatient sigh broke the silence.

"Good heavens, people!" Isabella scoffed. "Are we listening for a bird to sing?" She chewed her last bite of egg and reached for her cane. "It's always this way after a night of revelry—no one has the strength for conversation." She stood holding her cane and tapped it along the edge of the hearth as she left the room.

John leaned forward and watched Isabella walk into the parlor. "Lydia, come sit down." He propped his elbows on the table as Lydia walked back to the table. Levi stood. John reached up and touched his son's arm. "Stay," he commanded, and Levi sat back down.

John's eyes scanned the three of them. "Since Connor's arrival he has carefully studied the Land and our history. He has a great knowledge of the sky and technology and science. For the past several nights he has been out charting the stars. It has come to his attention that there is something in the atmosphere that he believes helps keep the Land hidden from the rest of the world. This appears to be a great blessing from God, considering the condition of the world at present. However, Connor's observations have indicated that if people in the Land ever develop certain technologies—using electric devices—we could be detected by other nations. He says if the Land were invaded, other nations would likely consume or destroy our resources. When Lydia traveled she heard mentions of experiments with electricity." He looked at Connor. "Do you believe this must be stopped to ensure our survival?"

"Yes, sir, I do."

"Are you willing to assist us in alerting the other villages?"

"Yes, sir." He didn't hesitate.

John nodded. "Then you must go to the elders in each village and speak to them about this matter."

Lydia shifted in her seat. "The news of an outsider in the Land will be a disturbance in our own village, let alone other villages. We don't know how people will react to Connor's message. I will go with him."

John shook his head. "You cannot go."

"He cannot go alone!" she protested, drawing a disgusted look from Levi.

John looked at her. "Your village needs you here. You cannot go. And I cannot leave the village for a journey of that length." He turned his head a degree toward his son. "Levi, you must go with him."

John's announcement stunned Connor, and by the chorus of raised eyebrows and darting glances, he guessed Lydia and Levi were surprised as well.

John seemed to perceive their trepidation. He put his hand on Levi's shoulder. "The overseers will receive you because you are my son. You can introduce Connor and verify his message to the elders. I have seen Connor work diligently to protect us since the moment he learned of the Land. It appears he has no way to return to his people, so he has made it his personal mission to ensure the Land is not invaded."

Connor waited for refusal, but Levi was silent. Levi pushed both hands through his hair, leaned back in his seat, and audibly exhaled. They all waited for his response, and he seemed to know it. He stared at his hands as he drummed his fingers on the table's edge.

Finally, he looked at his father. "I don't share your trust in Connor. However, if I go with him I'll be able to keep my eye on him. Fine. I'll go."

"Thank you, Levi," John said. "You should leave tomorrow. I will write letters of introduction for Connor and explain that he came to the Land by accident and cannot safely depart. I will mention he is a knowledgeable man of the sciences and has information that might enable the Land to remain at peace. Levi, put the top on the wagon today. You should embark to the southern villages first, as it will be cold there soon. We can plan your journey this evening. Lydia, if you are free this afternoon, please ready provisions for their journey."

"I will, Father. But there is a matter to attend to in Good Springs first..." Her cheeks flushed and she wiped her hands on her dress. It was like she was trying to clean something that wasn't dirty. "There's the matter of Frank Roberts."

Levi threw both palms into the air. "What does that pervert have to do with anything?"

John ignored his son's reaction and turned to Connor. "Have you found the device yet?"

Connor shook his head. "No, sir. I saw Frank with my boots, so I know he was there at my arrival. I need to search his cabin."

"Very well. I will permit it because there is evidence against him and for the safety of the Land. But you must only remove the electronic device. Leave everything else just as you find it. I prefer you enter his home while he is not there. We must avoid violence."

"He'll be at the market this morning," Levi said. "He's always there on Saturday mornings, lurking about, hoping to see Lydia."

Lydia pressed her fingers to her temple. "The thought makes me ill, but Levi is right: I should go to the market. Levi and I will stay there long enough that Connor has time to go and search Frank's cabin."

The thought of Lydia having a stalker made Connor ill too. "We shouldn't use you as a decoy."

The red in her cheeks deepened. "If I can't go to warn the other villages and help protect the Land, at least let me do this. I'll be fine. Levi will be with me. And Frank isn't going to hurt me."

Levi nodded once in agreement.

John tapped his fingertips on the table and studied each of them. "Very well. When you see Frank at the market, Connor, go search his cabin for the device and be quick about it. If a villager needs Lydia's attention, Levi, you stay where you can observe Frank until Connor returns to you. I trust each of you will give your best effort for the Land. Now if you will excuse me," John stood, "I have bread to bake."

As Connor and Levi walked out the back door, Lydia held up a finger. "I will be right there. I want to check on Aunt Isabella before we go." She turned and hurried toward her great-aunt's bedroom. But as Lydia stepped into the parlor, she saw her aunt sitting in the armchair around the corner from the kitchen with her knitting needles clenched in her frozen hands. "Aunt Isabella! How long have you been here?"

"Long enough. Not to worry though, dear girl. I have heard a lifetime of secrets in this house, and I have kept them all."

The knowledge of Connor's origin and the threat of invasion might be too much for her aunt to handle. Lydia knelt in front of her and took her hand. "How much did you hear?"

"All of it, child." Isabella smiled. "I have known for a while now where the young man is from. I heard him sneaking out of his room each night. He was looking for a way home. It is a pity he cannot get back to his own people—for their sake anyway. It is good for us. I'm rather fond of him."

"Oh, Aunt Isabella! I'm glad you aren't frightened by all of this. Connor and Levi will do everything they can to protect the Land. They will warn the other villages, and everything will be fine."

"They are good men, Lydia." Isabella's mouth moved between words. "There is something I want to give you, dear."

Lydia glanced back at the kitchen. The men were waiting for her and she had an unpleasant task ahead. Her stomach knotted. "What is it?"

"Oh, never mind. It can wait." Isabella patted her hand. "Go and do your part to help them. When you return, I shall delight in hearing your report."

Though Isabella gleaned every detail she could from the conversations in the house, she was still unaware of the bulk of the situation. Lydia couldn't burden the elderly woman with any more information. She patted her aunt's hand. "I must go now." She rushed back through the

kitchen and outside, where Levi and Connor
were waiting.

Chapter Eight

The bright sun quickly warmed the autumn morning, but it was more than the weather that changed the air between Connor and Levi. A common enemy gave Connor a purpose for their partnership, and he hoped it would give Levi a productive place to focus his aggression.

The two men walked with Lydia to the market just as they had planned. As they passed the pottery yard, Bethany called Lydia over to look at something she was making. Connor and Levi waited for her on the road. Connor looked ahead into the village where the people were gathering in the open-air market. Then he glanced back over his shoulder. Frank was a short distance behind them, walking into the village on the road.

Connor nudged Levi. "Here comes the dirt bag now."

Levi waved Lydia back to them. As she rejoined the men, her gaze landed on Frank. "I want to get this over with as quickly as possible. It is terribly unpleasant business."

Connor stayed at her side as they walked along the cobblestone street between the church and the library. Part of him wanted Frank to do something—anything—to give him a reason to beat the pervert's face in. He let the scene play out in his mind and enjoyed every second of the imagined beating.

When they entered the market, Lydia wrung her hands and glanced from side to side while she made conversation with friends. If Frank detected her odd behavior, he might leave. While Levi hovered close to Lydia, Connor moved around the merchants' booths. He tried to appear interested in the displays as he tracked Lydia's stalker.

Frank plucked an apple from a produce stand when the vendor was distracted. He tucked it into the pocket of his oversized coat and then found a place in the shadows to eat the stolen fruit. He stared at Lydia all the while.

Connor's fists tightened and he caught Levi's attention. Levi nodded in recognition and positioned himself where he could keep Frank under surveillance. Connor didn't want to leave Lydia there in front of Frank, but Levi was fully capable of protecting her.

Connor walked back down the cobblestone street and hoped he had gone unnoticed. He increased his pace where the cobblestones ended and the gravel began. Once he passed the Colburn house, his stride accelerated from a jog to a steady run. He sped through the tall grass and into the forest, following Frank's well-warn path to the cabin past the bluffs.

The cabin appeared unlivable. Its wood siding was rotten, its roof held a puddle of rainwater where it bowed in the center, and several tree saplings waved from its gutter. The steps on the outside of the one-room structure creaked as Connor climbed them. Though Lydia had said Frank lived alone, Connor stood still and listened with his ear at the door before he reached for the knob. His pulse accelerated as he imagined a fight. Once he felt certain the place was empty, he opened the door.

The acidic stench of the unkempt cabin stung his nose. He wished he could leave the door open for fresh air, but decided against it. Enough light came through the grease-filmed window for him to see. He spotted his boots under the edge of the bed and started searching there for the rest of his gear. He pulled out a stack of gray paper to look behind it but stopped when he noticed the top page was a sketch. It was an intricate drawing of Lydia. Her likeness had been captured with artistry and perfection. He flipped through the rest of the pages. Each page was another drawing of Lydia—different poses and settings, but each sketch portrayed her beautifully.

He pulled a second stack of papers from under the bed—again, more sketches. Lydia looked younger in the sketches at the bottom of the stack. There were hundreds of the drawings, and she hadn't posed for a single sketch. When he saw a drawing where Lydia's skin was bare, his nostrils flared and he shoved the papers back under the bed. He remembered John's instruction not to cause any damage, and that order was the only thing that kept him from tearing the cabin apart. He ran a hand over his hair and took a deep breath, but it did little to calm him.

He continued to search the room. The beacon had to be there somewhere. He went to a dresser and rummaged through the drawers, but only found a foul-smelling mess of clothing items that had never been washed. He inspected the only bookshelf in the room. It held jars of shark teeth, empty spools, and chipped dishes full of rusted fishhooks, but not a single book.

He moved past a blackened fireplace—its hearth overflowed with ashes—and noticed a bench seat at the table. It was not a seat; it was a wooden trunk. As he lifted the lid, he found his balled up parachute inside the trunk. Beneath the parachute lay a pile of cables and carabineers, his watch and helmet, a flashlight, and a few small scraps of plastic that were probably a part of the ejection seat.

He turned on the flashlight and used it to look in the corners of the trunk. Underneath it all, he spotted the locator beacon. It had not been activated.

He popped the plastic backing off and removed the battery. He put the battery in one of his trouser pockets and the beacon in the other. He wanted to take his watch and the flashlight too but—remembering his orders from the overseer—he fought the desire and only removed their batteries. He put the rest of the equipment back in the trunk the same way he had found it and left the way he came.

His feet hit the gravel road in pounding thuds. The thick scrub on either side of the road muffled the sound of his rapid stride. The passion that fueled his anger also increased his energy. He shifted into a near sprint, eager to get back in the village, eager to get Lydia out of Frank's sight.

The visit to Frank's cabin to retrieve the inactivated locator beacon was supposed to bring him relief—maybe even a sense of control—knowing the Land would remain undetected, or at least it would not be detected due to his equipment. The people would be protected and their unique culture preserved. Lydia wouldn't be harmed by the technology he'd brought to the Land. However, seeing Frank's sketches of Lydia burdened him with a whole new dread. Frank wasn't just an annoying admirer—he was obsessed and had crossed the line.

And Connor and Levi were using her as the lure to keep Frank occupied.

Desperate to see Lydia was safe, he didn't slow his pace until his feet hit the cobblestone streets.

When he arrived at the market, he scanned the crowd but couldn't find Lydia. He marched through the vendors and artists, then he spotted Levi near a weaver's loom. Levi's gaze wasn't on the weaver but fixed on the shrubs at the back of the sandy lot.

Levi glanced at Connor and pointed at the tree line behind the market. "Frank is hiding back there."

Connor moved only his eyes in the direction Levi indicated and saw Frank sitting on the ground behind a shrub, peering out like a depraved imp. "Where is Lydia?"

"She had to go to the cottage. Someone needed her. Frank is probably waiting for her to come back."

Connor clenched his fists but left them at his sides. "Man, I want to go over there and—"

Levi lifted a hand. "I have dealt with this for years. If anyone gets to take him apart, it's going to be me."

Lydia examined the burned skin on her patient's hand then went to the cabinet to get a fresh jar of ointment. "It could have been much worse, Cordelia," she said as she walked back to the patient cot where the woman sat. "If you keep the skin covered in this salve it should heal completely in a couple of days." She opened the jar, and the aroma of pure gray leaf tree oil filled the air.

She was used to the strong smell and barely noticed it, but her patient let out a little cough and blinked rapidly. "It's a bit pungent."

"Yes, but it will heal the burn in the fraction of the time it would take to heal naturally."

"I'll do whatever you say, Lydia. I've never felt such pain as I did today. I'm sorry I took you away from the market," she apologized as Lydia spread the medicine on her burned skin. "I saw when you were called out of the Fosters' party last night to help someone, and I wondered if you ever get to have a life of your own. Then today I went and spoiled your time at the market by getting myself burned."

"Oh now, you did not spoil anything at all." She was glad someone had taken her out of Frank's view but couldn't say it. She wrapped a thin piece of muslin around her patient's hand then smiled. "I am always happy to help."

She carried the ointment to the worktable and got an empty jar from the cabinet. While filling the jar with the medicinal salve for her patient to take home with her, she wondered what was happening with Connor at the cabin and Levi at the market. When she had left the market to treat Cordelia, Levi had stayed to watch Frank. Had there been trouble?

Trying not to think of the situation while she was with a patient, Lydia stepped to her desk, picked up her pen and a piece of paper, and wrote instructions for her patient. As she walked back to her patient, she glanced out the window. Levi was walking onto the property from the road. Connor wasn't with him.

"Lydia?"

She looked at her patient. "Yes?"

"You looked a thousand miles away. Is there something wrong?"

Lydia couldn't answer truthfully, but so many things were wrong. A man had fallen from the sky and couldn't return to his people. His people would ruin the Land if they knew about it. He was putting himself at risk to protect the Land and all she could do was watch and wait.

Lydia chose not to answer her patient at all. She smiled at Cordelia and held out the jar of gray leaf ointment. "Put this salve on the burn twice a day. The skin will shed itself a few times as new skin grows. Let me know if you need any more of this." Her patient took the jar and stood. Lydia walked with her to the door. "Do you need me to help you home?"

"No, no. Joshua is in your father's house. I thought he'd rather spend his time speaking with the overseer instead of watching me get bandaged up."

Lydia held the door open for Cordelia and followed her out. The woman's husband was standing near the open door of the kitchen and saw her coming. Lydia waved to him as she stepped back into her cottage.

She closed the door and sat at her desk, trying to focus on her notes. Her mind was distracted with worry about Connor, causing her to release her pen and stare blankly at the door. A figure passed the window, but she couldn't see who it was through the curtain. Before she could get up and look out, Levi tapped on the door and turned the knob. He opened the door a fraction. "Are you alone?"

"Yes. Is Connor back?" She stepped to the door, pulled it open, and looked out but didn't see Connor.

Levi smelled of sweat and straw. He sat in the chair beside her desk. "He came back to the village just after you left the market."

"Did he find the device?"

"He said he did. It hadn't been activated. I figured that would make him happy, but he was pretty angry."

"Angry? Why?"

"Because Frank Roberts is a pervert and deserves to get his face punched in."

"No, that's why you were angry. What did Connor say?"

Levi's eyes narrowed a degree. He didn't answer.

She wanted to go to Connor. She wanted to know he was all right. She didn't know why she felt that way, but she couldn't ignore it. "Well?" she questioned again.

Levi inclined his head. "Why are you so worried about Connor?"

"I am not worried about Connor," Lydia lied. She was more than worried. She held herself responsible for him and for anything bad that might happen to him because of Frank. She felt responsible for the Land and its possible endangerment because of Connor. She had drawn Frank's vulgar attention, and she had found Connor when he arrived. Whatever happened in any aspect of the situation, it would be her fault. She shook her head then sat at her desk. "I'm just concerned."

"Connor is a grown man, Lydia. And he is a warrior. I don't think he needs your concern." Levi laced his fingers behind his head and leaned back in the chair. "Don't you have more urgent matters to fret over… responsibilities that concern your work, not his?"

"There might be people generating electricity in other villages and it could alert the outside world to our Land. This is a very concerning situation for me."

"No, it's not… not for you. This is your work." Levi looked around the room as he spoke. "Connor and I will go to the other villages and speak to the overseers. If anyone is experimenting with the technology Connor mentioned, the elders will handle it. But I don't think anyone in the Land has the kind of inventions that Connor is worried about. After our journey to the southern villages, we'll stop here before we travel north. The whole business will only take a couple of months. Then we'll be home. I'll be home, anyway... maybe Connor will meet some pretty girl in another village and leave us in peace." Levi smiled when he said it.

Lydia didn't smile back.

"Oh, I see." Levi brought his arms down and leaned onto her desk. "That's what is really bothering you: you want Connor to come back."

"Yes, I do." Lydia looked at her brother. "Don't you?"

Levi snickered. "Not particularly. He has brought us nothing but trouble." When Lydia was silent, Levi's eyes widened. "I see. I know Father enjoys Connor's company, and Bethany and her friends like to look at him, but I hadn't realized you were forming an attachment to him as well."

Lydia waved a hand, dismissing the notion. "I am not forming an attachment to Connor." She paused for a moment but could not grasp a rational thought. "I find him fascinating. That's all."

"Of course you find him fascinating—he's from another land." Levi put his hands back behind his head, effusing nonchalance. "You're happiest when you're acquiring knowledge. Connor's from another place and speaks of things you've never known. There's much to learn from him, so it makes sense that you find him fascinating. That's probably why Father spends so much time with him, too. Oh, you should hear them discuss theology. They can talk for hours." Levi chuckled and looked at the door. "I should get back to work. I have to put the top on the wagon and clean the horse stalls before dinner. Father wants to discuss our journey this evening. Will you be joining us?"

"Yes, so long as I don't have a patient." Lydia opened the drawer on the right side of her desk and placed her notes with her other patient charts. "I'll prepare your provisions now—starting with medicine." She stepped to her cabinets and took out a few things as Levi rose and walked to the door. "I'll send dried gray tree leaves with you and some bandaging in case you need it. And, Levi?"

"Yes?"

"I appreciate your insight. You helped clarify a matter that might have otherwise caused me confusion." Lydia smiled when Levi simply nodded and walked outside.

The more she thought about it, the more she felt Levi was right. Though Connor's arrival had brought a great deal of tension and concern, it had also brought excitement and mystery. He knew about all kinds of things she'd never imagined.

Her mind had reeled with fascination since the moment he fell from the sky. It was logical that she had become captivated not by him, but by his knowledge. The thrill was new and confusing. She was trained to assess a situation and determine a course of action, but nothing like Connor's arrival had ever happened before. It had caught her off guard.

Levi was right: she should let Connor do his job and she should focus on her work. She breathed a sigh of relief and began to gather the supplies for Levi and Connor when there was a knock at the door.

"Lydia?" John opened the door but didn't come inside. The sadness in his blue eyes made her brace for bad news.

"Yes, Father? What is it?"

"Doctor Ashton's granddaughter is here from Woodland. Doctor Ashton has not been awake in two days. Mrs. Ashton believes his time has come. She asked if you would make sure he is comfortable."

"Yes, I… I'll go now."

John waited by the door while Lydia processed the news. She had been at the deathbed of several people in her time as a physician. She could keep a professional demeanor and was always gentle and respectful to the family, but never emotional. It would be hard to see Doctor Ashton die and harder still to remain impassive, but he had trained her well.

She wiped her hands on her skirt even though they weren't dirty. Picking up her medical bag, she took a steadying breath before she walked out the door.

After the evening meal, Connor sat at the kitchen table with John and Levi while they planned the journey. John copied maps and wrote the names of the overseers of each village. Levi watched with his usual reticence. Connor listened carefully and made notes as John listed the potential helps and hazards they might encounter along the way.

John instructed him and Levi to leave at dawn. They would take the covered wagon—pulled by two horses—and drive south to Woodland, inland to Riverside, south to Stonehill and finally, on to Southpoint. They'd have to stay overnight on the road between villages—two nights between some villages. After their journey south, Connor and Levi were to return to Good Springs before embarking to the three villages to the north.

Connor was surprised to learn how large the Land was—and John only had maps of the portions that had been explored. John spoke of a mountain range about three days' journey inland, which no one had ever crossed and returned to tell about it.

Connor glanced at the kitchen's back door every few minutes. He had hoped Lydia would be there for the planning. It had only been three years since she traveled throughout the Land, and he valued her input. But he hadn't seen her since he left the market that morning.

It bothered him.

Whenever he asked Levi where she was, he only answered with a surly grunt.

When they finished planning their trip, the day was gone and darkness filled the space where the kitchen door stood open. Connor gathered his papers from the table, rolled them tightly, and took them to the barn where the wagon was packed and ready for the trip. He usually enjoyed preparing for a mission, but the thought of leaving Lydia after he had seen inside Frank's cabin filled him with apprehension. The journey sounded like it would be a camping trip through a pristine country that reportedly didn't have predatory animals. If he could simply get some assurance Lydia would be all right, he could relax and enjoy the adventure.

Connor opened the barn door and stepped inside. He climbed onto the front of the wagon and put the papers under the cushion of the bench seat. He sat on the bench and looked around. How had he gone from the cockpit of a fighter jet to the bench seat of a covered wagon? Now that he was here, he intended to do everything he could to protect these people and their land.

Lydia walked into the barn, carrying a bushel basket full of food.

He jumped down from the wagon. "Here, let me help you with that."

Lydia let him take the basket. "It's for your journey."

"Thanks, Doc." He set it on the back of the wagon and turned back to Lydia. Strands of light brown waves had escaped the tie that held her hair back. She didn't bother to move them off her face like she usually did. "Are you okay?"

"Hm?" She gazed vacantly at him.

"What's wrong?" He stepped closer to her, but the distance between them only seemed to grow. It made him want to reach out and hold her. She was a strong woman and he loved that about her, but he had a strength she needed. He wanted to gather her into his arms but she wouldn't want him to. He sank his hands into his pockets.

"Doctor Ashton is close to death. I have known him my whole life. He trained me to be a physician." She blinked and looked away. Connor instinctively drew a hand out of his pocket and reached for her hand. She pulled it away and smoothed the front of her skirt. "He has lived a good, long life. Still, it's… hard for me."

"I'm sorry." He understood the pain of loss. In his life before coming to the Land, tragedy transpired daily. When he'd first learned of life in the Land he thought it would be simple—too simple—to hold any challenge for him. The Land was unspoiled, plentifully resourced and beautiful, with a small, barely-governed society. Yet even here the days were woven with the threads of the common experience. He wanted to spare her the pain and protect her from the effects of life in a fallen world. He couldn't take away her grief, but maybe he could shield her from danger.

She stepped to the back of the wagon where he'd set the basket. She pulled a package off the top of the basket and held it up. "This is medicine. Levi knows how to use it. Hopefully, you won't need it. Um… I think Father wrapped some bread for you." Her fingers shook slightly. "It might still be in the kitchen. I'll go and get it."

Her ability to focus on the task at hand no matter how she felt was admirable. He had to do it every day as an aviator. He would have to do it when he left Good Springs if he was worried about her safety the whole time he was gone. She started to walk to the door. At any moment someone could come to her for help, and he wouldn't see her again before he left. "Listen, Doc… " He rubbed his whiskered chin, not knowing what to say. "This morning, at Frank's cabin—"

"Oh, yes. Levi said you were able to retrieve the beacon and it hadn't been activated." Lydia grinned faintly, but it didn't reach her eyes.

"Yeah, that was a relief, but I saw some things that were… troubling. Remember when you first told me about Frank? And you said he was a man of poor character?"

Her smile vanished.

He continued speaking. "There is more to it than that. I know he's followed you around for years, so you don't think much of it. But you need to know that the man is obsessed with you in a bad way. He's dangerous."

Her cheeks grew pink and she looked away. "Yes, well… I should get back to work."

He hadn't meant to embarrass her. "I only wanted to warn you that Frank is a real threat to your safety."

"Frank Roberts has been lurking in the shadows since I was a girl. I know this is new to you, but it isn't new to me. He isn't going to hurt me. He only wants my attention. I worry that he will someday do something outlandish enough to make me look foolish to the village, but he won't hurt me physically."

"I want you to be careful while Levi and I are gone."

Lydia squared her shoulders and raised her chin. "I can take care of myself."

"No, you really can't," he said.

Hers eyes bulged in shock but he didn't mind. He wanted her to know the truth and stepped closer to her. "Last night when you bumped into me behind the house, I barely held you and you still couldn't move."

"I would have thought of something. Besides, you bumped into me."

"Face it, Doc, you couldn't fight off a man. Especially a crazy pervert like Frank."

She huffed and turned to the door, but she didn't leave. She mounted her fists on her hips and took a few loud breaths. After a moment her shoulders wilted. Then she spoke and her voice sounded unsteady. "As an unmarried woman I'm still under the protection of my father. That's the custom here. I'm safe because I still live with my father, and he has dealt with Frank."

He understood the custom but came from a culture where stalkers and rapists were commonplace. "You live in your cottage alone. People knock on your door at all hours of the night, and you open it to them."

"Because they need me." She spun around and faced him. "I am committed to caring for the health of this village. I must remain available to them." Her voice grew in fullness and volume. "I would never lock myself away— not out of fear or any other reason. The foremost purpose of that cottage is for the village to have a place to go for medical care. It isn't mine but theirs—the people of Good Springs. It is only secondly my home."

"Look, I know you have a heroic reputation around here, but you should be more careful."

"What are you so afraid of?"

"It would be so easy for him to—"

"To what?"

It was the first time Connor had seen her angry. He wasn't sure how he'd managed to get her upset. It produced both a dull weight of regret and a sharp ping of delight. His purpose was to protect her from that creep, but she didn't understand his intention. "You have to consider the possibilities."

"I will not live in fear!" she shouted.

"Just promise me you will lock your door."

"I promise you nothing." Lydia turned and stormed out.

As she disappeared into the darkness, Connor put his hands behind his head. He turned to pace the barn floor and kicked a clump of dirt, venting his frustration. It smacked into the wagon wheel with a thud and crumbled to the ground.

He hadn't expected her to find his concern offensive. There had to be something he could do to make sure she was safe while he was gone. Something besides taking Frank Roberts apart and burying the pieces. He could teach her self-defense, but she wouldn't want to learn.

She was right—she was responsible for herself, and maybe her father still had some obligation to protect her. John knew about Frank. He might not know about the sketches, but he knew the danger Frank posed.

Connor had to leave Lydia's safety to John, but the thought of Frank Roberts would plague him the entire time he was away.

Chapter Nine

Lydia climbed the stone steps and walked back into the chapel. Both of its tall doors were propped open. She yearned for the quiet inside the church now that all of the people were gone. Her footsteps tapped lightly on the wood-planked floor as she followed the center aisle. She let her fingers trail over the arm of each pew as she passed it, then she stopped near the front of the chapel—third row from the podium—where Doctor Ashton sat every Sunday.

She sat in his habitual seat and leaned her back against the wood. It was still warm from the mourners who had just left. She wanted to see the chapel from Doctor Ashton's perspective only this once. She was taking his place professionally, and that was enough.

She gazed at the podium in the front of the room and the large wreath of flowers leaning against it. One of nearly every flower in the Land was represented in the wreath. The colors of the flowers started to mix together in a blur until she blinked back her tears. Crying would be a childish thing to do. She needed to swallow her tears and avoid the headache inevitably brought by crying. Think logically, as Doctor Ashton always said.

He was in Heaven now. He was perfect and without pain. There was no reason to cry.

The words spoken by his family and the elders during the memorial service played through her mind. Doctor Ashton had been a faithful husband and a gentle father and grandfather. He was compassionate, generous, wise and careful. Lydia knew him to be a good teacher, patient and forgiving, intelligent and forthright. He also had a witty sense of humor. She remembered traveling with him during her apprenticeship and hearing the entertaining stories he told to pass the time as they rode between villages. She owed her profession to

Doctor Ashton and daily recalled his wise instruction as she cared for her patients.

The tradition for her profession was much like that of overseers in the Land. Every village needed one, but the training was long and the life so demanding there was usually only one per village. She had studied and trained for four years under Doctor Ashton and had worked alone for over a year. Surely the elders would soon bestow upon her the title of doctor. Receiving the title made his passing no less painful. It simply meant the village officially recognized her position.

Doctor Lydia Colburn—the thought made her smile. She needed that distinction. It would have made her mother proud. Would she be told the news in Heaven? Maybe Doctor Ashton would tell her himself.

"I thought I saw you come back in here." Mandy's voice echoed from the high chapel ceiling. "It was a lovely service, was it not?"

Lydia scooted down the pew to make room for her best friend. Mandy pulled a long curl through her fingertips. She twisted it around and around as they sat in silence. After a moment Mandy spoke again. "Did Levi hear about Doctor Ashton's passing before they left?"

Lydia shook her head. "He and Connor departed at dawn on Sunday. Doctor Ashton passed away later in the afternoon. Levi knew it was coming. But they had to leave. Father felt the matter was urgent."

Mandy's eyes were fixed on the flowers. "Yes, I suppose it was. My father told Everett and me about Connor last night. I knew there was something peculiar about him, though I never imagined he was from another land."

Lydia looked back at the flowers, but they had lost their charm. She turned to Mandy. "It caused quite a stir in our home too."

"How long have you known he was from another land?"

"Oh, since he arrived." Lydia bit her lip.

Mandy stopped twirling the ringlet of hair and held it laced between her fingertips. "Is he going to stay here?"

Lydia shrugged. "He says he cannot safely leave the Land. I don't know if he plans to live in Good Springs or not. I don't think he knows either." She smiled, thinking of her brother's reaction to Connor. "Levi is hopeful Connor will fall in love with a woman in another village and not come back here."

"Levi has never been quick to welcome strangers." Mandy resumed her curl twirling.

Lydia remembered her last conversation with Connor. "I am afraid we did not part on the best of terms."

"You and Connor?"

"Yes. I know he meant well. I'm not even sure why I got so upset." Lydia looked at her hands folded in her lap. She remembered how Connor had reached out to her and she had pulled away. "Connor seemed to have some personal interest in my safety. He warned me to be careful while he was gone. He wanted me to promise I would lock the door of the medical office. He was concerned about—"

"Frank Roberts?"

"Yes."

"So Connor noticed the same danger we all see and he tried to warn you."

"Yes, well… it doesn't sound so problematic when you say it, but it felt intrusive when he said it. I had just come from Doctor Ashton's house and I was worried about Connor and Levi's journey and it probably does not make sense, but Connor reached out to me and I just did not want his concern."

"I see. You don't mind if he needs you, but you don't want to need him."

"That is just it, I don't need him. He's certainly pleasant and I enjoy his company, but I don't need him. By custom, I'm still under my father's protection, and Levi's protectiveness of me is no secret. I don't need another man telling me to be careful."

Mandy put her arm over the pew. "Is it possible his personal interest in your safety comes from his personal interest in you?"

Lydia chuckled. "I doubt it."

"I saw how he watched you at my family's party. It looked to me as though he's intrigued with you. And that beautiful dance had to mean something to him."

Lydia refused to speculate about Connor's intentions, and she had no romantic intentions of her own. She dismissed Mandy's observations with a wave of her hand. "It hardly seems appropriate to speak of now."

Mandy grinned. "I can think of no better time to speak of hopeful things than in the wake of sadness."

Footsteps scuffed the entryway. John closed one of the chapel doors and stood waiting to close the other. Lydia and Mandy shuffled out of the pew and walked down the aisle to the door. Lydia glanced back at the flowers one last time and walked out.

After leaving the Colburns' home, Connor and Levi traveled south for two days on the road through the gray leaf forest before they arrived in the village of Woodland. Though smaller than Good Springs, Woodland's residents were no less hospitable. Levi was acquainted with the overseer of Woodland, who welcomed them into his home. When Connor presented the letter from John Colburn, the man quickly gathered the elders to hear the warning.

The only inn in the Land was situated halfway between Woodland and the village of Riverside. After a full day of travel, Levi stopped the wagon there and offered the owners of the quaint country house a full jar of

Lydia's gray leaf salve for one night in the last remaining guest room.

Connor enjoyed spending the evening among the travelers over a feast in the communal dining hall. The seasoned traders told stories of traveling to all the villages in the Land, but he kept his origin to himself. Still, it felt good to be around people who were jovial in nature and open to whomever gave an ear.

Levi was quiet but courteous with the strangers. His infrequent—albeit constructive—responses proved he was prone to deeper thought than Connor had previously accredited him. When the owners of the inn called it a night, Connor taught Levi the game of rock-paper-scissors to determine who would sleep on the single bed in the small room. After a practice round, the men played the game in earnest, and then Connor spread his bedroll on the guest room floor.

The village of Riverside was active with trade and smelled like stewed beef. Most of the elders were busy gathering their harvests, but when the overseer heard Connor's message, he immediately sent word for the elders to meet. After departing Riverside, a three-day journey took them to the outskirts of the village of Stonehill.

Perched on the front bench of the wagon, on the eighth day of what was a much smoother trip than he'd anticipated, Connor enjoyed the long day of travel through the Land. Levi wasn't much of a conversationalist, but he was less surly than he had been at home. Connor didn't mind that they had to sleep on the ground when they camped between villages. The nights grew cooler the farther south they traveled, and he was looking forward to arriving in Stonehill.

Shadows played across the horses' backs as they pulled the wagon beneath a tall tree. Comfortable with the primitive vehicle's rattle and sway, Connor folded his arms and relaxed while Levi drove toward Stonehill. As they passed the entrance to a salt mine, Levi said they were not far from the village.

A falcon drifted overhead. It made Connor miss flying. He thought less about his old life with each passing day. He preferred to stay focused on the present, and at present he was on a peaceful wagon ride through beautiful country.

Certain places in the Land reminded him of other parts of the world, though differences remained. The forest near Good Springs made him think of southeastern Australia. The country around Riverside with its big sky and mountains rising in the distance resembled the American West. And as they traveled toward Stonehill, he thought of the North Atlantic coast in Canada.

Still, no matter where he was in the Land, he could not shake the feeling that he was at the end of the earth.

Outside the village of Stonehill, the wagon meandered atop cliffs near the coast. The road veered high above the ocean with no guardrails or warning signs and only a few feet of packed earth between the wagon wheels and the edge of the cliff. A cabin on the bluffs in the distance reminded him of Frank Roberts.

His concern for Lydia flooded back. She was never far from his thoughts anyway. He had plenty of time to think during the journey, and he spent most of the time thinking of Lydia.

Connor appreciated how peaceful life was without the constant interruption of technology, but he also found himself wishing for some way to contact Lydia. He hated that they fought the night before he left. He'd missed many hours of sleep wishing he could talk to her and know they were still friends.

The road veered away from the cliff and to the village ahead. They passed one house, then another. A woman was hanging wet clothes on a line strung from the side of her house to the trunk of a thin pine tree. Levi pulled the wagon near her yard. Its wheels sent chickens scurrying in all directions. Levi asked the woman about Overseer Vestal. She pointed at the parsonage.

The Vestals were friendly and eager to welcome Levi and Connor into their home. Overseer Vestal insisted they call him Wade. He was the first person in the Land that Connor had considered portly. Mrs. Vestal seemed exuberant to have guests and disappeared into the kitchen, humming while pots and pans clanked.

Wade ushered Connor and Levi through a narrow hallway and into a formally decorated sitting room. He motioned for them to sit on chairs upholstered with thick, red velvet. Then Wade popped up again and shouted back down the hallway. "Hazel! Send for Phillipa! Tell her we have gentlemen guests!"

"Right away, dear!" Mrs. Vestal's response had a singsong quality.

Wade shifted his ample weight in the chair. "So you have come from Good Springs with news?"

Levi handed John's letter to the overseer. Wade chewed his cheek as he read it, his eyes widening all the while. Then he asked Connor for his report. Wade folded the letter in half and creased it between his thumb and forefinger several times as he listened to Connor. All at once, he seemed to realize he was creasing another man's paper and handed the letter back to Levi.

Connor explained about the people from other lands that were scouring the world for resources. He'd already given the speech several times before they reached Stonehill. He explained the Land was currently undetectable to outsiders, but the people of the Land must refrain from certain technologies to help keep it that way.

Levi asked about the inventor whom Lydia had met years ago. Wade said he knew the man and nodded his head. His plump jowls jiggled rapidly. "Yes, yes. This matter does sound pertinent, gentleman. I'll gather the elders. And I'll speak to Jeremiah Cotter—though I doubt he has gotten very far with his inventions. His heart troubles him, and he spends most of his days in bed." Wade looked at Connor then.

"Such is the course for the ailments a man is born with. No amount of gray leaf tea will heal those afflictions."

The front door of the parsonage creaked open, then footsteps and whispering came down the hall. Mrs. Vestal appeared in the doorway. "Excuse me, gentlemen," she said while wiping her hands on a flower-print dishtowel. "May I present my daughter, Miss Phillipa Vestal."

A young woman stepped into the doorway. She looked to be in her late teens and had an attractive figure. Connor's eyes moved from her ribbon-laced shoes up to her face, and then he had to look away quickly. She had a thick line of dark hair above her upper lip and only one eye that focused directly ahead.

"I'm pleased to make your acquaintance," she said.

Connor glanced at her and nodded politely.

The young woman smiled, revealing a flock of yellow teeth that darted in every direction. She closed her lips but one snaggletooth refused to be concealed.

Levi stood and introduced himself.

She shook his hand but kept one eye pointed at Connor.

After dinner and a long evening of conversation, Mrs. Vestal showed Connor and Levi to the guest room. Relieved to see two beds, Connor walked to the bed nearest the window and kicked off his shoes. He lifted the heavy-framed sash window. Fresh air blew through the room. Levi tossed his satchel on the other bed and began to rifle through it.

As Connor reclined on the bed, he stretched his legs to the end of the mattress and rested his hands behind his head. He wondered what Lydia was doing at that exact moment. He imagined her riding her horse, rushing to someone who needed help. If she were in any modern society, she would probably be an emergency room doctor. He tried to imagine her wearing scrubs and using computerized medical equipment to check vital signs, but the image didn't suit her. A thought occurred to him and he sat up. "Hey Levi, what is the custom here when a man is interested in a woman?"

Levi's eyes shot open and he grinned. "Yes, right, well," he fumbled for words and seemed pleased with Connor for the first time since his arrival. "First, you must go to her father and ask his permission."

That sounded a bit serious to Connor. He raised a finger. "What if you aren't sure you want to marry her yet… you just want to get to know her? We call it dating. What do you call it?"

"Do you mean courting?"

"I guess."

"You still must ask her father first. Otherwise, your intentions would seem questionable."

That sounded fair. "All right. Let's say I talk to the girl's father and he's fine with it. Then what?"

"Then you visit her and spend time with her. Go on walks, picnics, that type of thing."

"What if I spend some time with her and realize I don't like her as much as I thought I would... am I obligated to marry her?" He doubted that would happen, but it was best to know all the facts before he got himself into something serious.

"No. I don't think so." Levi looked deep in thought for a moment. "Of course you shouldn't ask for her hand in marriage unless you are sure."

"Right, thanks." Connor reclined on the bed. He felt confident he could handle their customs and imagined going to John Colburn to ask permission to court his daughter. John was a fair man and seemed to like him, so he guessed his chances of approval were good. As he began to plan exactly what he would say to John, Connor sensed Levi was still looking at him.

"Well?" Levi asked.

"Well what?"

"Are you going to go speak with Wade?"

"About what?"

"Phillipa."

"Wade's daughter?"

"Of course. Isn't that who you were speaking of?"

"Seriously?" Connor would have found Levi's miscalculation humorous if the overseer's daughter were less pitiful. During dinner Connor had felt something rub his ankle several times, and when he finally looked under the table he saw it was Phillipa's foot. He had glanced up at her and she tried to give him a seductive look.

He shuddered. "No, not her."

Levi pushed his hands through his hair. His friendly smile was gone. He marched to the door. Connor hoped Levi would leave the room without asking any more questions, but Levi turned back around and crossed his arms over his chest. He lowered his voice an octave. "What exactly are your intentions with Lydia?"

Connor appreciated Levi's willingness to fight for his sister's honor. He doubted Levi would believe he was willing to fight for it too. "My intentions?" Connor repeated, unsure if he wanted to answer Levi's question.

"Yes. I know you have wishes for my sister. What are they?" Levi demanded.

"I have wishes for Lydia? Yeah, yeah, I do." Connor sucked in a breath and sat up. "I wish that stalker of hers would spontaneously combust. I wish the village would acknowledge her worth and start calling her Doctor. I wish she owned a pair of jeans. Those are a few of my wishes for Lydia."

Levi turned and stormed out.

Connor lay back down on the bed. The front door opened and slammed shut. So much for camaraderie. Levi could deal with the horses and wagon by himself for one night. They still had to travel to Southpoint before retracing the road back to Good Springs, and there wouldn't be many occasions for giving each other personal space.

Chapter Ten

A wagon rumbled on the road in front of the Colburn property. Lydia stepped to the kitchen window to look out. The wagon passed the house and continued driving toward the village. Lydia shuffled back to the kitchen sink and began peeling potatoes.

John walked out of the pantry holding a handful of green beans. "Who was that?"

"William McIntosh, I believe." She stopped what she was doing, took a ceramic bowl from the cabinet, and placed it on the kitchen table in front of Isabella. Then she returned to peeling potatoes at the sink.

John laid the green beans in a pile on the table in front of Isabella. She reached to the pile and began snapping the beans. As she dropped the pieces into the bowl, her lips twitched. "Shouldn't the boys be back by now?"

Lydia looked at her father and waited for his reassuring response.

John filled a large pot with water and set it on the stove. "It depends on how long it takes them to meet with the elders in each village. I expected them to be away for at least three weeks."

"It has been nearly four, has it not?" Isabella asked.

"Tomorrow." Lydia peeled the last potato and set it aside with the rest. "Four weeks tomorrow."

"Now ladies, worry accomplishes nothing." John gathered the potatoes and carried them to the stove. "Rest assured, they will be back any day—"

Another wagon rolled down the road. It turned toward the Colburn house. Lydia pulled her apron off and rushed outside to meet the wagon.

"Mr. Cotter. Mrs. Cotter." Lydia saw the couple on the front seat of the wagon and thought something was wrong. "Where is the baby?"

"He's home. We have a neighbor girl looking after him," Mark Cotter said as he climbed down from the wagon. He walked around to the other side. "It's Doris who needs to see you." He held his hand up to his wife and she took it as she carefully stepped down to the ground. "I'll wait out here," he told Doris.

Mark's cheeks were flushed and he wore half a grin.

Lydia looked at his wife. "Yes, Doris. Do come in." She led the woman into the medical cottage and closed the door behind them.

While attending her patient, it sounded like another wagon outside. She was probably just anxious for Levi and Connor to come home. Her contentment hinged on their return and it alarmed her.

Perhaps it was her argument with Connor or Doctor Ashton's death or simply that she missed them, but everything seemed a bit dreary lately. And the dreariness was interspersed with apprehension because of Connor's warning about Frank. Though she truly believed Frank wouldn't do anything to harm her physically, Connor's caution echoed in her mind every time she stepped outside or heard a knock at her door. Levi and Connor's return would renew her sense of security and lift her spirit.

While her patient dressed, Lydia sat at her desk and made notes. She turned the pages in her calendar to check a date and made another note. Doris's baby had been born on the morning of the autumn equinox in March— the same day Connor had arrived in the Land.

Men's voices murmured outside the cottage. It was probably her father and Mark.

Doris buttoned her dress as she walked to the desk. "Thank you, Lydia." Her chin began to quiver and tears came to her eyes. "I'm happy about this, really I am. I don't know why I'm crying."

Lydia inclined her head as she touched her patient's arm. "There now, Doris, your husband will be pleased when you tell him the news."

"It's just that little James is not yet three months old." Doris drew a handkerchief from her sleeve and dabbed at her tears. "Neither Mark nor I thought this could happen quite so soon."

"James and his new brother or sister will probably grow up to be good friends. My brother is just ten months younger than me, and we've always been very fond of each other." Lydia opened the door. "You have a lot to look forward to."

She followed Doris outside to Mark's wagon. Behind it was her father's wagon. The men stood near the back door of the main house. Bethany was hugging Levi, and John was shaking Connor's hand while Mark watched the welcome party.

Lydia stood still at the threshold of her doorway. Everyone became quiet when Doris walked toward her husband. Doris smiled at Mark and took both of his hands in hers as she whispered something to him. His face lit up. He looked over his wife's shoulder to Lydia for confirmation, and Lydia nodded.

"We are going to have another baby!" Mark announced. He laughed and wrapped his arms around his wife. Then he pulled away and put his hand on her belly.

John and Levi stepped forward to congratulate Mark. Bethany beamed and started chatting with Doris about the exciting news. Lydia looked through the happy crowd. Connor was watching her. His whiskers were longer and he looked tired, but his eyes were still warm. A faint smile curved his lips. With the crowd between them, Connor simply mouthed hi.

Lydia returned his gesture. "Hi." She blinked and looked away before anyone else could notice.

Levi scooped her up with one arm and swung her in a circle. He set her back down and she smiled up at him. "I am so glad you're home!"

"I'm glad to be back." Levi grinned and reached into his coat pocket. "I got you something in Southpoint."

Bethany overheard him and furled both arms around Levi's chest. "What about me?" She pretended to pout. "Did you bring me something too?"

"Yes, you too." Levi chuckled and drew a small package from his pocket. He opened it and removed two bracelets made of delicate silver links. He handed one to Lydia and one to Bethany. Lydia wrapped the silver bracelet around her wrist and clasped it securely. Bethany did the same, giggling all the while.

"That's not all." Levi emptied the contents of the paper into his hand. "This one is for Bethany." He placed a small silver charm in her hand.

Bethany examined the charm closely. "It's a little vase, like the ones I made when I was first learning to make pottery. Oh, thank you, Levi!"

Levi took the other charm and placed it in Lydia's palm. Her eyes widened as she studied it, and she closed her hand over the tiny charm. "It's shaped like a gray leaf. How thoughtful!"

Levi secured the charm to Lydia's bracelet and did the same for Bethany. The sisters admired each other's bracelets. The Cotters waved goodbye as they pulled away.

Lydia glanced up from her bracelet to see Connor lift his satchel from the wagon. He smiled at her and followed John and Levi into the house.

Elated to set six places for dinner, Lydia hummed as she carried a stack of plates to the table. The little silver charm dangled at her wrist all the while.

Connor awoke at first light. He didn't need a clock to tell him what time it was. He rolled out of bed and onto the floor, where he counted off fifty push-ups. After getting dressed, he left the guest room and walked through the hallway, taking great care not to make a sound near Isabella's door. Though the Colburn house wasn't his home, it was good to be someplace familiar. He passed through the kitchen and walked out the back door, closing it behind him.

He followed the dirt path from the house to the gravel road in front of the property and stopped to stretch his calf muscles before he began to run. His breath streamed out in visible puffs in the cold morning air as his stride settled into a good rhythm. Since it was no longer a secret that he was from another land, he was free to run. Though he would never be able to return to military service, he intended to stay in shape no matter the expressions his running drew from the occasional onlooker.

His feet pounded the road comfortably in his new shoes. They might not have been designed with advanced athletic technology, but the shoemaker Lydia bartered with had crafted something far better than he'd expected. His feet had callused from the borrowed shoes, and he was pleased to see the new shoes waiting for him when he returned from his trip to the southern villages.

He had one more day to break in the new shoes before he would have to leave Good Springs again, which meant only one more day to see Lydia. He wanted to talk to John about her, but after Levi's display of disapproval, it was best to give it some time. He didn't expect the same opposition from John, but he did not want any more misunderstandings before he had to leave again.

The time between trips was going too fast. He'd spent Saturday evening giving John a report of their journey and had spent Sunday at church, where he sat on the back pew in the chapel and listened while John preached. Lydia had come into the church halfway through the sermon and sat in the seat next to him. He'd automatically slipped his arm over the pew behind her shoulders. When she didn't seem to mind, he left it there. It had felt natural to sit there next to her. Had she thought anything of it at all?

He instinctively turned around on the road where he calculated a mile and a half and ran back. He jogged the last few yards of the road, turned toward the Colburn house, and walked from there.

The kitchen door was open when he returned. John was making coffee and Bethany was sitting at the table with a well-worn schoolbook open in front of her. Connor poured himself a glass of water. He drank it standing at the sink then refilled the glass and turned to the table.

"This is dreadful, absolutely dreadful," Bethany huffed as she slammed her pencil into her book. The pencil bounced to the floor. With exaggerated gestures she pretended to collapse onto her school papers and heaved a sigh. Her long lashes fluttered from the edges of her twitching eyelids while she faked a dramatic death.

Connor rolled his eyes at the teenager's shameless performance and bent to the floor to pick up the pencil. Bethany cracked one eye open and peeked at him. Connor used the pencil to point at the book. "What are you studying?"

Bethany came back to life and blew out a breath. "Algebra. I'll never understand it. Schoolwork is just dreadful and absolutely useless." She straightened in her chair and looked at her father. "Must I go to class today? After my apprenticeship at the pottery yard, I will never need math again."

John eyed his fifteen-year-old daughter as he brought the coffee pot to the table. He exuded the unsympathetic calm of a man who had raised five children, four of them girls. "You must finish your schooling, Bethany. You know that."

"Oh, but it's utterly useless. I never use what I learn in class when I'm at the potter's wheel," she grumbled.

Connor sat at the table beside her and turned the book where he could see it. He scanned the page and turned the book back to Bethany. Pointing to the section where her frustration had resulted in a deep pencil groove through the page, he got her attention. "Okay, see the parenthesis here? They mean you should treat these terms as a group. So you first add these two numbers, then you multiply the sum by this factor here." He glanced up at her and she appeared to follow what he was saying.

He offered her the pencil. She took it and worked the equation on a piece of gray leaf paper. The kitchen was silent except for the sound of the pencil scratching on the paper. When she was finished, Connor took the pencil and wrote a similar equation with different numbers. "Now try this one."

He checked her work. She had the correct answer. He took the pencil and scribbled out another equation then handed the pencil back to her again.

John drummed his fingers on the table in light, rapid thumps. "The teacher of our secondary students hopes to return to his family home in Riverside soon, but we have been unable to find another teacher to fill the position."

He glanced at John then looked back at the page. "That's too bad."

"Connor, have you ever thought of teaching?"

The idea took Connor by surprise. He leaned back in the chair and looked at John. "Teach what—high school? No, sir."

"It might be something to consider."

"Oh, I don't think I could teach."

Bethany lifted her page and showed them another correct answer.

John gave half a smile then he looked at Connor. "It looks like you just did."

Lydia tidied her office and was ready to leave when she remembered her gloves. She climbed the stairs to her bedroom and retrieved a pair of leather gloves from the top of her dresser. Then she hurried back down the stairs and to the door. She opened it and startled. Connor stood on the other side with his knuckles raised.

He smiled. "Oh, hi. I was about to knock."

Lydia stepped out of her cottage and closed the door behind her. "I was just leaving. Do you need something?"

He held up a book. "No, I came to return this."

"Thank you." She took the book and set it on her desk. She turned to go back outside, but Connor had stepped in behind her. "I planned to be at Mark and Doris's farm by noon, so I really must be going."

He pressed his lips together and raised a palm. "I'm sorry."

"Please, don't apologize. Actually, if you have the time, maybe you could walk with me."

He rubbed the back of his neck and looked away. "I have the time. I'm just not sure that we should… I mean that I should…"

She waved a hand, dismissing the idea and her disappointment from his rejection. "That's fine. I just thought an extra pair of hands might be helpful, but I can manage the horses by myself."

"Horses?"

"Mark Cotter is a horse breeder. He originally offered me a four-year-old gelding for my service to Doris during the delivery of their firstborn. But after the news that another baby is on the way, Mark said he would go ahead and make it a pair of horses." She lowered her volume. "I thought maybe the new horses would be a pleasant surprise for Levi and he could use them on the trip north tomorrow."

Connor looked relieved, though Lydia wasn't sure why. "So you want me to walk with you to the Cotters' farm and help you bring the horses back here?"

"That probably sounds boring to you." She shook her head. "Never mind. Your time is best used on less tedious tasks."

"No, it sounds great. I'd love to walk with you." He smiled and backed out the door, holding up a finger. "Wait just a second, though. I want to tell your dad where we're going. I'll be right back. Wait for me, okay?"

His sudden enthusiasm puzzled her. She followed him out of the cottage and closed her door. "Okay," she repeated as she waited on the path in front of her cottage. While he was in the house speaking with her father, she considered the strange words he used. She liked the things he said.

Connor came out of the main house a moment later. He smiled and briskly rubbed his hands together. As they walked to the road she used her hand to shield her eyes from the sun and looked up at Connor. "Have you always been interested in horses?"

He chuckled. "Not until recently. Tell me, did the founders bring all the animals here?"

"Yes. They brought horses, cattle, sheep, goats, chickens, dogs, and cats. They also had a team of oxen, but the oxen died at sea. They brought the seed for grain, vegetables, fruit trees, and cotton."

"All on one ship?"

"All on one ship." She loved the history of the founders. "Fifty-seven persons and all those animals."

"Where did they get the ship?"

"Charles Weathermon, a retired shipping tycoon. He was widowed and had no children, and he offered the use of his ship if the founders agreed to take him with them." She had slowed her pace as they walked. "They planned everything in complete secrecy. Then before they departed America they quarantined themselves for several weeks to ensure no contagious illness was carried to their new settlement."

"So no one in the Land has encountered a communicable disease for seven generations?"

"That's right."

"Good thing I didn't have a cold when I arrived. It could have wiped out the entire population."

Lydia considered the possibility. "I suppose so. The founders were more concerned with having to endure illness during the voyage."

"Where did they plan to settle?"

"We don't know for sure. My primary school teacher always said he thought they were probably going to South America. All we know is that after nearly four months at sea, the schooner made landfall here. They found no signs of human life ever having been here, so they settled and simply called this place the Land."

"Do you know why they left America?"

"Not for certain. The founders' journals don't mention much about life in America before they sailed. They were a highly adventurous group. I believe they simply wanted the challenge of finding a new land and establishing a settlement."

"Your dad told me the founders arrived here in March of eighteen sixty-one and they were at sea for four months. That means they left America just before the start of the Civil War."

"The Civil War? Is that when America changed its name?"

"What do you mean?" He reached up and snagged a leaf from the low-hanging branch of a gray leaf tree as they passed it.

She watched out of the corner of her eye to see what he was going to do with the leaf. He examined it closely then peeled its flesh from its stem piece by piece and dropped it to the ground.

"Well, the founders referred to your country as the United States of America but you call it the Unified States of America. Did the war cause that change?"

His demeanor changed when she mentioned the Unified States. He forcefully blew out a breath and looked away. Why did he find the history of the Land fascinating, yet seem uncomfortable when she asked about his country?

He slid his hands into his pockets. "I heard Doctor Ashton passed away. I'm sorry. I know you were close to him."

Lydia allowed his change of subject. "Thank you. I suppose I feel a bit orphaned professionally."

"That's understandable." He looked at her as they walked. "I hope you realize you're a completely competent physician."

Lydia appreciated hearing that, especially from Connor. She tucked a wave of hair behind her ear. "Thank you."

"Who will take care of Mrs. Ashton?"

"Her granddaughter came from Woodland just before Doctor Ashton died. She and her husband have moved into the Ashtons' home. They will care for Mrs. Ashton and inherit the house one day." She found his thoughtfulness refreshing. In the midst of all he was going through, he cared what would happen to an elderly woman he had never met. "It's very considerate of you to ask."

He shrugged. "I admire the way you all take care of each other. I feel like I've gone back in time since I arrived here. People in my country take care of each other, too. It's just… simpler here. It's nice."

As they approached the gate to the Cotters' farm, Lydia pointed at several horses grazing in the distance. "Here we are."

"Yeah, I noticed this place Saturday when Levi and I passed it on our way back to the village. It's a beautiful property."

"It's been in Mark's family for generations. Over the years they cleared more than a hundred acres for pasture." She lifted the latch on the wooden gate and it squeaked as Connor pushed it open. "Mark is my mother's third cousin."

He closed the gate behind them and followed her into the pasture. Mark waved from the barn. She waved back and then watched the ground as she walked beside Connor through the pasture.

Lydia and Connor were at Mark Cotter's horse farm for less than an hour. As they walked back to the Colburn property, they each held a rope with a horse at the other end. Lydia was glad Connor had gone with her. She liked watching him as he spoke with Mark and the farmhands. He acted differently now that he no longer needed to be secretive. He initiated handshakes and patted backs and looked people in the eye when they spoke. She liked how people responded to him. It made her want to know him more.

With the sun behind them, Lydia looked up at Connor as they strolled along the road. "What was it like for you arriving here and being thrown into my family with hardly a choice?"

"It hasn't been all that bad. In fact, I'm rather fond of your family."

"As am I. My father and Bethany adore you. Aunt Isabella does too, but Levi has not been very welcoming."

"He is only trying to protect his family. I understand. The guy has four sisters. I guess he has his work cut out for him." Connor rubbed his chin. He had shaved his whiskers. She missed them.

She was staring. She tried to peel her eyes away, but it took effort. He was from a different world, yet she was drawn to him. Levi had said it was just her thirst for knowledge. At first that made sense, but it was more than that.

Looking at Connor stirred a hope in her she'd never known. It was illogical to feel so happy and terribly confused all at once. She couldn't trust those feelings and willed herself to focus on their conversation. "Since my eldest sisters, Adeline and Maggie, are both married, Levi only worries over Bethany and me. No matter his motive, he hasn't shown you the best in himself. But you've handled it graciously." She switched the rope to the other hand and the horses breathed loudly. "I believe you and Levi will be good friends once he gets to know you."

"I like your optimism." Connor grinned a little. What was he thinking?

They were walking in a slow stride.

She asked, "Do you come from a large family?"

"No." He cast his gaze into the distance and remained quiet. Maybe his family was a sore topic. She gave him time to reply and had nearly given up on a response when finally he spoke. "I'm an only child. My mother died when I was young. She'd been sick for years, so it was really my grandmother who raised me."

"I'm sorry." She knew all too well what it was like to lose a parent. "How did your father cope with losing her?"

"I have no idea."

"What do you mean?"

"He wasn't exactly in the picture. I never knew my dad."

"Did he die?"

"I don't know. When I was a kid, my mom told me that he was a pilot. Whenever an airplane would fly over, she would point at it and tell me that my dad might be flying it. She talked about him like he was a hero. I guess that's why I wanted to be a pilot."

He grinned but it didn't reach his eyes. "My grandmother came to visit me when I finished flight school. I asked her about my father. She said it didn't really matter. I wanted to tell her it mattered to me, but I could tell by the look on her face that I should let it go. She died a few months later."

Lydia thought about what it must be like to have no family at all. She couldn't imagine it. "It sounds like your life was lonely."

"I never thought of it that way. But being a guest in your dad's house is the first time I have ever been with a large family." He chuckled and raised his eyebrows. "It's been a whole new experience for me."

He could lighten the mood instantly. She smiled and wished they had more time together before he had to leave again.

He stopped walking and turned to her. The horses stood still and sniffed the air. Lydia stopped too and looked up at Connor. His gaze was fixed on her, and his expression held a sober vulnerability. "I feel honored to be here… with your family… in your village. I feel honored to be with you, even walking a couple of horses down the road." He was quiet for a moment but didn't look away. He was calculating his words carefully. "When I was traveling to the other villages, I missed this place. I missed you, Lydia."

He hadn't called her Doc. Though she liked his nickname for her, she also liked the way he said her name. Caught by his stare, she understood what her giggly little sister meant when she'd said Connor's deep brown eyes were full of mystery and passion.

Lydia felt dazed and illogical. How did she look to him? Was her hair a mess? Was she blushing? Her hands were sweating inside her gloves. If this feeling was what Mandy meant when she spoke of intrigue, it wasn't nearly as enjoyable as she had made it sound.

Connor reached his hand toward her. She thought he was going to touch her and she held her breath. But he only took the rope out of her hand.

She let her empty hands fall to her side.

He flashed his confident grin and emitted satisfaction. "I have to leave again tomorrow. I want you to know I'll miss you while I'm gone."

He had control of both horses and started to walk again. He clicked at the horses and they followed him.

She brushed her gloved hands together, aware of their emptiness and the unease that came with having nothing to hold on to. She walked beside him and, as they approached the barn on the Colburn property, he looked at her, still grinning. "Do you think these two would like to go for a run?"

"Possibly." Lydia glanced at the two horses then back at Connor. "Would you like to ride? I can teach you."

He chortled. "Thanks, Doc, but I know how to ride a horse. I heard that you're the fastest rider in the village. I would like to see it for myself."

She liked the challenge. "Oh, I see. Let's take them to the barn for saddles, and then we can ride to the paddock across the road and have a run." She mirrored his grin and squared her shoulders. "That is, unless you're afraid of riding fast."

He laughed. "The last time I rode fast, I was at Mach one point eight."

"I'm not sure what that means, but I hope to find out." She took one of the ropes out of his hand and walked the horse to the barn. He was watching her, and she liked it. After she brushed one horse, she heaved a saddle onto it and glanced at Connor as he saddled the other horse. He knew what he was doing.

Connor lowered himself into the saddle and held the horse's reins. Lydia mounted her horse with swift grace. The hobby of his youth was her daily experience. Her skirt bunched in front of her thighs, exposing her legs. He stared until she caught him.

He grinned and pointed at the field across the road from the Colburn property, but before he could ask, she turned her horse and led the way. She flashed a pretty smile over her shoulder. "Follow me."

His competitive spirit tempted him to fire a challenging retort. Instead, he kicked the horse and caught up to Lydia. As soon as they crossed the gravel road, she tore through the open field and left him momentarily surprised. He urged the horse to gallop but was only halfway across the field when she pulled on the reins and turned her horse around.

She chuckled as Connor reached her. "What Mach was that?"

"You're funny, Doc." His horse snorted and fidgeted, while the horse Lydia rode seemed perfectly content beneath her. Connor tugged the reins and turned the nervous horse toward the road. "Race me back."

Lydia grinned and accepted his challenge. His chances of winning were slim, but he rode hard as he crossed the field. He was only a few feet behind her when she made it to the road. He considered his quick improvement a hopeful sign of a future victory.

She threw her head back and laughed when she turned and saw him behind her. She had once seemed delicate and serious, but he was now familiar with her strength and her fervor. She could challenge him for the rest of his life. The thought of spending his life with her appealed to him deeply. The desire was foreign to his plans, and the weight of it stunned him. As he rode next to her, her expression changed. The seriousness of his thoughts must have been obvious on his face.

Lydia drew her brows together. "What's wrong?"

"Nothing." He forced himself to smile but all he could think was a life here in the Land with Lydia Colburn—not because the rest of the world was at war, but because he had met his match and would have no peace without her.

Someone called her name from across the road. Bethany was running from the Colburn property, waving her arms over her head. "Lydia, come quickly!" she shouted. "There's a man at the cottage looking for you. He said they need you at the school immediately. One of the children has been hurt."

Lydia popped the reins and took off. In a matter of seconds, she was out of sight.

As Connor watched her disappear, he realized she had held back during their race. He shook his head in amused disbelief then swung down from the saddle and walked Levi's new horse into the barn.

Chapter Eleven

"And then what did he say?" Mandy asked as she lowered herself into a chair at the Colburns' kitchen table. Lydia carried a porcelain cup full of fresh cream to the table and offered it to Mandy as she sat across from her. Mandy put up her hand. "No, thank you."

Lydia drizzled the warm cream into her afternoon cup of coffee. She raised the cup to her lips and glanced at Mandy through the steam. Mandy leaned forward and propped her elbows on the table while she waited for Lydia's reply. Lydia had already made sure there was no one in the parlor, but she kept her voice low just in case Isabella was listening. "Connor said that while he is gone he would miss me."

"He will miss you?" Mandy furrowed her brow and pulled a curl of auburn hair through her

306 • KEELY BROOKE KEITH

fingers. "I suppose it could mean something. It's certainly a friendly thing to say." She dropped the curl and tapped her thin fingers on the side of her cup. "The men I have intrigued are more obvious than that when they declare their romantic notions. But Connor might have a different way of handling it. How did he look when he said it?"

"I prefer not to read too much into a person's demeanor, especially since I was feeling struck blind by my own infatuation at the time." Lydia thought back a day and pictured Connor as they walked home with the horses. "It was as if he wanted me to know something, but he couldn't say it." She waved her hand. "See, my own interpretation cannot be trusted."

"And maybe your impression of him was accurate." Mandy put her finger to her bottom lip as she thought for a moment. "Did he touch you at all while he was speaking?"

Lydia shook her head. "He took the horse rope out of my hand and then he smiled and kept walking."

"What kind of smile?"

"Oh, I don't know."

"Of course you do."

Lydia set her cup on the table then hid her face in her hands and laughed. "Can you believe I'm having these feelings? This giggling over a man—this is your forte and maybe Bethany's, but certainly not mine."

Mandy beamed with delight. "Truly intrigue is the most magnificent part of life, Lydia. You should enjoy it."

Lydia mocked a grimace. "Enjoy it? I can barely tolerate being in my skin feeling this way. I cannot believe you enjoy this sensation!"

"What could possibly be undesirable about falling in love?"

Lydia could have listed manifold discomforts about the situation. She sighed and gazed at the ceiling. Her eyes traced the wooden rafters high above the kitchen table. "If I'm wrong about Connor's feelings, then I'll feel humiliated. If I'm right, then my whole life could take course in a new direction—a direction I neither want nor feel suited to fulfill."

Mandy leaned back and brought her cup to her mouth with both hands. "Perhaps now you understand why I stick to intrigue and refuse commitment. Well, that's part of my reasoning anyhow. Just enjoy falling in love and when it's run its course, which it always does, return to yourself unfettered."

Lydia chortled. "You almost make your hobby of toying with men's affections sound logical." She thought of Levi and how painful it was for the person on the other end of that rejection. "I prefer not to enter a situation destined to end in broken hearts. I suppose it's for the best that Connor is gone right now. I should use this time to sort out my feelings. I've never wanted to marry. I'm still not sure I do, but I must work that out on my own time and not on someone else's heart."

"So you're intrigued by Connor, the mysterious traveler. You're certainly not the first in the village for that." Mandy grinned briefly, then her serious expression returned. "Is he worth further consideration to you?"

"Yes... I believe he... he would make a good husband. He's intelligent and considerate and protective, and when someone is speaking to him he stops whatever he's doing and gives that person his attention." She was getting swept away as she thought of Connor's qualities. She shook her head. "But that isn't what is important right now. What I must decide is if I could be a wife."

Mandy drew her head back in surprise. "Of course you could be a wife."

"Really? What man would appreciate his wife leaving home at midnight to rush to someone's aid? Or what if I became a mother? How would it affect the village if I were so encumbered being with-child that I couldn't help a person who needed me?" With only brief consideration of her profession and its importance to the village, her romantic feelings all but dissipated. She blew out a breath. "There's more to consider than whether or not he's likable. I have to consider if this is even possible. Connor said he and Levi would be away for three weeks. I want to have an answer prepared by then—even if the question is never asked."

Mandy tilted her head to the side, and a curtain of curls dropped over her cheek. "You were always so resolute that you would never marry. Even you must admit it's humorous you should become intrigued by the first man to fall from the sky." Mandy smiled over the top of her cup. "Whatever you decide, you have my support. And if you decide that you can't marry, do send Connor my way."

Lydia lingered in the kitchen long after Mandy went home. She remained at the table but turned her chair so she could look out the window. Her eyes fixed on the grass outside but focused on no particular point. As the sun sank lower in the sky, she watched shadows stretch across the yard. Finally, she stood and walked into the parlor.

Isabella emerged from her afternoon nap and tapped her cane along the floor as she stepped into the parlor where her knitting basket awaited her. John came home as the sun was setting. He sat near the fireplace in a winged-back armchair and propped his feet on a wooden footstool. Isabella's knitting needles clicked as she worked.

Lydia sat on the plush rug that spanned the parlor floor and sorted through her aunt's basket of yarn balls. As she untangled knots, she studied her father's face. His head was angled toward the fireplace, and the warm light illuminated the faint creases at the corners of his eyes. They looked deeper than usual.

John stared into the fire. "It is nearly one hundred twenty miles north to Pleasant Valley.

The boys should be there by Sunday afternoon if all goes well."

"Yes," Lydia agreed. "I hope the weather remains favorable for them." She found a knot in a ball of light green yarn and began to pick the tangle apart. Her fingers stayed busy while she thought about Connor.

She had to decide if she could get romantically involved with anyone before Connor returned, but her thoughts only drifted to him as a person. Maybe the two concepts were inseparable; only the love of the right man could make her want to marry. Still, she couldn't believe any man would want a woman whose profession would always be her prominent duty. The men she knew preferred women who were devoted only to domestic interests. She wanted to ask her father's advice, but the matter should go no further than Mandy… unless Connor made his feelings known. If he even possessed those feelings for her, which she had no reason to believe he did. She shook her head out of frustration.

"Have you got a tough one?" John asked.

"Pardon?" Her attention snapped from her thoughts. Had she spoken out loud?

"The knot." John pointed at the yarn she was holding. "You looked frustrated."

"Oh, yes... perhaps. I don't know."

"I see." He furrowed his brow. "You will work it out, Lydia. I know you will."

She nodded, thankful for her father's encouragement even if they were thinking about two different things.

Someone tapped lightly on the front door. Most people in the village went to the Colburns' kitchen door. Lydia glanced at her father as she set the yarn in the basket. She straightened her skirt as she walked to the door. Its rarely-used knob squeaked when she turned it. "Mrs. Owens. Please, come in."

A slight woman in her mid-thirties, Ruth Owens wiped her boots politely and stepped across the threshold. "Thank you, Lydia. Is your father home?" She looked past Lydia. "Oh, hello, Mr. Colburn. May I have a moment of your time?"

John removed his feet from the footstool and stood. "Of course, Ruth." He motioned to the divan across from his chair. "Please, have a seat."

"I'll only be a moment. I have to hurry home and cook dinner." Ruth sat on the edge of the divan and folded her hands in her lap. "It's my boy Luke. His father and I are concerned about him. I'm more concerned than his father. That's why I came to you, Mr. Colburn."

Lydia started to leave the room, but Ruth held her hand up. "Stay, Lydia. I have no secrets. Mr. Owens and I rarely see eye to eye on things, especially Luke's upbringing, but this time I think Luke is headed for real trouble."

John nodded to Lydia, and she sat beside Ruth on the divan. John sat back down in the armchair. "Please, continue."

"Luke was always a good boy, you see, doing his chores and minding us." She gestured continually with one hand while she spoke. "Then not long ago, he started having some trouble in school, mostly with the other boys. I spoke to his teacher about it. He says Luke only has one friend, Walter McIntosh. The teacher said Luke and Walter usually keep to themselves. Then last month Luke started coming home from school later each day. Now he gives his father lip about the chores and refuses to answer when we ask why he is late. I understand it's natural for a fourteen-year-old boy to want his independence, but this sudden rebelliousness seems odd for Luke. So I went by the school one afternoon last week when I knew he should be getting out of class. I watched from a distance as my son and Walter left the school yard with Frank Roberts."

Lydia shot her father a look.

He glanced at her and returned his attention to Ruth without changing his expression.

Ruth put up both hands. "Frank Roberts is a grown man, and an odd one at that. Pardon me, Mr. Colburn, if that was wrong to say. I just don't like my son being influenced to ignore his chores and sass his parents. They are up to no good. I just know it."

John shifted in his chair. "Did you tell your husband that you saw Luke with Frank Roberts?"

Ruth nodded. "He said it's Luke's way of showing us he is growing up. He said I shouldn't worry about it, but I have been losing sleep over this. Luke is my son."

"Your husband is right, Ruth. Luke is growing from a boy into a man, and it is normal for him to challenge authority. And you are also right. Adolescence is a time when young men easily make bad choices. From the behavior we have witnessed from Frank Roberts, I would consider it a bad choice for a young man to spend time alone with him."

"Will you speak to my husband then?"

John leaned an elbow onto the arm of the chair. He rubbed his fingertips against his thumb for a moment as he turned his face toward the fire. Ruth and Lydia waited silently for his response; Isabella's knitting needles clicked in time with the clock.

John looked back at Ruth. "Yes, I will. I can encourage your husband to guide Luke away from Frank, but whether Mr. Owens acts on my advice or not is up to him. Is tomorrow afternoon all right?"

Ruth put a hand to her heart. "Yes, thank you."

While John saw Ruth to the door, Lydia excused herself and walked to the kitchen. Her mind filled with dread. The thought of boys Bethany's age befriended by Frank Roberts made her stomach churn. Was Frank planning to do something to the boys or with them?

Feeling the need to busy herself, Lydia pulled a pot from the kitchen shelf. She filled it with water and set it on the stove to boil. Then she stepped into the pantry and picked up an armful of sweet potatoes to peel and cook.

Bethany walked into the kitchen and started working beside her, but Lydia didn't speak a word. Her mind was fixed on Frank Roberts influencing Luke and Walter. Ruth Owens had come to John about the problem because he was the overseer of the village, and Lydia just happened to be in the house at the time of Ruth's visit. Still, how many people in the village knew about Frank's attraction to her? Maybe Ruth knew about it and associated her with Frank when she discovered the despicable man was influencing Luke. Any mention of Frank Roberts caused her to fluctuate between embarrassment that she would be associated with him and guilt that she was to blame for sparking his desire in the first place.

Darkness fell early as the autumn sunset quickly ended the day. She stepped close to the kitchen window to look out, feeling eerie and exposed. Maybe she should make curtains for the kitchen window.

As she glanced at her cottage, she wished Levi and Connor were home. Connor had tried to warn her about Frank weeks before, and it had irritated her. He said she couldn't fight off a man. Her eyes found her reflection in the window; she was thin but not frail and she never considered herself weak. She often rode her horse on the forest paths at night to get to the ill and injured. Her volition gave her strength beyond her physical form.

She cursed her fearful thoughts and walked back to the stove. Frank wouldn't hurt her. He was up to no good and might embarrass her, but he wouldn't hurt her. She needed to make dinner and think no more about the darkness or Frank Roberts.

She would keep busy the rest of the evening and the next evening and the next until they were home… until Connor was home.

In the forest outside of Good Springs, the gray leaf trees stood tall and packed together like marching soldiers frozen in time. Connor and Levi traveled for two days along the narrow road through the forest. Then the road curved north and led them alongside the river. At times the worn dirt trail veered close to the riverbank, and other times the water could only be heard in the distance. On the fifth day of travel they reached Pleasant Valley. Though the area lived up to its name, when their business was completed, Connor was ready to move on.

The topography of the Land changed as they traveled farther north toward Clover Ridge. Connor estimated the Land was about thirty-five degrees south of the equator, yet the northern region had distinctly sub-tropic characteristics. The agriculture reflected the difference with fewer sheep farms and more citrus groves. Between abundant outcrops of volcanic rock grew banana trees, lush fern, and acres of bushy, dark green shrubs in carefully weeded rows.

After a night camped beside the road, Connor and Levi arrived in the village of Northcrest. The overseer welcomed them into his home and accepted Connor's message, as the other overseers had. The letters from John Colburn made his work easy. Only minimal explanation of the issue was ever needed, and never did anyone demand proof—all of which increased Connor's respect for John and his appreciation for the simplicity of life in the Land.

They remained at the overseer's home in Northcrest for three nights and helped the elders locate the man who had once told Lydia about an electric motor. They spoke with the man, and he explained he'd only read an ancestor's story of seeing an electric motor, but he had no plan to recreate such a machine.

Connor was relieved to know the elders in every village of the Land now understood the possible dangers of developing certain technology. He'd been able to spread the message without having to report many details of the outside world. His mission to protect the

Land was almost complete. Soon he could return to Good Springs and protect Lydia.

He was beginning to think the only real danger in the Land stalked through her village and lived in a dilapidated cabin past the bluffs.

After leaving Northcrest, Connor and Levi retraced the road south. They stopped to camp for the night beside the road halfway back to Clover Ridge. The campsite was a clearing between the road and the bank of the river. A wooden bridge barely wider than a wagon spanned the river beyond the clearing. A well-used fire pit marked the center of the campsite. The fire pit, surrounded by gravel and sand, overflowed with fresh ashes and bits of animal bones from the last campers.

Connor and Levi were the first to stop at the campsite for the night and built a fresh fire. Later a trader, traveling on horseback, pitched his tent in the grassy field beside Levi's wagon.

The elders in Northcrest had supplied Connor and Levi with baskets of produce, packages of salted meat, and wrapped loaves of bread. They shared dinner with the trader and, after eating, as Levi unhitched and fed the horses, the trader warned of leeches and advised them to sleep in the back of the wagon since they had no tent.

Connor emptied the supplies from the back of the wagon to fit the bedrolls inside. He stacked the goods beneath the wagon and expected it all to be there in the morning.

He awoke at the first light of dawn, opened the cover at the back of the wagon, and climbed to the ground, which was wet with dew. The trader stood by his horse, strapping his rolled-up tent to the back of the saddle. Sacks bulged on either side of the horse. The air was filled with the thick scent of coffee.

The trader nodded at Connor. "I'm off to the north. Will you be staying here another night?"

"No." Connor stretched his neck and it popped. "I'm ready to get back to Good Springs."

"I know a few folks in Good Springs," the trader mumbled as he pulled straps across his horse and fastened a few buckles. The horse's back sagged under the weight of multiple bulging sacks.

Connor pointed at the overstuffed sacks. "What do you trade?"

"I have eighty pounds of fresh coffee leaves in each of these bags. I'm taking it to Northcrest for cotton cloth."

"Coffee leaves?" Connor grinned. "You mean coffee beans."

The trader poked his stubby fingers into the top of one of the sacks. He withdrew a pinch of dark, green leaves from the bag and held it out to Connor.

Connor took a piece of leaf and sniffed it. It smelled like coffee. "How do you make coffee from these leaves?"

The trader drew his head back. "You dry the leaves and brew it, of course. Don't tell me you've never had coffee to drink." He contorted his face and resumed checking his saddle.

"I've had coffee. I've just never prepared it— not like that anyway." Connor rubbed his hand over his hair and realized it was longer than it had been in years. He turned to walk into the woods. "Have a safe journey."

When Connor returned to the campsite the trader was gone, and Levi was climbing out of the back of the wagon. They ate breakfast, after which Levi took the horses off the lines staked to the ground and hitched them to the wagon. Connor pulled the bedrolls out of the back of the wagon and tossed them to the ground. Then he dropped the satchels on the ground beside the bedrolls. He jumped down, gathered the goods from beneath the wagon, and lifted them into the back. Then he climbed inside to make more room.

As Connor arranged the cargo inside the wagon, horse hooves stamped across the bridge.

Levi knocked on the side of the wagon. "Get out here. We have trouble."

"What is it?" As Connor jumped down from the wagon, three men rode horseback from the bridge to the campsite.

Levi glowered at them with his nostrils flared and his fists clenched.

Connor slipped his hand inside the wagon and picked up one of the metal stakes Levi had just pulled from the ground. He tightened his grip around it and slowly positioned his hand behind his back.

One man pulled ahead of the other two as they approached. A blend of black and silver hair hung behind his shoulders. His eyes shifted rapidly between Connor and Levi. His horse stamped a hoof as he pulled it to a halt by the wagon and waited for the other two men.

They seemed to be younger versions of their leader—same shifty eyes and desperate need of a comb. One had his dirty, black hair tied back in a ponytail. He jumped down from his horse and handed the reins to the other man, waiting for his cue.

They were empty handed, so Connor loosened his grip on the tent stake he held behind his back and stood shoulder to shoulder with Levi.

"What do you want, Felix?" Levi's question flowed out like a growl.

Felix parted his lips, revealing crowded brown teeth. "Step away from the wagon." His mustache curled into his mouth when he spoke. He looked back at his sons and nodded once. "Take it, boys," Felix commanded as he moved his horse between the wagon and Levi.

The hulking horse pushed its head at Levi aggressively.

The ponytailed man rushed to the front of the wagon. In a heartbeat Connor dropped the tent stake, slipped past Felix's snarling horse, and charged to intercept. The ponytailed man had one leg up to the wagon bench when Connor reached him. Connor grabbed him with both hands and pulled him down, throwing the first punch before the man hit the ground.

The other young man leapt down from his horse. Connor fought them both and evaded every punch until Felix rode by with Levi hanging onto the back of the angry horse. It tore through the campsite toward the bridge. Levi held onto the horse's saddle with one hand and was trying to pull Felix down with the other. Halfway across the bridge the horse bucked and Levi was thrown off.

As Levi rolled over the edge of the bridge, a fist planted firmly into the side of Connor's mouth. His head snapped back and to the side. He let the momentum propel him away from the men and toward the bridge.

Felix kept riding and was already to the other side of the river when Connor got to the place where Levi had disappeared. He looked down over the side of the bridge. Levi's fingers were digging into the edge of the wooden planks. His feet were swinging as he dangled from the bridge high above the rushing river.

Connor dropped to his stomach and reached down. He tried to get a grip on Levi, but Levi was kicking frantically. The bridge trembled beneath his body and the other horses rumbled past. The robbers whooped in victory as the wagon passed mere inches from Connor's body.

He struggled to hold onto Levi. "Hang on, Levi! I've got you!" He sank his feet between the wooden slats of the bridge and hoped it would hold him.

Levi looked up at Connor with eyes full of fear. Perspiration dripped from his jaw and his muscles shook as he strained to pull his body up.

Shards of the old wooden planks splintered into Connor's skin while he reached both arms down. "Stop kicking!" He locked his hands around Levi's arms and pulled with every ounce of strength he had. His back burned as his muscles contracted and he heaved Levi onto the bridge.

Levi crawled to the middle of the planks and curled his legs beneath his body. He let out a yell like a wordless curse and pounded his fist into the wood beneath him. He got to his knees before giving in to the exhaustion and lay on the bridge, panting.

Neither man moved as they caught their breath. Felix and his sons drove the Colburns' wagon into the distance on the west side of the river. After a moment, they were alone with only the rush of the river. Their wagon and horses were gone.

The metallic taste of blood filled Connor's mouth. He sat up and spit over the edge of the bridge. From high over the river he watched the water rush by. He faced Levi. "You okay?" His jaw ached when he spoke. He stood and wiped his split lip with the back of his hand.

"No." Levi forcefully exhaled and made it to his feet. He rested his hands on his knees and breathed through his mouth. He cast his gaze to the other side of the river and frowned, broken in spirit.

The robbers were gone, along with their transportation and food. Connor understood the agony of defeat, but he remembered the war that raged around the globe and decided this battle was insignificant. "It's just a wagon." He turned and started to walk back to the campsite. "You can build another one when we get back to Good Springs."

"It's more than the wagon." Levi's words came in short bursts as he trudged beside Connor.

"Right—the horses. You can barter for a couple more."

As Connor's feet stepped off the bridge and onto the solid ground of the campsite, he pointed at the bedrolls and satchels still lying in the grass. "Good thing I'd just thrown these out of the wagon before the robbery." He picked up his bedroll and handed the other one to Levi.

Levi didn't take it. He stared back at the bridge. "No, you don't understand. That was my chance. For ten years I have dreamed of the chance to kill Felix." Levi spit in the grass. His eyebrows pulled together, carving a crease between them. He shook his head. "Felix knew not to get off that horse. He knew I wanted to kill him."

Connor nodded to show support for Levi, even though he didn't know the story. As he waited to hear the explanation, he dug through his bag and found a length of leather cord. He strung the cord through the center of the bedroll and pulled it over his head so that it hung across his body. He drew its strap over his head, hanging the bag across his chest on the opposite side. He cut another length of cord and strung it through Levi's bedroll then held it out to him. "So you heard about that guy when you were young and always wanted a shot at him?"

Levi took the bedroll this time. He hung it from the cord across his body as Connor had done. "No, I didn't hear about him. Felix and his sons came into our home. They robbed us… and killed my mother."

Connor clenched his teeth and swallowed hard. Levi's words hit him with more intensity than any punch. That was why Levi had clung to the horse and tried to pull Felix down.

Connor looked back across the bridge. The desire to hunt Felix down and deliver justice started to overwhelm his logic. He took a deep breath and folded his arms across his chest. "I knew your mother died. I didn't know she was murdered."

"My parents were in the kitchen one afternoon. Felix and his sons marched through the door and started snatching everything they wanted." Levi lifted his satchel from the ground and held it by its shoulder strap. He picked at the lacing on the strap while he spoke. "Lydia and I were in the parlor and heard the commotion. We ran into the kitchen in time to see our mother try to stop Felix. He shoved her and she fell onto the hearth. Her head hit the stone and she didn't move. Lydia rushed to her.

"I remember looking at my father. I thought he was going to do something to Felix for that, but he just stood there. He didn't do anything. When Felix saw my mother was hurt, he and his sons took off. My father knew Felix somehow, but he refused to discuss it. My mother died two days later. Lydia didn't leave her side until it was over. We never saw Felix or his sons again, but I always imagined if I got the chance someday, I'd make Felix pay for what he did."

Levi pulled his satchel over his shoulder. Connor didn't know if Levi wanted to say any more, and he certainly was not going to press him on the matter. With nothing left at the campsite, they started to walk south on the road.

"Did you say you are John Colburn's son?" A lanky, middle-aged man with a booming voice and a stern jaw shook Levi's hand with two forceful pumps. "There is plenty of honor in that name. When I was a young man, I once traveled with my uncle, a land trader, to Good Springs, and your father insisted we stay with him. Yes, I remember John Colburn well. He'd just taken his father's place as overseer and was quite eager to do his best in the position. That might have been before you were born. I recall little girls in the Colburn house but not a boy. Do come aboard, gentlemen."

He pulled his hand away from Levi and motioned to a long board wedged into the ground. The thick plank linked the bare dirt of the riverbank to a small, double-masted schooner anchored in the deep river.

Wanting an introduction, Connor glanced at Levi then at the boat's captain.

Levi put his hand on Connor's shoulder. "Mr. Roberts, this is Connor Bradshaw, a friend of mine."

"Arnold Roberts." The man stuck out his long hand. His skin was thick with calluses. He raised a wooly eyebrow. "Bradshaw? I haven't heard that name before."

"I'm from another land," Connor replied. "I've heard the name Roberts in Good Springs. Are you related to a Frank Roberts?"

At the mention of Frank, Levi's eyes darted to Connor.

Connor didn't care. He preferred to know if the captain were related to Lydia's stalker before boarding the man's ship.

"Frank Roberts? No, that name is not familiar. My relations are all in Riverside." Arnold withdrew his hand and scratched behind his ear. "You're from another land you say?"

"Yes, sir." Connor waited for a reaction while the man studied him. He briefly wondered if his alien status would ruin the chance of a quick journey back to Good Springs—a chance that had been secured by John Colburn's good name.

"I've never met a man from another land. You must have plenty of interesting stories to tell," Arnold chuckled. "I want to hear all about your land after we set sail. Yes, I imagine you have great stories to tell. It's a pity we will deliver you to the bank near Good Springs by morning."

"By morning, Mr. Roberts?" Levi asked.

Arnold walked the plank to the schooner with the graceful ease of a man accustomed to balancing on moving objects. He jumped over the ship's rail and then looked down at Levi and Connor. "We will have the current and the wind in our favor tonight."

Levi followed the veteran river trader onto his vessel, and Connor walked up the wobbly board after him.

Arnold motioned to the back of the boat. "We're full down below. You'll have to make do in the stern tonight. My men are almost ready to sail. Keep out of the way and watch for the boom."

Connor and Levi stepped to the stern of the small ship and dropped their satchels and bedrolls against the back wall. Connor leaned his shoulder against the taffrail and watched the crew prepare to weigh anchor. It made him think about the last ship he was aboard. The schooner held an old-world charm lacked by an aircraft carrier, and it would cut two weeks off their journey back to Good Springs. Still, Connor missed the carrier—the constant rumble of the action on the flight deck, the noxious smells of men and metal, the terrifying thrill of the catapult launch.

Levi planted his palms on the wooden railing and looked down at the river below. Connor glanced down briefly, but because of the tight space he kept his attention on the boom while they were standing. Arnold walked to the stern, handed Connor a paper package, and whirled back around, yelling orders to his men. Levi removed his hands from the railing and looked at the package as Connor unrolled it. The contents appeared to be some type of dried meat. Levi pulled a piece of the meat from the package then lowered himself to the deck and began to eat.

Connor also sat down. He drew a chunk of the meat out of the package and smelled it. Then he took a bite, not wanting to appear picky. His jaw ached when he chewed. The salty meat's tough texture reminded him of beef jerky, but he didn't recognize the flavor.

"Beef?" He asked Levi.

Levi shook his head and kept chewing.

"Lamb?" Connor guessed again.

Levi grinned slightly as he shook his head once more.

Connor was out of guesses. "What is it?"

Levi swallowed the bite he had been chewing and reached for another piece of the salted meat. "It's venison."

"That was my next guess." Connor drew his legs close to his chest to stay out of the way when a crewman walked by.

The ship began to move as the crew worked to guide the vessel to the center of the wide river.

Chapter Twelve

The white cross on the chapel's steeple rose above the gray leaf trees, energizing Connor for the final mile to the village. He and Levi would be walking the cobblestone streets through Good Springs within minutes.

"I don't think I have ever been this grateful to see my own village," Levi grinned. "If I never sleep on the soggy, wet ground again it'll still be too soon."

"I agree." Connor brushed the growing hair off his forehead. "I will forever be grateful to Arnold Roberts. It would have taken us weeks to walk home if it weren't for him."

Levi raised an eyebrow. "Home?"

"The village," Connor corrected himself.

"Do you plan to stay in Good Springs?"

At once it hit him: Good Springs felt like home. He gave Levi a sidelong glance. "Are you okay with that?"

Levi didn't immediately respond. Connor waited, knowing Levi thought before he spoke. He respected Levi for it. The friendship they'd forged in the battle transcended all previous misconception.

Levi drew a deep breath. "You have a place here. You've worked hard to prove yourself, and you're important to my family."

That meant something coming from Levi. Connor needed the affirmation. "Thanks, man."

The path turned from gravel to cobblestones as they stepped into the village of Good Springs. An elderly woman peeked through her curtains as they passed her house. Across the street stood the library where Lydia came in the day he was reading the founders' journals. He couldn't look away from her then, and he was desperate to see her now. Next they passed the chapel. Its doors were closed. John had already gone home for the day.

Levi nudged him. "Do you still want to talk to my father about Lydia?"

"I plan to, yes."

Levi kept his voice low and aimed at Connor, but he looked straight ahead. "You don't need my blessing, but I want you to know that you have it."

"Thank you. That's good to know." Connor agreed that he didn't need Levi's permission, but he didn't want to sow discord in the family.

"My sister is stronger than most women and independent too. She needs a man who is stronger than she, but meek enough to support her, not stop her. She's never been interested in courting, but that's because there wasn't a suitable man in Good Springs. I'm not sure what your chances are, but if she accepts you, I know you will be good to her."

"Yes, I will."

Lydia worked all day and had missed lunch. Her stomach growled incessantly as she walked her horse into the barn. It was long past dark, so she lit a lantern and hung it near her horse's stall. She removed the saddle and blanket and brushed the horse before she took off the bridle and slung it over a rusted hook on the wall. After checking her horse's hooves, she walked it into the stall.

The horse snorted as Lydia put out the lantern's flame.

"Good night to you, too." She picked up her medical bag, closed the barn doors, and walked through the darkness to her family's house.

Her warm breath puffed in little clouds in the cold night air. As she neared the back door, she looked through the window and into the kitchen. The low fire of a gray leaf log glowed in the fireplace. Bethany approached the door and stepped outside carrying a milk pail. She closed the kitchen door behind her and flinched when she saw Lydia.

"Oh, my!" Bethany sucked in a breath. "Thank goodness it's you! I'm glad you're home."

"I'm sorry. I didn't mean to startle you." Lydia glanced at the milk pail. "It's a little late to go milk the cow, isn't it?"

"Oh, you won't believe what happened!" Bethany gripped Lydia's forearm as she spoke. Her dramatic enunciations came with every report, so they rarely piqued Lydia's curiosity. "You simply will not believe it."

Lydia was exhausted and hungry, but Bethany wouldn't be ignored. She inclined her head. "If it is gossip, Bethany, I don't want to hear it."

"I don't think it's gossip. It's not a secret or slanderous anyway. It's simply all too exciting! You will be shocked."

"Fine, what is it?"

"Levi and Connor were robbed." Bethany froze as if she wanted a dramatic response from Lydia.

Lydia tried to process the news. She glanced at the road but only saw darkness. "Have they returned? The wagon wasn't in the barn. What do you mean robbed?"

"That's just it—the wagon was stolen by the robbers. And after the robbery, Levi and Connor had to walk all day to Clover Ridge, and a river trader let them ride on his boat down the river. Then they still had to walk three days to get from the river to Good Springs. I tried to hear the rest, but Father keeps sending me to do chores." Bethany glanced at the pail then back to Lydia. "Can you believe it? Robbers! Isn't that exciting!"

"Levi and Connor are here? Now?" She wanted to see him. Her stomach fluttered. "Are they inside?"

Bethany smiled and nodded. "They're in the parlor with Father."

Lydia dropped her medical bag and rushed past Bethany for the kitchen door. Just as she did, Levi opened the door from the other side and stepped out of the house. She threw her arms around his neck. "Levi!"

He kissed the top of her head.

She drew back and looked up at him. "Bethany said you were robbed. Are you all right?"

"Yes, I'm fine." He smiled down at her.

"Who robbed you?"

Every trace of happiness withdrew from his expression. He moved only his eyes toward Bethany. Their younger sister was waiting, wide-eyed, to absorb all the details of his misadventure. He squinted slightly as he looked at Bethany. "Don't you have a cow to milk?"

Disappointment washed over Bethany's face and she nodded at Levi.

"Then go," he ordered.

Bethany turned and stomped toward the barn.

Levi watched her until she was out of earshot and then he looked back at Lydia. "It was Felix—"

"Felix Colburn?"

Levi nodded and Lydia audibly drew a breath and put her hand over her open mouth.

"Felix and his two sons. They're older now, but I recognized them instantly."

One thousand anxious thoughts flooded Lydia's mind. She had not heard Felix's name mentioned in years. Even when she traveled during her medical training, she wondered if she would hear of him, or worse yet, encounter him on the road, but she never did. She squeezed Levi's forearm. "Did they recognize you?"

Levi shook his head. "I don't think so. They were planning to rob whoever was at the campsite. It just was by chance that it was me and Connor."

"How did it happen?" She kept her hand on her brother's arm.

"One morning on our way home, we were breaking camp near the river. I looked up and saw them riding across the bridge. I warned Connor and he stood with me as they approached. Felix told his sons to take the wagon. Connor fought both of Felix's sons while I tried to pull Felix off his horse. Felix took off while I was halfway on the horse and I ended up going over the side of the bridge. I was barely able to hold onto the edge. All I saw were the rocks and the river below. My fingers dug into the wood, but I couldn't get back up. Connor pulled me onto the bridge. He saved my life. The men got away with our wagon and horses."

She searched his face for any signs of injury. "Was anyone hurt?"

"Connor took a punch to get to me, but I'm sure Felix's sons got the worst of it. You should see Connor fight."

"Is he all right?"

"He was hit in the mouth. It bled for the rest of the day. We still had our satchels and I reminded him of the medicine you sent, but he said he didn't need to numb his whole body for a busted lip."

She tried to imagine Connor brawling with two men then refusing medicine. Her face softened. "He would say something like that." She smiled a little. "I'm so relieved you are both safely home. Where is he? I would like to see him."

Levi looked over his shoulder through the kitchen window. He turned his head back toward Lydia but didn't move out of the way. His expression relaxed, which immediately aroused her suspicion.

She peered through the window. No one was in the kitchen. She raised an eyebrow at him. "What's going on?"

He blew out a breath. "I was wrong about Connor."

"How do you mean?"

"When he arrived, I thought he was dangerous. I thought he would ruin us. Now I see he has done nothing but try to protect us… the Land… you." He grinned, trying to hint at something.

She quickly discerned his meaning. "Is Connor in the house?"

Levi nodded.

She tried to keep her excitement to herself, but her smile gave her away. "Is he speaking with Father?"

Levi nodded again.

She pressed her palm to her stomach. "If you have any objection to us courting, you should probably say it now."

"No, Lydia, I have no objection. I respect Connor. He wants to spend time with you, and I told him he has my blessing." He shrugged, his grin holding steady. "I believe he will treat you well, and if he doesn't, he knows I will hold him accountable."

Bethany walked toward them from the barn. She had a full pail of milk and a sour expression on her face.

John opened the kitchen door. "Bethany, Levi. Come inside, please." He held the door by its knob as his grown children walked inside. When they had passed, he looked at Lydia. "Connor would like to speak with you, and I have given him my permission, but it is up to you if you would like to spend time with him… alone."

John waved for Connor to come outside. Then he disappeared into the parlor with Levi and Bethany.

Lydia tried not to shiver from the cold. She waited until her family was out of sight before she spoke. "Levi told me what you did."

Connor's eyebrows arched slightly as if he wasn't sure what she meant.

She smiled. "About how during the robbery you saved his life." In the dim light that came through the kitchen window, she could see the mark on his lip. "Were you injured?"

Connor touched his mouth. "Not badly. I'm fine. Thanks, Doc." He grinned with the confidence she had come to admire. "Look, it's late and you have worked all day, so I won't keep you out here long." He raked his fingers through his hair. "I talked to your dad and he gave me permission to spend time with you. I thought about you the whole time I was gone. I want to get to know you more. Come with me tomorrow night. There is that thing—your dad mentioned it—the festival."

She nodded. "The Squash Festival?"

"Yes." He chuckled. "That. Let me take you."

He was asking to begin something she'd never imagined but now desperately wanted. She wouldn't enter into it lightly. And she would make sure he didn't either. "Connor, I'm flattered and I would like to spend time with you as well, but you must understand my plans are frequently interrupted by someone needing—"

"I can deal with that."

"No, I'm not simply speaking of tomorrow night." Aware of what she could give and what she couldn't, she looked into his eyes and searched for a way to make him understand. "I mean every day. My life is devoted to my profession. I couldn't be a good physician and put myself in a position to where I'm unavailable to people. And I couldn't be a good wife and constantly disappoint a husband." Her priorities were unusual for a woman in the Land, and she expected Connor to be shocked by her devotion to her profession.

Connor tilted his head, unfazed. "I would never expect you to give up your work. Not tomorrow, not ever."

A wave of loose hair blew onto her face. Before she could push it away, he tucked it behind her ear. "Where I'm from, most women—most people—have commitments in addition to relationships and family. You're a committed physician. You're passionate about medicine and saving people. Life is pitifully mediocre without passion. Never let anyone take your passion away from you. I certainly won't try to take it away from you or take you away from your village. These people need you." He reached for her hand and lightly held her fingers. "Plan to go with me tomorrow night, and if that plan is interrupted we will make another plan and another. Eventually it will happen."

"You make my burdensome complication sound like a simple inconvenience. All right, I will go with you tomorrow." She liked the feeling of her hand in his. His palm was wide and warm. She left her hand there until he let go. "Good night, Connor."

She picked up her medical bag and walked to her cottage. The floorboards creaked as she stepped inside. She felt his gaze on her until she closed the door.

Leaning her back against the door, she felt as though her whole body might melt right there on the doormat. She needed to absorb the moment. Connor wanted her. His words rang in her head and confirmed it was more than intrigue. He had given serious thought to this, just as she had.

It would take more than biological desire or social expectation to move her to join her life to another. It would take a certain man. One who captured her curiosity and held it. One who proved his strength through action, even when no one was around to see his choices. One who understood her passion and wouldn't try to take it away from her.

Connor was the only man who could ever fit at the end of that equation for Lydia, and she was willing to accept his offer to court. More than willing, she was elated. He had initiated the journey she had always assumed she would never have to take.

Too exhausted to eat and too excited to sleep, she lit the lamp on her desk and carried it upstairs.

Lydia sat on the cushioned chair in front of her dressing mirror while Mandy primped her like a favorite doll. Mandy held several hairpins between her lips as she combed out a small section of Lydia's hair. She braided the long strand from behind one ear, wrapped it over the top of Lydia's head, and pinned it behind the other ear. Then she began the process on the other side, rhythmically intertwining Lydia's hair. The braids held Lydia's hair off of her face and revealed her light brown eyes, bright and unpainted.

Mandy took the last hairpin from between her lips. She studied Lydia in the mirror and gauged where to place the pin. "When is Connor coming for you?"

"At sunset."

"Have you seen him today?"

"Not once." The rest of Lydia's hair was pinned in circles around her head where it had been held for an hour. Mandy began removing the pins on one side as Lydia worked on the other. Long, loose ringlets dropped below the neckline of Lydia's dress.

"Do you think this dress is appropriate?" Lydia asked as she smoothed the fabric at her waist.

"Of course. You always look lovely in dark blue." Mandy released the last pin and arranged the ringlets behind Lydia's shoulders. "Connor is in love with you. I doubt it matters to him what you wear."

Lydia touched the silver bracelet around her wrist and fidgeted with the tiny gray leaf charm. "That may be; however, we are going to a festival and the entire village will see us."

"They will not simply see you, they will watch you all evening—both of you. Every young woman in the village will wish she were you tonight. There," Mandy said as she arranged the last ringlet. "Stand up." Mandy stepped back and studied the result of an hour's work. "Perfection. Now I must go to the festival. Mother has lined the street with two hundred luminaries carved from gourds and I promised to help her light them at dusk."

Lydia checked herself in the mirror and was delighted with her transformation. Though she always tried to look respectable, her motivation in dressing was rarely beauty. She felt pretty and girly and nervous.

She followed Mandy to the door.

Before leaving, Mandy hugged her and said, "The next time a warrior falls from the sky, bring him to my house to recover." With a wink she was gone, and Lydia was left alone in her cottage to wait for Connor.

She ascended the stairs to her room and selected soft black gloves from a drawer atop her dressing table. The leather dress shoes she seldom wore uncomfortably restricted her feet. After loosening their laces, she tied a bow at each ankle.

Maybe she'd have one night without a call for her help. As she stood to face the mirror for one last assessment, a knock echoed from downstairs.

She opened the door expecting to see Connor, but didn't expect the catch in her breath that came from seeing the admirable man at her door—not because he needed something—because he liked her.

Despite her attempt to remain logical, her heart was drawn to his. The realization produced an exquisite ache in her soul. She found the foreign feeling both delightful and dreadful and hoped it would never go away.

Connor wore a new woolen coat tailored to a perfect fit, attesting to his ability to navigate life in the Land without her. The collar of a white cotton shirt rose in a sharp peak between his neck and the coat. His face was clean-shaven and his dark hair combed and damp. As it dried it would fall onto his forehead.

He flashed a happy but nervous smile. "You look beautiful."

"Thank you."

He glanced into the cottage. "Are you available?"

"I am." She lifted the front of her heavy dress an inch and stepped over the threshold.

He pulled the door shut then offered his arm. She took it and walked close to him as they stepped away from her cottage and past the empty Colburn house. Her family was already at the festival, and she absorbed the thrill of arriving somewhere public with a man.

The sun sank behind the forest to the west and left the sky streaked with pink and orange. The cold air made Lydia appreciate Mandy's admonition to wear her hair down. The moon, full and oval, slowly climbed in the sky over the ocean to the east. Mrs. Foster's gourd lights twinkled along the road in the village ahead.

She felt safe walking with Connor. He frequently scanned the thick darkness that settled on either side of them along the road, yet his attentiveness to her never seemed divided. He was gentle and controlled, but it had only been a week since he fought two men using only his fists. The thought excited her.

He tucked her fingers around his arm. "Tell me about this festival we are going to."

"Well, we call it the Squash Festival. People make everything you can think of out of squash." She pulled a loose ringlet through her fingers, but let it go when the action reminded her of Mandy. "Do you like squash?"

Connor pursed his lips. "Not particularly. Do you?"

"Not particularly." She smiled. "But the festival is more of a social opportunity. Many of the women spend days preparing the food and crafts for tonight. Young people get dressed up and come to flirt with one another. The children enjoy the games, and the elderly huddle together and exchange opinions on the whole spectacle."

Connor planned to absorb every detail of his date with Lydia, from the delicate clicks her heels made on the cobblestones to the bounce of the loose ringlets draping her shoulders. How had he managed to get a woman like her to go out with him?

The gourd lights along the street lined the way to the festival. He checked the darkened road behind them. Frank Roberts was probably watching. Connor didn't want that creep ruining their first date.

The crowd gathered in the village ahead. He wouldn't get much time alone with her once they arrived. He'd spent several months living with her family, but there was much left to learn about her. She was the kind of woman he could study for a lifetime and still not know completely.

He scanned the thick shrubs on either side of the road as they walked toward the village, then he gazed at her again. "I know you apprenticed to become a physician, and you're passionate about your work, but I don't know why you became a doctor. Most doctors say something inspired them during their childhood. What about you?"

Lydia smiled then looked at the festival ahead. "I suppose it was both being helped and being there for someone in need. I always admired Doctor Ashton and was fascinated by the way he helped people. When I learned of the medicinal power of the gray leaf, I was mesmerized by it." She became quiet for a moment. "When my mother was hurt, I stayed by her side for two days and nights until she died. Doctor Ashton did everything he could for her, and I helped him with all her care. I remember when he left one day I sat on the bed beside my mother and thought there just had to be something else I could do for her.

After she died, I read every medical journal in our village's library. I never found any reason to doubt Doctor Ashton's treatment of my mother, but I understood what I read and began to ask Doctor Ashton medical questions. He realized I had a natural inclination for medicine and encouraged me to keep studying." She reached to her hairline to tuck her hair behind her ear out of habit, but her fingers stopped when she touched the braids that held her hair off her face. "I want to save every life I possibly can. I can't imagine doing anything else with my life. I feel like I'm doing what I was made to do."

Connor remembered her care when he was her patient. He smiled at her. "And I'm personally grateful for your dedication."

As they walked into the center of the village, Connor received nods from people he recognized and a few stares from others on the outskirts of the assembly. He and Lydia were soon engulfed in the greetings and glances of the crowd. Booths with games lined the street, and tables of food filled the open-air market.

As they strolled through the festival, Connor managed to decline the offer of a cup of squash soup and a sample of squash and oats, but when Lydia graciously accepted a squash muffin that he knew she didn't want, he surveyed the festival for a less conspicuous place. He spotted the unoccupied church steps on the other side of the street and led Lydia to the chapel.

They walked to the stone steps and into the lantern light that escaped from the church's tall, open doors. Lydia climbed one step higher than Connor. She turned and faced him, eye to eye. He wanted to kiss her, but the restrained society reminded him of the camp counselors of his youth who fussed about public displays of affection.

He looked down at her gloved hands, which held the orange-tinted muffin. "You don't want that, do you?"

Her mouth curved at the edges. "No."

"Are you going to hold it all night?"

"No."

"Throw it away."

"I wouldn't dare." She didn't mind that her maturity and high manners left her holding a stinky squash muffin. Her smile reached her eyes as someone familiar walked past them. She held the food out to Mandy's brother. "Here, Everett, try this."

Everett stopped and took the muffin. He pinched one bite off the top and his face contorted into a scowl as he chewed. "Who made this?"

"The shoemaker's wife is giving them away." She chuckled as Everett turned to the wooden rubbish bin beside the steps. He threw the muffin in it and walked away wiping his lips.

Connor tightened his gaze on her. When she looked at him, he raised an eyebrow at her and her smile faded.

"Oh, was that mischievous?" she asked.

"A little."

"Are you shocked?

"Stunned."

"I'm sorry."

"Don't be. I thought it was well played. I just didn't know you were capable of mischief."

"I am." She brushed her hands together as if to loosen any crumbs left behind by the muffin. "Though I rarely find use for it."

"We need to change that," Connor joked. He watched Lydia's face as she laughed.

Several children streamed out of the chapel wearing matching choral robes. They followed a man who was completely bald on top but had a full, silver beard. Connor took Lydia's hand and moved away from the church steps. The bearded man herded the children and arranged them on the steps to prepare for their performance.

In front of the library, Connor found the empty end of a long table and they took a seat. The choir director rang a bell and directed the crowd's attention to the children. Two young women Connor recognized from the Fosters' barn party sat beside Lydia. They fawned over her hair and the silver charm bracelet Levi had brought her from Southpoint.

Someone gripped his shoulders from behind and he looked up. Everett smirked then sat beside him. The teenaged boy leaned in close as if he had a clandestine message. "Bethany told me you fought robbers on your journey. Is it true?" His eyes widened, eager for the answer.

Connor glanced at Lydia. She was still chatting with the young women. "Yes, it's true."

"Can you teach me how to fight like that? I don't have anyone to fight, but if I did I would want to—"

Connor raised his hand to halt the young man's enthusiastic request. "How old are you, Everett?"

"Seventeen."

Everett was tall compared to most of the boys his age in the Land, and he had a solid frame, but he seemed younger than seventeen. Each time Connor had encountered Everett, the young man was acting goofy. But if he earnestly wanted to learn to fight, he might grow to be a good sparing partner. "What does your father have to say about fighting?"

Before Everett could answer, he had a friend join him and then another. More young men joined them at the table. Everett didn't mention fighting in front of the other teenagers, and Connor appreciated his ability to keep the matter private.

As the boys claimed Connor's attention, Lydia's friends chirped enthusiastically around her. Then Mandy sauntered over to join them. When Connor's eyes met Mandy's he expected her usual eyelash batting, but she only gave a friendly smile and looked away. At least Mandy knew to show Lydia that respect. He wondered if there were more substance to Mandy than he had accredited her.

Connor grew impatient with the crowd they had acquired. He gazed at Lydia sitting across from him at the narrow table. He wanted to reach across and take her hand. She might not appreciate the gesture with people watching.

He moved his leg under the table until it pressed against hers. With a look she acknowledged his touch. She gave no expression of disapproval, nor did she move away.

Lydia feigned interest in the glib conversation around her but focused on the warmth conducted through the physical connection with Connor. The children's choir had come and gone, and the cooking competition results had been announced. Someone brought a tray of non-squash related food to the table and they all shared it.

The tray was empty now, and Lydia wanted to be alone with Connor.

It cost her more energy to ignore her desire for his attention than it would to acknowledge it. Finally, she let him catch her eye.

He stood, wearing his confident half-grin, and came around to her side of the table without decreasing the intensity of his gaze. The voices around her blended into a gentle hum and lowered in significance as she rose above the crowd.

He offered his arm and she accepted; their steps synchronized in a harmonious gait as they strolled away from the crowd. When he stopped near the last flickering gourd light, she glanced back at the dwindling festival. People cleared off tables and escorted the elderly home. A group of youngsters, including Bethany, shuffled down the path that led to the beach and disappeared, giggling. Villagers packed their small children onto wagons, and men carried whatever the women stacked into their arms.

As Lydia turned to Connor and considered how she should word her gratitude for the evening, a sharp boom pierced the air. A flash of sparks shot over the treetops. She jerked reflexively and entrenched her fingers into the wool of Connor's coat sleeve.

He coolly turned his head in the direction of the sound and let out a heavy sigh.

All motion among the villagers paused, followed by a flurry of questioning glances, unsettled by the distant explosion. John stood at the top of the chapel steps with his hands on his hips and looked in the direction of the sparks that dissolved in the night sky. Concern marked his brow as he descended the steps. Levi and a few other men met him in the street.

Connor took Lydia's hand and kept her a step behind him as he hurried toward John.

"Do you know what that was?" she asked Connor as they approached the others.

"Just stay with me." His serious tone made her look from the sky to the concerned men to the path that led to the beach.

As the group gathered in the street, Bethany sprang from the sandy path nearby. She rushed to John and the others just as Connor and Lydia met them. Bethany panted and pointed back at the ocean. "Father, come quickly!"

At once, John rushed to Bethany and she led him along the path to the beach. Levi and the others were right behind them. Connor followed, still holding Lydia's hand. She felt desperate to catch up to Bethany and find out what had happened, but the momentum of the whole group pulsed forward ahead of her.

John put his hand on Bethany's back as they moved into the moonlit clearing on the sand. Bethany was explaining the commotion to her father as they hurried, but Lydia couldn't decipher Bethany's words.

She glanced at Connor. He knew the source of the sound and the flare of lights. She wanted to ask him about it, but she trusted him enough simply to stay with him as he had instructed.

The ocean reflected the light of the full moon. The light provided ample illumination but little explanation for what was happening at the water's edge. The tide was going out, and near a sandbar Frank Roberts stood on a makeshift boat with his arms crossed and his chin lifted in defiant pride. Two young men with their pants rolled above their knees were climbing aboard the wobbly craft. Frank handed them each a paddle.

Lydia pushed between John and Levi and took Bethany's elbow. "What is Frank doing?"

Bethany's high voice rose above the sound of the ocean waves. "When Everett and I came out here with our friends, we saw Frank push that boat out to the sandbar. Luke and Walter were with him. We asked what they were doing, and Luke said Frank told him and Walter there is a place just beyond the horizon that is filled with treasure. They said if they row out far enough they could reach it."

"What? They know the current is too strong for a boat." Lydia grappled to understand. "Why would anyone believe Frank Roberts?"

"We tried to talk them out of it, but they wouldn't listen. Luke just kept saying Frank has shown them some of the treasures and everyone in Good Springs wants to keep them from getting more."

"What treasures? Where did Frank get treasures?"

"Frank has items from Connor's land." Bethany's chin quivered, afraid for her young classmates as they went farther into an ocean known for its deadly currents. Bethany glanced at Connor, who was speaking with John and the others behind them. She looked back at Lydia. "Frank shot that thing into the air and it made fire in the sky. Luke said Frank even has a magic cloth that will carry them safely home." Bethany turned her face toward the boys as they began to paddle out to sea, and she dragged a knuckle under her eye to catch her tears.

Lydia followed Bethany's line of sight and understood her sister's fear. It was a shock for all of them to see Luke Owens and Walter McIntosh being deceived to their demise. Ruth Owens had been afraid Frank would get her boy into trouble, and she'd been right. The two young men knew as well as everyone in Good Springs to stay out of the water. Its currents ripped visibly below the surface with an angry appetite.

Lydia had never witnessed anyone venture so far from the shore. She watched Walter and Luke on the boat as Frank stood aboard with his arms crossed in satisfied insolence.

She spun around to the men. John was talking with Connor and Levi. She pushed between them. "Father, this is ridiculous! Tell them to come back to shore. They will be killed."

Connor and Levi stopped talking with John and looked at her. She watched their faces for response, but none was given. She turned to the one young man there who seemed to know the most about the situation. "Everett, why is Frank doing this?"

"He said it's all for you."

Lydia stepped closer to Everett. "What is for me?"

"The treasure." Everett drew a breath to relay Frank's words. "Frank said he could get treasures and fly back here on some magic cloth. Somehow he convinced Luke and Walter to go with him. He just kept saying over and over, 'This will make Lydia love me.' I'm sorry, Lydia."

Everett's report raked Lydia's conscience, leaving deep grooves of guilt. The heels of her dress shoes sank into the sand as she staggered back a step. Frank was doing the very thing she had always feared, though she never imagined he would endanger others in his attempt to get her attention. She covered her mouth with her hand.

"Everett, no," Levi groaned.

Lydia felt the eyes of her father and brother and the man she was beginning to love all looking at her. She couldn't discern if their expressions held pity or blame, and it left her speechless. Her pulse raced and her ears rang from the increasing pressure.

Feeling caged by the crowd, she walked to the water's edge then stopped on the last inch of hard packed sand. It was still damp from the waves that departed with the tide. She had to rescue the two young boys being coaxed to their death by a man obsessed with her, but how?

Backlit by lightning, the faint silhouettes of the boys and Frank and the boat were barely visible on the near horizon. After a moment they were only a blur.

She couldn't stop them. There was nothing left for her to do but suffocate in the reeking sludge of humiliation that buried her spirit. Frank had exposed his desire for her in the most public and destructive way he could devise. The young people who had heard his words were relaying the details to the curious crowd that gathered on the beach.

Misery hammered in her chest as she heard them recount Frank's intention. His selfish desire to get her attention would cause the death of two naïve boys. Frank's actions would dissolve the reputation she worked hard to build and protect. And she would lose the respect of the only man she'd ever considered sharing her life with.

Voices murmured behind her. Her father trying to calm the crowd, Levi consoling Bethany, Everett explaining to Connor he hadn't meant to blame her. She ignored them all.

A gust of wind came from the sea and blew her ringlets behind her shoulders. She gathered all of her hair and swirled it together then held it bound in one hand over her chest. Her heartbeat pounded through the bodice of her dress. Her pulse had steadied some, though her nerves had not.

Another burst of wind whipped Lydia's skirt behind her with a snap. Shadows marched across the water as freshly formed clouds rolled in from the horizon. The unexpected squall brought neither chill nor rain but threw a salty mist into the air, pelting the onlookers. The gusts grew in intensity and, when lighting cracked, the crowd began retreating from the sandy shore.

John stepped beside her. "There is nothing to be done for them. A storm is coming. We must go home."

"No." Her voice cracked with angst. "If I'm here when they're washed ashore, I can try to revive them. It might not be possible, but I will try. I must. I am the cause of this."

"Come home, Lydia," her father commanded.

"I will take care of her, John. I brought her out tonight and I will take her home." Connor raised his voice over a clap of thunder and Lydia flinched.

She briefly took her eyes off the ocean and then tried to refocus on the horizon, but the spray from the sea forced her to turn her face away.

John left them and corralled Bethany and the others to the path away from the beach.

"I am not leaving." Lydia's protest was muffled by the tempestuous groans of the wind. Her hand clung to the twist of her hair as lightning clawed at the ocean. She couldn't bear to stand on the shore and watch for another moment. Frank might get what he deserved, but she could still rescue the boys. She had watched her mother die and had since vowed to save every person she could for the rest of her life.

She bent one knee and, raising her ankle to her hand, untied her shoe's ribbon. Then—

after a glance in Connor's direction to confirm he had not noticed her action—she furtively did the same to the other shoe. Beneath the secret cover of her long dress, she stepped out of her shoes.

Sucking in a breath, she dashed into the surf, holding her dress high as she ran through the shallows. The stinging saltwater quickly deepened as she rushed into the ocean. She paused briefly when she reached the first break of a wave and braced for the new experience. The mild crest spat brine and foam across her body, soaking her from navel to neck.

Connor's anxious voice came from behind her. It dissipated on the wind before she could understand his words. She wouldn't look back until she reached the boys.

She let go of her dress and pushed farther into the ocean. Its depth covered her chest. As the next wave approached, the sand withdrew beneath her feet, and a malicious current gripped her body and pulled her into the deep.

Arms flailing, she held her breath, helpless in the cumbersomeness of the drenched dress. Wrapped in the surge of a violent wave, her body rose with its crest. She gasped the moment her face was exposed to the air, only to be pulled powerfully under the water again.

Her hands frantically tugged at the dress as she tried to rip the fabric apart. The weight of the dress held her in the water, but her fingers found the seam between the skirt and the bodice. The threads snapped as she blindly yanked her fingertips along the stitches. Her lungs began to burn from the breath she held.

The surge of the water returned to toss her body upon another wave. Determined to save herself so that she could save the boys, she willed her hands to work. She tore the seam and ripped the skirt away from the bodice while the ocean drew her to its churning surface. She raked in a breath and coughed. She held her chin above the water while she kicked free from the skirt's heavy fabric, then she arched her back and attempted to float on the water's tumultuous surface.

She treaded the water with her splayed arms and tried to get her bearings. When she heard a voice, she bent her body and craned her head. While she strained to see where the voice came from, a swell drew her body up and she spotted the boat some twenty feet away. With sudden visual acuity, she focused through the darkness and saw Luke's face.

"Luke!" she screamed.

He was clinging to the edge of the makeshift boat, now overturned in the swells. With each bob of the waves between them, Luke moved in and out of her line of vision. She paddled through the breakers and was almost close enough to reach him.

"Luke! Hang on—" She tried to yell reassurance to the boy, but choked on the saltwater that lapped into her mouth.

The wind whipped over the sea and cracks of thunder shook through the undulating water. She anticipated the rhythm of the swells as they passed beneath her. Expecting to rise with the waves again, she prepared to clutch the boat. As the swell lifted her, the rhythm broke and the undercurrent sucked her bare legs into the spiral of a churning wave. She kicked violently against the water as the ocean's fury whipped her body and swept her along the swell. She tightened her arms against her chest as the current's force spiraled her with the wave until the crest carried her back into the shallows.

Sand shifted beneath her hands as she crawled through the seaweed, using the last of her strength to save herself from the next wave. Finally clear of the ocean's grip, she collapsed on the foamy beach, coughing.

Thunder cracked in the clouds roiling overhead as she curled her naked legs beneath her body. Thin dregs of seawater lapped around her and drew sand from under her limbs. Opening her stinging eyes, she tried to focus her vision.

She panted for breath as she lifted her head, hoping to see the boys nearby. She scanned the beach. They weren't here. The sea had hurled her back to the shore but not the boys.

The image of Luke's frightened face was burned inside her mind. She wasn't able to save him. There was nothing she could do, just like there had been nothing she could do to save her mother.

Overcome by her abject failure, she rose to her knees and looked back at the ocean. Someone approached behind her, but she didn't look away from the roaring waves. "I could not save them. I could not save them." The words fell from her lips between jagged breaths.

She began to shake, disoriented with ignominious disappointment. Hands moved around her, wrapping her in a coat. Its woolen lapel pressed against her damp skin. Scooped from the sand, she fell limp in Connor's arms as he carried her away from the shore.

Chapter Thirteen

Lydia borrowed a dress from Bethany and cuffed its long sleeves as she descended the stairs of her family's home. She willed her aching legs to walk across the parlor floor. Though aware that her father and Connor were outside closing all the shutters, she jumped when the wooden planks banged across the window beside her. A draft came down the chimney and caused the slow-burning gray leaf tree log to spark, just like the lights in the sky that had commenced Frank's horrid plan.

Levi was in Bethany's bedroom trying to console their younger sister. Her sobs drifted down the stairs. Though not close friends with Luke or Walter, the boys were Bethany's classmates, and their deaths would traumatize her sensitive heart.

Maybe this folly could have been prevented if Lydia had done something after Luke's mother visited them. Ruth Owens had warned them that Frank was planning something, and she was right. John had gone to Mr. Owens about it, but their efforts changed nothing. Luke and Walter had been determined to continue their association with Frank. Maybe if Lydia had treated Frank differently the boys wouldn't be drowning. Maybe she had driven Frank to lunacy; after all, he had said this was all for her.

The gravity of each anxious speculation pushed the guilt deeper into her heart.

A crack of thunder rumbled the floor beneath and the wind's groan increased outside. Between the storm's violent sounds, Isabella's door creaked open.

"Lydia, come here, child," her great-aunt summoned.

"Coming." Lydia picked up a ceramic oil lamp from the mantle. She lit the flame and inched her weary legs down the corridor and into Isabella's bedroom. It was pitch black in the room. "Yes, Aunt Isabella? Are you all right?"

"Of course, dear." Isabella used her cane as she shuffled back to her rocking chair. She wore a long, cotton nightgown and her silver hair coiled stiffly behind her back. "I overheard your brother and sister. It seems there has been an incident."

"Yes, there was."

"Are you all right, child?"

"I am," Lydia lied as she set the lamp on the dresser near the door. It cast a faint light across the room. She approached her aunt's chair. "Has the storm frightened you?" She knelt on the floor beside Isabella's chair. It was the first time she'd rested since she sat with Connor at the festival. Though only hours before, that felt like a lifetime ago.

"No, dear. I've heard many storms in my lifetime. However, this storm is full of wind and fury but lacks rain. It's different." Isabella silently moved her lips between sentences. "It isn't a natural storm, you see. It is an act of God."

Lydia thought of the gullibility of the two young men and the guile of Frank and decided to refrain from considering the storm's divine wrath. She didn't have the strength to dispute her aunt's theory.

Isabella cleared her throat. "Go to my wardrobe, dear. Open the bottom drawer. At the back, beneath the scarves, you will find a book wrapped in a pillowcase." The elderly woman's voice was weakened by the evening of socializing in the cold air.

Lydia obeyed, and as she returned to her aunt, she pulled the ancient journal out of the embroidered pillowcase. The journal's binding was that of the old printer's method from the generation who founded the Land.

"Here it is." She touched the book to her aunt's hand.

Isabella didn't take the book. She folded her thins hands in her lap. "It is for you, child. Open it."

Lydia's legs burned as she knelt on the floor again. She looked at the old journal and lifted the cover. The first page was spotted with age and in pencil was inscribed: Lillian Colburn, 1899. The people in the Land shared their books of history and wisdom, and copies of each of the founders' works were printed and distributed among the villages. "Why isn't this in the library?"

"It is the private journal of our ancestor, Lillian Colburn. She wrote it during a shameful time in our history. After the trouble passed, the elders of that time agreed never to speak of it again. They wanted to record only the pleasant and noble portions of their experience. Lillian secretively disagreed and recorded the details of the disgraceful event. She hid the journal, but when she was near death she gave it to her great-grandson. He promised to keep the contents confidential and only bring it to light if the same type of situation ever loomed again.

He was my Grandfather Colburn. Before he died, he read the journal to me and placed it in my keeping." Though her eyes roamed, Isabella turned her head in Lydia's direction. "God commands the wind and the waves. He controls entrance to the Land and refuses departure. The storm is God's voice reminding us He judges rebellion."

John and Connor's voices came from the kitchen. They were safely inside the house. Would they disparage her for her attempt to save the boys? Her aunt wanted her to focus on the journal and some potential lesson therein, but she was preoccupied with the unfolding crisis.

John's footsteps ascended the stairs. Connor passed Isabella's door and walked briskly through the hallway toward the guest room.

Lydia closed the cover of the ancient journal. "Thank you, Aunt Isabella. I will cherish this heirloom."

"And read it."

"Yes, of course." She stood and stroked her aunt's folded hands. "I cannot now—please understand—but I will read it." She tucked the old journal under her arm and collected the oil lamp from the top of Isabella's dresser. "Good night, Aunt Isabella."

The closed shutters on the outside of the window rattled in the wind that beat against the sturdy old house. "I will stay in the parlor tonight in case you need me."

Lydia carried the lamp as she walked down the hallway and into the parlor. She set the lamp on the mantel and lowered her tired body to the divan. The loose sand that chafed her toes sprinkled onto the rug. She curled herself into the seat and blanketed her feet under the borrowed dress. Her heart ached for the young boys and for their families and for her reputation. She reclined into the corner of the divan and used her arm for a pillow.

Moments later, Connor came from the hallway wearing the only shirt he had from his land. It was thin and white with short sleeves and no collar. It reminded Lydia of the first few days he was in her life. He had been her patient—at first unconscious and inexplicable. Then he wanted to court her. He couldn't possibly find her desirable after what was transpiring now. She would not blame him if he'd lost interest in her. She certainly would have.

Connor walked to the armchair across from Lydia. He sat down and sighed heavily. He leaned his head against the high back of the chair and stretched his hands along its arms, wrapping his fingers around its wooden ends. His hair was clean and damp. It fringed loosely across his forehead.

If she looked at him for long she might cry. She commanded her eyes to stare at the fire and hoped he didn't consider her rude.

He didn't ask her how she was, and for that she was grateful. He simply afforded her the silence she needed. If only the wind would be as merciful.

She would rest until the storm blew over. At its first sign of passing, she would return to the shore. Maybe the boys had been ejected from the sea on the crest of a wave like she was. That was unlikely.

The light coming from upstairs grew dim. Maybe Bethany had finally cried herself to sleep. The gears clicked inside the clock on the wall behind the chair where Connor sat. Lydia looked at it even though the old clock only made that particular sound when it struck midnight and noon. When she looked away from the clock, Connor caught her eye.

"What time is it?" His voice was quiet and gruff.

"Midnight," she replied as she shifted her body on the lumpy divan.

"You shouldn't go out to your cottage yet. The wind is full of sand and sea foam."

"I didn't intend to. I told Aunt Isabella I would stay here until the storm is over."

"You can take my bed. I'll sleep out here."

"I'm only waiting until the storm passes. Then I will go back."

"To the beach?"

"Of course."

"No, you aren't." Though his body was relaxed, his gaze was intense. "Not tonight."

At present, Lydia desired neither his attention nor his concern. She looked back at the log in the fireplace and returned to her cognitive dissection of the problem at hand.

She would go back to the shore as soon as the storm settled. It was her duty. Connor himself had promised to never interfere with her work, and she expected him to keep his word.

As she watched the fire for what seemed like an eternity, she became lost in her thoughts. The flame dimmed and she blinked. Her thoughts were simply a dream, and for an instant she wondered if the whole evening had been a dream also.

Connor had changed positions in the chair but was still awake. And the wind still lashed against the shutters.

Lydia remembered standing with Connor at the edge of the village as the festival ended and how he had taken her hands in his. He had looked as though he were about to say something. She briefly wondered what it was and then remembered the interruption of the blast and the sparks in the night sky. He hadn't been disturbed by the commotion at all—in fact, he looked as though something he expected had finally happened.

"The blast… the sparks in the sky… Bethany said Frank caused it." Her voice was hoarse. "What was it?"

Connor leaned forward, propping his elbows on his knees. He folded his hands in front of him and looked at Lydia. His eyes were kind but serious. "It was a flare from a flare gun."

"What's the purpose of a flare?"

"To get someone's attention."

"Could it have alerted your people?"

"I doubt it."

Lydia sat up. "Could it have caused the storm?" She spoke the words as they occurred to her and immediately realized her logic was obviously drained.

The edges of Connor's mouth curved up. "No." He seemed delighted by her half-awake supposition, but she felt idiotic. She laid her head back down on the arm of the divan.

Connor stood and walked to the linen closet. He opened its door as if he had lived in the house his entire life. After pulling a blanket from the upper shelf, he closed the closet and stepped back into the parlor. He shook the blanket open and spread it over her. Then he kissed the top of her head and returned to the chair by the fire.

Thin strips of yellow light sliced between the long rectangular shutters and beamed into the living room. Connor yawned and stretched his neck to either side. His muscles ached and told him he would regret the night spent sleeping upright in an armchair, but he'd been determined to make sure Lydia stayed in the house during the storm. She had slipped past him at the beach and nearly drowned, and he vowed never to underestimate her again.

The room was washed in silence; the only movement came from specks of dust that swam in the shards of sunlight. The air outside had stilled.

Connor fixed his eyes on the blanket folded neatly on the empty couch opposite him. Lydia was already gone. The old journal that she had held most of the night was now on the rug beneath the sofa. He picked it up and left the living room.

His footsteps echoed through the empty kitchen as he walked to the back door. He marched to Lydia's cottage, entered without knocking, and called out her name. When there was no answer, he laid the old journal on her desk and left her office. He rounded the main house and took a shortcut on a path through the edge of the forest to the shore.

The sea folded calmly under a cloudless sky, and the sun formed a crenulated circle as it climbed from the horizon. Its reflection off the water was already too brilliant for naked eyes. Connor squinted as he trekked the last length of sand-strewn forest. He cleared the wind-whipped grasses and descended a steep bank of sand.

The tide had come in, and with it three bodies, lifeless and inert. Their clothing was dark and soiled, and it caught the seaweed and foam that failed to wash out with the waves. Lydia was kneeling in the wet sand, hunched over the body of Luke Owens, the young man whose rebellious choice had inflicted her with the most despair.

Connor knelt beside her in the wet sand. Luke's face was bluish-gray. Lydia closed the boy's eyelids with the palm of her hand. She turned to Connor and dropped her forehead onto his shoulder.

She shook silently.

He wrapped his arm around her and anticipated violent sobbing, but it never came. He understood death and loss. She had encountered those things before and surely would again, but he wanted to make it all go away for her.

He would take it on himself for her in an instant if it were possible. As a naval aviator, he frequently put himself in harm's way for a greater good, but this desire to sacrifice his wellbeing to secure one particular individual's contentment was foreign to him.

Sitting mere inches from the empty shell of a recently departed soul, Connor's purpose bound to the life of another. This tragedy would not break Lydia, and he wouldn't rest until he saw her through it. In that moment, on the shore of a land the rest of the world did not know existed, he relinquished his allegiance to his former life and directed his devotion to Lydia Colburn of the Land.

John arrived and Luke's mother with him. Others came and wept too. Lydia pulled away from Connor without looking at him. He stood and held out his hand to help her up. She moved directly to the other bodies and confirmed their deaths as the resident doctor, wearing the stoic expression of a physician at work.

Levi stamped through the grass pulling a wooden cart. He motioned Connor over to one of the bodies. The onlookers around that particular corpse were only gawking. No one wept for that man. Connor helped Levi lift Frank's body onto the cart. He glanced at the military-issued boots on the corpse and was glad Frank Roberts was dead, though the torment of knowing that Lydia took the blame made him wish he had killed the creep himself. He let the thought simmer as he helped Levi move the cart over the sand to the path that led through the forest.

He didn't want to leave Lydia on the beach. He thought of practical logistics and considered suggesting they load all three bodies on the cart at once. But when he saw more of the boys' family members arrive, he was astonished at how the coldness of war had calloused his heart to human remains.

As Connor and Levi moved the cart toward the path, John stepped close and whispered something to Levi. Levi nodded and continued away from the beach while John walked back to the mourners. Connor followed the cart as Levi pulled it along the forest path and into the center of the village.

A young woman and her small child were walking down the cobblestone street. When they noticed Frank's body on the cart, the woman drew her child close to her and turned back around.

The cart's wheels rattled as Levi pulled it across the cobblestones and to the back of the chapel. He directed the cart to an outbuilding that Connor hadn't noticed before. He'd given little thought to the graveyard that lay dark and quiet behind the chapel.

Levi unlatched the rickety wooden door on the shed, and the extent of his duties as the overseer's son became clear. Frank Roberts had no family, so they would have to take on the role of undertaker.

Levi pulled the cart into the shed, and Connor helped him move the body onto the dirt floor. The shed smelled of mildew, and the morning light that came through the cracks in the wooden walls illuminated several spades. They left the corpse in the shed and pulled the cart back to the beach to retrieve the other bodies.

When Connor and Levi returned to the shore, Walter's family had already removed his body. Luke's covered remains had been moved from the edge of the encroaching water. John informed Connor that the boy's father was on his way with a wagon.

Bethany and many of the teenagers whom Connor recognized from the festival had gathered. Lydia stood near Luke's body, expressionless. Luke's father arrived and scooped his son from the sand. He looked at Connor, his eyes thick with sadness, before he turned and carried his son away to be buried.

As the mourners filed behind them to leave, Luke's mother turned to Lydia and said something in a shrill tone then continued walking. Connor couldn't hear exactly what Mrs. Owens said, but once everyone else was gone, Lydia buried her face in her hands. Before Connor could get to her, she composed herself and followed the others away from the beach.

Levi trudged past Connor. "Come, Connor. We have a hole to dig."

With the gruesome task of burying Frank's corpse complete, Connor left the graveyard early in the afternoon. Exhaustion and hunger reduced his senses and clouded his mind, but his anger against the dead stalker drove him past the Colburn property and down Frank's well-warn path through the forest to the dilapidated cabin on the bluffs. With every shovelful of dirt Connor had dumped into the fresh grave, he had thought of the ways Frank had violated Lydia without ever touching her. As he stomped to the cabin, Connor anticipated the cathartic release of destroying anything that could cause her further harm.

Connor threw open the cabin door. It crashed into the wall behind it and sent dust and splinters into the air. Leaving the door agape, he charged to the bed and dropped to the floor. He dragged the stacks of sketches from beneath the mattress and carried them to the fireplace.

After tossing a lit match onto the first stack of gray leaf pages, Connor squatted by the hearth. He watched the hungry flame grow and slowly fed it more of the drawings of Lydia. She probably had no idea that Frank had sketched a single picture of her, and Connor wanted to make sure she never knew. As he dropped the last page onto the fire, he stood and walked to the old trunk where he had found the locator beacon when he searched Frank's cabin weeks before.

The trunk was empty now. Frank had taken all of Connor's gear with him out to sea—the helmet, the parachute, the flashlight—because he thought those things had the power to get Lydia's attention. Now Lydia was in agony because of Frank's stupidity. But Frank wasn't the only one to blame.

If Connor's parachute had not carried him to the shore in front of Lydia, maybe none of this would have happened. His hungry gut tightened with guilt. Maybe he should have left the Colburns as soon as he'd recovered. Maybe he should have told John about Frank's sketches, or even burned down the cabin when Frank was still alive. He should have died when his aircraft malfunctioned and spared them all this misery.

He glanced at the pile of ashes that whispered as they moved in the hearth. On the other hand: if he hadn't landed where he did, Frank would still be alive, stalking Lydia. Connor took one last look around the vile cabin. Frank would have eventually lost patience with simply watching her and sketching her.

Lydia deserved to be free of him. If Connor's arrival had led to Frank's demise, it was worth it all in the end.

Connor closed the cabin door and brushed the dust from his hands. No one would ever know about the sketches of Lydia. Frank Roberts would never bother her again. As he walked back to the Colburn property, his guilt dissipated along with the anger.

Chapter Fourteen

Lydia stopped outside her cottage and shook all the sand from her dress that she could before she stepped inside. The borrowed dress was now stained with saltwater. She closed the door and leaned against it, letting her head fall back to the doorframe.

Her whole body ached. She couldn't deny her fatigue any longer. Everyone and everything else in the world would have to wait for her to recover. She turned the lock on the door of the medical cottage for the first time in broad daylight.

With shaky fingers she unbuttoned the row of pearl buttons down the front of the dress. The dirty, borrowed garment dropped to the floor at her feet. She left it where it fell and climbed the stairs.

She sat at her dressing table and looked with disgust at herself in the mirror. She unraveled the little braids Mandy had fashioned in her hair the evening before. The braids were knotted, and the sea had washed out most of the pins. She picked a piece of seaweed away from her scalp then bathed and combed her clean hair with rigid, mechanical motions.

When she got into her bed, eyes half closed, she couldn't remember coming home. She crawled under the covers and fell asleep without stirring for a comfortable position. Despite being in a bedroom flooded with sunlight, a dreamless sleep smothered her.

She awoke late in the afternoon. Her eyes shifted occasionally from one aspect of her bedroom to another, but her body remained motionless. Her mind wouldn't focus. She hated sleeping during the day.

Each moment she tried to rest another torturous thought burst into her awareness. Each image brought with it the emotions she had felt in those moments—emotions she usually buried in order to carry on effectively. Now those feelings bubbled to the surface and threatened to shadow her existence unless she dealt with them.

She stared at a miniature vase on the corner of her dresser. The late afternoon sunlight illuminated the thick layer of red glaze used to make the clay vase look more beautiful than it actually was. Bethany had made the vase when she first started working at the pottery yard. The clay was rough and poorly molded. She only displayed the imperfect item because her young sister's effort made it seem special. The shiny glaze held her gaze but not her attention.

She thought of Ruth Owens. The grieving mother had poured words poisonous with blame on Lydia as she left the shore that morning. Luke had made a series of bad choices that led to his death. So had Walter. Lydia had tried to save the boys, nearly losing her life in the process, but that didn't loosen the grip of guilt from her heart.

She thought of Frank's death and regretted her attitude and actions toward him while he was alive. She had spent years afraid—not of him—but of what others might think about her because of his attention. She had inwardly despised him and the embarrassment his unwanted affection brought upon her. Her outward portrayal of utmost purity was simply a glaze over her prideful heart like the glaze on Bethany's substandard vase.

As the sun lowered in position, its light struck a pattern in the quilt on her bed. The colors caught her eye. She moved her head slightly and noticed the pillow under her face was wet. She wiped her eye with the back of her hand and moved a stream of tears that flowed without permission. She neither tried to stop it nor encourage it but allowed herself the natural release of crying.

It was dark outside when Lydia emerged from her bed. Unconcerned with the hour, she poured a glass of water and sat on top of the rumpled bedcovers. As she sipped the tepid fluid, she remembered seeing something on her desk that morning. The memory seemed blurry, like a dream; still, she went down the steps to her office to confirm it.

She tiptoed to her desk as if making a sound in her own home would alert a needy village to her wakefulness. There on her desk—just as she had pictured—was the journal Isabella gave her during the storm. Lydia knew she left it in the parlor of her family's home and realized Connor brought it to her cottage when he searched for her that morning. The magnitude of his concern struck her deeply.

She took the ancient journal upstairs and lit an oil lamp on her bedside table. She climbed into bed, and her cold feet were thankful to be back under the covers. Pulling the quilt to her waist, she relaxed against the headboard and opened the old book.

Despite the years since the journal's completion, the penciled writing was still bold and easy for Lydia to decipher. The journal detailed a painful division in the third generation of Colburns in the Land and a freak storm that followed their feud. Lydia understood the correlation Isabella drew between the storm in the journal and last night's storm—both were harsh and rainless, and both occurred after rebellion in the village.

Still, Lydia refused to dwell on pointless speculation or call the storm divine judgment. There would always be some tragedy in life, some rebellion, some mistake—whether malicious or accidental—but she refused to live trapped by fear. Anymore.

After Lydia soaked in every morsel of the ancient details, she curled the old book into her arms. She'd read many journals written by Lillian Colburn and considered her writings to be the standard in matriarchal wisdom. She hadn't found the prophetic voice in the secret journal that her aunt did, but she was honored nonetheless to be trusted with the private heirloom.

After Lydia put out the light, she thought of Connor and how he'd remained with her through her ordeal. She recalled his actions and his questions and his palpable concern. He'd demonstrated his commitment to guard her physically, and at the same time he also showed his desire to guard her heart.

As with her treatment of the storm's cause, she would not speculate if she needed Connor's protection, because she wanted it. She'd been so afraid of what joining her life to another might take away from her that she had not considered what it could bring. Dreaming of those possibilities was perhaps what caused the feeling her peers referred to as intrigue. Though the feeling was becoming more enjoyable, mere infatuation of Connor wasn't enough to change her life and his.

It would take more than that. It was his heart— the immaterial substance of his existence— that assured her of his merit. However, it did little good to consider marriage now. He wouldn't want her anymore. Frank had revealed his deadly stunt was because of his affection for her. She had failed to save the boys. The ordeal would tarnish her image in the village and ruin her chance of receiving the title Doctor.

What respectable man would court a disrespected woman?

Connor would probably go on to another village, as far as he could get from the foolish spectacle of her and her village. She preferred to distance herself from anything less perfect and so she would understand if he did.

Connor was the last person in the Colburn house to arrive at the breakfast table. Lydia hadn't emerged from her self-imprisonment in nearly twenty-four hours, and it caused his mood to fluctuate between annoyance and alarm. No one spoke as the dishes of food were passed around the kitchen table. He stretched his arm reluctantly over Lydia's empty seat to accept the bread basket from John. Both he and her father had tried knocking on the door of her cottage to no avail.

The food passed from one person to the next, and John held another dish out to Connor over Lydia's empty plate. He pictured her in her cottage either mournfully broken or immaturely wallowing in self-pity. If the former, she needed his comfort. If the latter, she needed his correction.

His patience ended.

He accepted the dish from John then stood and filled Lydia's plate with food. He picked up the filled plate, dropped an open napkin over it, and looked at John. "Unless you object, sir."

John shook his head.

The others watched Connor, their eyes wide. How long would they have gone without doing what he was about to do?

He walked to the cabinets by the pantry, opened a drawer that was stuffed with tools and old utensils, and found two long nails. The nails chinked when he dropped them in his shirt pocket. The Colburn family silently watched him as he stepped past the table.

Cold air gushed into the kitchen when he opened the back door. He quickly closed it and walked to Lydia's cottage. With the plate of food in one hand, he knocked firmly on her door with the other hand to allow her one last opportunity to open the door herself. When he received no answer, he crouched to inspect the keyhole. He set the plate of food on a pavestone, took the two long nails from his shirt pocket, and proceeded to pick the antediluvian-style lock. With one nail he easily found the internal pin and with a quick turn of the second nail, the lightweight lock clicked open.

Her dirty dress was crumpled on the sandy floor. He stepped over it and walked into her office. He set the plate of food on her desk and immediately forgot about it. Though already mid-morning, the overcast sky made the medical office dim and gloomy.

He looked upstairs. The door to her bedroom was closed. "Lydia?" He stood still and listened but heard nothing. He took the stairs two at a time then pounded on her bedroom door. "Lydia?"

"Connor?"

He turned the knob and pushed the door open.

"Don't come in."

"Too late." He averted his eyes. "Are you decent?"

"Yes, but you should not be up here."

He looked at her lying in bed. Her room was dark and chilly. He walked straight to the small fireplace embedded in the long windowless wall opposite the door. The fireplace was clean and had obviously remained unused since the previous winter. He pulled back its metal screen, opened the chimney's flue, and set a quartered gray leaf log on the grate. The flames reminded him of the sketches he had burned in Frank's cabin the day before.

Lydia watched him light the fire. "My door was locked."

"Your dad knows I'm here." Relieved to see she appeared physically well, he closed the fireplace screen and meandered around her bedroom. Wanting to give her time to get used to his presence in her private space, he inspected the knickknacks on top of her dresser. Finally, he turned to face her. "Are you okay?"

"I'm fine, thank you. I simply needed rest."

"I understand," he said, but he didn't buy it. He put his hands behind his back and stood with his feet firmly planted beside her bed, looking down at the woman he loved. "I was worried about you."

"I'm sorry. I didn't mean to upset anyone by locking the door. I had to rest and… think." She sat up in bed and held the covers under her chin. Her hair was loose and had dried in wild waves forming untidy tresses. It gave her a thoroughly modern look, which she wouldn't even know about.

Not wanting her to think he was there to scold her, he lowered his voice. "This whole thing has been hard on you. I saw how Ruth Owens spoke to you yesterday and—"

She waved her hand as if it was nothing. "I am fine, really."

Regardless of her insistence, her eyes were red and swollen as if she'd spent as much time crying as she had sleeping. "No, you aren't fine. You nearly drowned trying to save those boys, and now you're hiding. You locked the door to the medical office, which you swore you would never do."

He sat on the edge of her bed. Surprise flashed across her face. He liked it. "You're in mourning, and there is nothing wrong with that. But you aren't the only one who was hurt by this. Your whole village is in mourning. They need you as much as you need them. Your dad has planned a memorial service for Luke and Walter this evening. He said the village would get through this together. You need to be there."

Lydia tucked her hair behind her ear, but it refused to be held back in its current state. She stared down at the quilt. "I can't go."

"Yes, you can."

"No, I can't face people after this."

He wanted to touch her but refrained, wanting her trust even more. "This wasn't your fault." Fire burned inside him at the thought of anyone hurting her in any way. He caught her eye to make sure she understood. "You know that, right?"

"Everyone will see me differently now." She dropped her hands to her lap. The bedcovers followed and revealed her buttoned flannel nightshirt. She folded a crease of the sheet between her fingers over and over. "I have worked very hard to make sure people think well of me. This incident and being associated with Frank Roberts will make people question my ability."

"People know that Frank was shady. If anything, they pity you because of what you have endured from him, but no one blames you."

Lydia lifted her chin. "What about Mrs. Owens?"

"She was distraught. You can't take that to heart."

"What about you? Do you blame me or pity me?"

"Neither."

"Only because you don't know the whole truth." She looked down at her fingers. "When Frank first came to Good Springs, I liked talking to him. I missed my mother and I felt like I had let her die. Frank didn't know my family or me personally, and it felt good to talk to an adult who didn't care that I wasn't perfect. I was very young, and I didn't realize his concern for me was corrupt. I just thought he was nice. My father saw Frank's true intentions and told him to stay away from me. It was the only time I ever heard my father call someone a bad word.

Father said I wasn't to blame, but I caused Frank's attraction somehow."

"That's ridiculous. You were a child and he was a grown man. Don't excuse his depravity."

"I will understand if you no longer want to court me after this."

"Are you kidding?" He wanted to scoop her up, carry her to the chapel, and marry her that very minute. "I want to be with you."

"Even now?"

"More now."

Of all the possible fallout from the tragic deaths of three villagers, she was afraid that he would admire her less. It was oddly flattering. He held back a grin. "Is that what you have been up here worrying about?"

"Mostly." She reached to the bedside table and picked up the old journal he'd left on her desk the morning before. Her fingers tapped on it in little drumrolls and she bit her lip, but said no more.

As he watched her, he became overwhelmed with the desire to hold her and kiss her and have her. He immediately got up and stepped to the door. "Get dressed and come downstairs. I brought breakfast. You need to eat." He stopped and put his hand against the doorframe. "Bring the book. You can tell me about it if you want. If you don't want to talk… that's fine too."

He looked at her for a moment and then went downstairs where he waited in her office. Footsteps moved lightly around her bedroom and soon she appeared on the stairs. She wore a pale green dress. Her hair was brushed and tied loosely behind her head. She handed the journal to him as she sat at her desk.

He sat in the chair beside her desk and scanned the book's cover. She peeled the napkin from the top of the plate of breakfast food. After eating half of a muffin, she put it back on the plate. "Aunt Isabella gave me that book during the storm. It's the private journal of one of my ancestors."

Connor leaned an elbow on her desk, ready to listen. He tried not to stare, but he couldn't look away. He would either spend the rest of his life with this woman or have to move as far away as possible and never see her again. One day without her solidified the fact that he could accept nothing in between. He laid the journal on her desk and waited for her to speak.

"It was written by Lillian Colburn. She was my fifth-great grandmother and the wife of Reverend William Colburn, the man who orchestrated the departure of the eight families from America. She wrote this journal in her later years. Her husband was already deceased. The journal is about a rift in the Colburn family that caused division and filled the settlement with strife.

"Her grandsons, Isaac and Peter, had been rivals since childhood. They were brothers, two years apart but incompatible in temperament. To the other members of the family, neither brother ever seemed overly correct in their squabbles. The family attributed the brothers' feuding to simple personality differences. By adulthood, as the elder son, Isaac, learned his father's profession and grew in favor, the younger son, Peter, grew in bitterness. A raging sense of entitlement swelled within Peter. He surrendered himself to its powerful control and put all his energy into gaining the sympathy of others in the village. The wickedness of Peter's heart became apparent to all and he found no ally—save one cousin. As Peter plotted revenge, a great storm grew over the ocean and battered the Land through the night. The rainless wind tore trees from the ground and ripped the roofs off houses.

"When the elders learned of Peter's evil plan, they emphatically believed the storm was God's wrath and the destruction was His divine judgment. They commanded Peter and his sympathetic cousin to gather their wives and children and leave the village. They were to continue traveling until they reached the mountains. They left and were never heard from again. Lillian wrote of her great despair over the situation but kept the journal hidden, since the founders had demanded that the incident never be mentioned."

Connor found the notion of selective history-keeping unsettling. He lifted a palm. "Why didn't the founders want the feud mentioned?"

Lydia shrugged. "Aunt Isabella said they wanted to record only the pleasant and noble portions of their experience. I suppose since they had left America determined to create a peaceful society, they must have thought it was best to conceal anything that implied failure." She looked at her hands for a moment. "I've always been inspired by the founders' writings. But now I see how their practice of recording only pleasant and noble experiences shaped my expectations of myself. This journal has given me much to consider, though probably not in the way that my aunt intended."

"What made Isabella give it to you now?"

Lydia turned her face toward the window, and the dim light trickling through the curtains highlighted her features. "My aunt thought the storm we experienced was similar to the storm in the journal. She was scared. She'd held this family secret her whole life as if it were prophecy and had waited for the right moment to reveal it. There aren't many disputes in the Land. Though not perfect by any means, most people here enjoy our peaceful way of life. The tragedy on the beach was the first Aunt Isabella had encountered since..."

"Since your mother's death?"

Lydia nodded. "I'm surprised Aunt Isabella didn't reveal this journal at that time, at least to my father. I was too young."

He touched the old book. "It's certainly an interesting piece of your history."

"Actually, it's more of an interesting piece to a puzzle that has long disturbed my family. When Felix intruded our home, I heard him tell my father he wanted what was rightfully his. He said he was a Colburn and he had the right to demand Colburn girls as mates for his sons."

"As in you and Bethany?"

"No, probably my two elder sisters. They're closer in age to his two sons. Of course, my father refused him. It infuriated Felix and he started taking things. Mother tried to stop him and he shoved her."

Connor had heard part of the story before. "Levi told me about it after we fought Felix and his sons up north. He didn't mention that Felix is a Colburn or that he had demanded your sisters, though."

Lydia sighed and looked at the ceiling. "Levi didn't hear what I heard. He's always blamed Father for Mother's death. We knew Felix came from a group that lives near the mountains. It was rumored they had settled out there several generations ago. They rarely go into the villages, and when they do it usually ends in violence. I never understood the cause for Felix's demand, but now I know. The rebellious brother in Lillian's story is Felix's ancestor. That's why Felix believes he has a right to whatever belongs to my family."

Connor thought of the three men he and Levi had fought and wondered if he would ever encounter the Land's biggest outlaws again. He tapped the cover of the old book. "Are you going to mention this to your dad?"

"Not right now. I don't see what good it would do. This ordeal has probably reminded him of losing Mother. I shouldn't add this to his sorrow." Lydia looked at the journal and back at Connor. "This piece of history has made me think about the demands I put on myself... striving for perfection and how it only makes things harder for me. And no matter how hard I tried, I still failed."

Connor put his hand on top of hers. "Your family loves you and your village loves you."

"I know."

"Good, because when you know you're loved, you know it's okay to fail."

Her eyes darted to his.

He was in love with her and wanted to tell her, but decided to focus on her needs first. "Will you be all right?"

She slowly nodded. "I will be." Then the corners of her mouth curled up. "Will you?"

It was good to see her smiling again. He chuckled. "Yeah, I'm fine. This is nothing compared to what I've seen. And that's good... I don't want that for you. Ever."

"What do you mean?"

He had said more than he meant to and pulled his hand away. Her eyes widened just enough to tell him his action had deepened her curiosity. His heart banged inside his chest. "I only meant that this situation will make history in the Land, but where I'm from... tragedy is everyday life, right now anyway. It didn't used to be that way."

He wanted to keep her removed from the atrocities of a world at war, insulated by the inexplicable bubble, safe in the Land. He waited for her to question him and expected her to prod. Would she sulk if he chose not to answer?

He let out a breath through pursed lips and gazed at the woman he loved. She didn't seem the least bit annoyed by his silence. She picked up the half-eaten muffin and finished it off while he thought of how to tell her the outside world reeked of despair.

Maybe he didn't have to tell her anything.

But he wanted her trust and that would require him to remove any mystery that might cause her doubt.

She wiped her fingertips on the napkin and folded her hands in her lap. Her gaze searched his face, making him feel exposed. He wanted to go back to worrying about her and trying to protect her and rescue her. More than that, he wanted to love her well, and that meant allowing her to love him. He had never felt so weakened in his life and was unnerved that an unarmed woman accomplished it.

"I know you are a warrior, and I realize that war spans the continents or you would not have fallen here so far from your home." Her voice was soft but confident. "You've been kind to spare me any ghoulish details of life outside of the Land. I'm sure my father had some persuasion in that." She smiled and looked toward the window. "Many women in the village find your mysterious past intriguing. However, I'm far more inspired by the knowledge you share than by your silence. When I ask a question, you may remain silent if you prefer not to answer, but you should understand silence will only hinder any possibility of intimacy."

He respected her forthrightness. It would be wise to take her advice to heart. He reached for her hand and rubbed his thumb lightly across her fingers. "What do you want to know?"

She raised her shoulders slightly as if the matter was not choosing a question but a chance for him to prove his willingness to trust her. "What is the cause of the war?"

With one finger he mindlessly traced her hand. Mentally he searched for a simple answer to her question. There was no simple answer. "There are battles raging on every continent. Each nation would probably cite a different cause for the war and would name multiple enemies. I can only tell you my perspective, and it's limited. My country's government gives information on a need-to-know basis."

She tilted her head, confirming her attention.

"It started three years ago. I was finishing my flight training and had already signed a six-year service contract. The government of my nation—like most nations—is a much bigger part of society than it is here. We have monetary systems that are complicated and interwoven with other nations. Our economy is built on debt—at least it was before the war. Other nations figured out how to use investment against us, and when they demanded repayment, it was too late. In a hurried response, our leaders basically bankrupted the nation. They changed the country's name and nullified our constitution in the process. This cleared our debt but angered our creditors and plunged our society into fear and chaos.

"At the same time, there were groups who purposed to inflict terror on our society, and they found a way to poison the fresh water supplies of North America and Europe. Millions of sick people needed medical attention, but there was no way to meet the demand. There were also tyrants who ruled in many places in the world, and their populations were weakened by starvation, disease, and slavery. It only got worse for them as the once-wealthy nations seized what few resources were left.

"After three years of world war, there are few clean fresh water supplies left. Millions of people died daily. My last few missions involved securing fresh water supplies for the Unified States. Now the battle is simply for survival, and that's why it is so important to keep the Land hidden."

He swallowed hard and waited for her reaction. It was a heavy load to hand someone from a society with a council of elders for a government, a bartering economy, no contagious disease, and a forest full of medicinal trees. He braced for her to react with shock or even disdain because of his part in the war. "What else would you like to know?"

"Nothing. Thank you." She looked him in the eye. "Should I have further questions, I simply desire the freedom to ask them."

"That's fair. I don't want you to spend your life afraid to ask me anything."

"Spend my life?" With eyebrows raised, a faint smile lit her face.

"Yeah." He grinned when he realized the words had slipped out. "I plan on spending my life here… in Good Springs…" He closed his mouth, wondering if it was too soon to say any more. No matter how sure he was about her, he wasn't sure what she thought of him. They had only been on one real date, the end of which was ruined by Frank Roberts.

Connor thought of the last moments of their date together, standing on the edge of the village after the festival, and how he had wanted to kiss her. He wanted to kiss her now, but after popping the lock on her door to get inside her home, he figured he would be wise not to touch her.

He looked at their joined hands and pulled his away. He wiped his sweaty palm on his pants. "I plan on spending my life here because I want to be here. I like it here. I like you. You're the most fascinating woman I've ever met. You are brilliant and beautiful and compassionate. You don't hesitate to risk your life to save others. You are passionate and kindhearted. I feel like I know you and yet there is still so much more I want to know."

Her lips curved into a sweet smile.

He leaned forward. "I want to know everything about you. I want to protect you and help you. I'm not just here because I have nowhere else to go or courting you because you live next door. I plan to build my life here, and I hope to spend it with you. I'm all in, but I'm not going to rush you. I will give you time to make sure that you want to build a life with me."

Chapter Fifteen

A thin layer of early-spring snow crunched beneath Lydia's boots as she walked with Mandy through the village. Lydia kept her eyes fixed on the school building ahead. Mandy was watching her, waiting for her answer. "Yes, if Connor asks me, I will marry him."

Mandy gave a muffled squeal and tapped her gloved hands in a noiseless clap. "I knew you were in love." Then she chuckled. "So are you admitting it is love or have you found some practical logic to claim as your reason for marriage?"

"I do love him, yes. And I could come up with many practical reasons to marry him, but it's more than that. At first, I could only suppose that he would make a good husband because of his qualities, but after what happened last month, I know I want him in my life always."

Bare deciduous trees reached their limbs to the sturdy gray leaf trees overhead. Their branches blended together, making Lydia smile. "I believe love and logic have interwoven in a way that assures me I could be a physician and a wife. But only because of Connor. If we don't marry, I will not look for another man."

A quick laugh escaped Mandy's throat. "I don't want to marry, but I'm always looking for another man."

She grinned at Mandy and looked at the school building ahead as they left the road. The quiet schoolyard was empty, but as they approached the building, the noise of the students bled outside. She stopped to readjust the scarf at her neck. "The students haven't been dismissed yet. We're early."

"No, we aren't." Mandy kept trotting through the snow. Her auburn curls—flattened beneath a knit woolen cap—fluffed over her shoulders and down her back. She threw the door open.

Lydia knocked the snow from her heels and followed Mandy inside the vestibule. "I haven't been in here in a while."

Mandy wrinkled her nose. "Do you remember the year we had that secondary teacher from Woodland?"

"Mr. Vestal?" Lydia remembered all too well. "I can't recall what was more distracting—the way he continually sent spittle across the classroom as he lectured, or the jumping of the startled students who were spit upon."

Mandy made a face. "That was the year I lost interest in academics." She stepped to the corridor that split the building into two classrooms.

Lydia was eager to see the new teacher of the secondary school, but she didn't want to interrupt his class. She reached for Mandy's sleeve. "Wait until the students come out."

Mandy winked at her and kept walking. She turned the knob on the familiar classroom door.

Lydia quietly stepped inside first and stayed near the door at the back of the room.

Connor had his back to the class and was writing physics equations on the blackboard. "...which equals velocity—" He turned and spotted Lydia. "—and that's all we have time for today. Class dismissed."

Lydia and Mandy moved out of the way as the restless group of adolescents reached for their coats and bolted for the door. Everett pinched Mandy's side as he passed her, and she followed him into the hallway with an insincere scolding.

Connor dusted the chalk from his hands and grinned as he walked toward Lydia. His sleeves were rolled into cuffs over his forearms. He motioned to the classroom with both hands. "So, what do you think?"

She thought he looked handsome and gave him a playful smile. "This suits you."

"It's better than cleaning gutters." He looked past her into the hallway. He ran his fingers through his hair and put his hands in his pockets. She knew his gestures well enough to know that meant he wanted to touch her but someone was coming.

Mandy popped back into the classroom. "Is he coming with us or not?"

Connor raised his eyebrows and looked to Lydia for an explanation.

"Levi has been granted the land he requested. He invited us to the building site before he starts clearing it. Mandy and I are on our way now. We thought you might like to join us."

"Yeah, I'd love to. I will be right out." Connor held up a finger and stepped back to his desk at the front of the classroom. He unrolled his sleeves and put on his coat.

Lydia turned and stepped into the hallway with Mandy, and they walked slowly to the front of the school building. When they reached the vestibule, Connor was right behind them. He reached his arm in front of them, opened the door, and held it as they walked through.

The snow in the schoolyard had been stomped into mud by the exiting students. While Mandy recounted a story from her school years, Lydia glanced at Connor. He buttoned the front of his coat and took her hand. She didn't hear a word Mandy said, but only thought of how sweet and natural it felt to be connected to the man she loved.

As they walked through the village and passed the Colburn property, Lydia considered how her family and her village were responding to Connor. His presence as a leader was evident, and his charisma was infectious. Not only did the classroom suit him, life in the Land suited him.

The property Levi had selected was directly across the road from the Fosters' sheep farm. As they passed the farm, Connor thought of the barn party there during the autumn and remembered the moment his interest in Lydia had taken root. Now he held her hand as they walked along the peaceful road in the village he was beginning to consider home. He glanced at her and grinned, wondering if they would one day tell their grandchildren the story of how they met.

Levi was waiting beside the road when they arrived. He proudly directed their attention to hatchet marks in trees indicating the boundaries of his land. The property was covered in loosely-packed gray leaf forest. Levi said he would clear only what he must and he would use every log for lumber.

They followed him through a path he had already cleared in the shrub to the place where his land rose in a slight incline. It was the closest thing to a hill in the area around Good Springs, and Levi planned to build his house on top of it.

While they stood on the hill and Levi and Connor discussed building plans, Mandy took Lydia's arm and led her away from the men. Mandy whispered something to her. Whatever it was, Lydia reacted with a surprised laugh and slight blush.

Levi stopped talking. He was watching Mandy.

Connor inclined his head a degree and asked, "Any reason you chose the property across the road from the Fosters?"

Levi shrugged. "My parents were close friends with Samuel and Roseanna Foster. I grew up spending as much time out here as I did at home. I guess I just always wanted to build a house on this hill."

Connor didn't quite believe it was only the hill Levi wanted, but he decided to drop the subject.

Lydia was still engrossed in her conversation with Mandy, so Connor took the opportunity to show Levi what he had acquired. He reached into the interior pocket of his coat and produced a small box.

Levi eyed the box. "Is that the ring?"

Connor double-checked that the women weren't looking. He opened the little box to reveal a delicate gold band with an oval ruby set in its center.

Levi gave an approving nod.

Connor grinned proudly before he closed the box and reburied it safely back inside his coat.

An occasional whisper echoed from the chapel ceiling as the congregation waited in the crowded pews. John Colburn—having already preached the Sunday sermon—rubbed the edge of his Bible as he stepped away from the podium. The front row of the church was filled with the village elders. They frequently turned their heads and looked at the chapel doors.

Connor sat behind them between Levi and Everett. He wondered if Lydia would make it to the church before John had to dismiss the congregation.

Mandy's heels clicked on the hardwood floor as she hurried down the outer aisle of the chapel. She scooted into the pew and lowered herself beside Levi. She whispered something to him, and he turned his head and whispered to Connor. In unison, they stood and walked the center aisle to the back of the hushed church then out the doors and across the thin layer of ice on the chapel's front steps.

Lydia was standing at the bottom of the steps with Mrs. Ashton holding onto her arm. Lydia smiled at Connor and Levi. "Thank you." She was late to a ceremony in her honor because she had gone to help the elderly Mrs. Ashton make it safely to the church. Connor's heart swelled with pride.

Mrs. Ashton hummed in delight as Connor and Levi came on either side of her and kept her steady while she climbed the icy steps. They escorted Doctor Ashton's widow down the aisle and stopped at the pew she pointed to on the left—third row from the front—before they went back to their seats.

John stepped away from the podium, and the elders stood as Lydia walked to the front of the chapel. Connor perched on the edge of the pew and wished he had a camera.

John explained the importance of honoring a skilled physician with the title of doctor. One of the elders confirmed Lydia's completed training and recited her qualifications. John read from an ancient text and charged Lydia with the responsibility of caring for the health of the village and all who needed her care, day or night. She accepted the charge and repeated the oath John recited, "…for the good of my patients to the best of my ability and my judgment and never do harm to anyone."

Then John motioned for Lydia to turn and face the audience. "People of Good Springs, I present your physician, Doctor Lydia Colburn." John's professional demeanor remained intact as he stepped back to allow Lydia to receive the applause she deserved.

After the ceremony ended, the townspeople lingered in the chapel. Lydia graciously accepted congratulations from many of the villagers.

Connor had grown fond of the way people in Good Springs took their time and acknowledged each other at every occasion. Six months of living in the village had elevated his gratitude for community and his patience for people. But today he had a ring burning a hole in his pocket.

It took great effort to focus his attention on each person who paused to greet him. He reciprocated their pleasantries, but his gaze automatically shifted to Lydia. She stood on the other side of the chapel with her back to a tall, narrow window. A line of people waited to speak to her.

Connor took a few steps in her direction, but as he passed the Fosters, Roseanna Foster put her hand on his back. "Mr. Bradshaw, I must let you know how thrilled we are that you are teaching the secondary students." She beamed. "Not a day goes by without Everett delighting us with some new fact he has learned in your class."

"Mother." Everett looked embarrassed.

"Thank you, Mrs. Foster." Connor glanced at Lydia. She was moving her silver bracelet in tiny increments around and around her wrist as she spoke to the villagers. "I'm pleased to hear it. Everett is a good student." He nodded to Mrs. Foster and stepped away.

At last, the queue for Lydia's attention began to diminish. Connor stepped behind the last couple in line as they moved forward to speak with her. He was taller than the well-wishers and looked over their heads to catch Lydia's eye.

She glanced up at him. Her quick, faint smile proved her connection to him without drawing attention to it. Satisfied, he leaned his palm on the back of an empty pew and waited his turn.

Mrs. Foster's cackle of a laugh echoed through the sanctuary as she left the chapel with the last of the congregants. Levi was following them out the door, speaking with Everett as they walked. His eyes were glued to Mandy. Bethany's voice chirped in melodic conversation with Adeline and Maggie outside.

He watched Lydia's three sisters, amazed he'd grown to consider these people family. He planned to make it official and already had John's approval. No custom of engagement rings existed in the Land, but thanks to Isabella's eavesdropping, Connor was now in possession of a thin, gold ring with an oval ruby embedded in its band.

The couple in front of Connor said goodbye to Lydia and moved away. John met them at the chapel door. He gave Connor a nod and walked out behind them. The chapel was empty except for Connor and Lydia, but the chorus of voices outside the church meant the gathering had not ended but simply shifted locations.

He stepped close to the woman he planned to make his wife. "Congratulations, Doc."

"Thank you, Mr. Bradshaw." She brushed her hands together and smiled up at him. "And congratulations on the teaching position. Everyone speaks of how effortlessly you capture the attention of the class. I have no doubt you will prove to be the most interesting teacher our village has ever had."

"Thank you." He slid his hand into his pocket and felt the ring. The certainty of his heart compelled him, but he briefly wondered if it was the right moment. The chapel was quiet except for the murmur of outside noise leaking through the single-paned windows. Time alone with Lydia rarely went uninterrupted. He abolished his hesitation. "Lydia, or, Doctor Colburn I should say—"

She smiled. "Lydia will suffice."

"Lydia, there is no reason why I, out of every man in the world, should find myself in this land with a new chance at life—a real and good life. I have done nothing to deserve it, nor do I deserve your affection. You saved my life, welcomed me into your village and your family, and then let me into your heart. I found myself at the end of the earth but, because of you, I have never felt alone. Now I can't imagine my life anywhere else with anyone else. I want to build a life with you and make a home with you and have a family with you. I want to wake up beside you every morning and spend my days adoring you. Will you marry me?"

Lydia tucked a wisp of hair behind her ear and smiled. She showed no hint of surprise at his proposal.

The voices outside the church made him nervous. "I don't want to rush your answer but you know as well as I do that at any moment some villager could barge in here screaming and bloody, needing your help, and if they do I will wait but—"

"I will. Yes, I will marry you." Lydia didn't pause to make her decision. Her answer was already prepared. She simply wanted to soak in the moment and the hope-filled future his question implied. Her life presented no lack before Connor arrived but now, having known him and loved him, she couldn't imagine contentment in life without him. Her response barely escaped her lips when he wrapped her in his arms.

"We can do the wedding and everything else by your traditions, but there is one thing I have to do." He reached into his pocket.

She watched him intently, wondering what tradition he desired to perform. He pulled his hand out and with it a ring, rare in metal and stone. It was a family heirloom. She held her right hand out to him.

"No, the other one." He slid the delicate, gold band onto the ring finger of her left hand and kissed her. If the gesture was intended to hint at the bond she should expect with him, it accomplished magnificent anticipation. It was a new experience for her, and her heartbeat rang in her ears. The kiss was brief but poignant, effectively assuring her it was not an end unto itself but a foretaste of the oneness their marriage would bring.

Her gaze moved up to meet his. Joining her life with him wouldn't detract from her contentment as she once believed, but it would fulfill her in ways she hadn't previously understood. She found joy in knowing she would provide the same fulfillment for him. In what ways and over how much time, she could not know, but the possibilities swelled her heart with contentment.

The summer sun rose early over the village of Good Springs. January's heavy rains left the mossy ground squishy with mud. Doctor Lydia Bradshaw leaned close to her horse to avoid a low branch as she rushed down the path through the forest. Glints of morning light sparkled in the dew on the foliage of the gray leaf trees that rustled around her. Green pastures rolled to the horizon as she raced to the Cotters' farmhouse. At the steps of the front porch, she dismounted and passed the reins to a waiting ranch hand. With her medical bag gripped firmly in one fist, she threw open the Cotters' front door and rushed inside.

Epilogue

Lieutenant Justin Mercer arrived at McMurdo Station on Ross Island, Antarctica at zero four hundred hours on a sunny Tuesday in the middle of January 2026. The thermometer outside the dormitory window measured precisely fifty-three degrees Fahrenheit. His new commanding officer informed him it would likely be the highest mercury rise he would witness for the duration of his assignment.

Mercer dropped his tattered duffle bag at the foot of his assigned bunk and asked to be taken immediately to his post. The once internationally celebrated scientific research station was now home to the only remaining Unified States military satellite communications system still operational on the Southern Hemisphere. Though Mercer missed flying, he planned to use his new assignment on the global surveillance unit to find the land his country desperately needed.

Convinced Lieutenant Connor Bradshaw's parachute had carried him to that land after their ill-fated flight, Mercer had spent the past ten months charting the atmospheric anomalies over the coordinates of the crash site using the data relayed from the monitoring unit left behind by the search crew.

Mercer sat in a lumpy office chair at his post—a short particleboard desk in the center of what was once a climate research lab. He placed the palm of his hand firmly onto the center of one of three touchscreens at his desk and allowed its sensors to verify his identity. Upon security verification, his first task was to upload his private files, which contained his models reconstructing the crash, emergency ejection, descent, and the possible landing sites ignored by the search and rescue efforts.

No matter what the Unified States Navy officials said, Mercer considered the vivid memory of watching Bradshaw's parachute drift toward the uncharted landmass definitive proof Connor could have survived. He had replayed that memory multiple times each day in the ten months since the crash, and he would continue to keep the memory alive until he found that land and Connor Bradshaw. Among the many scenarios he often mentally directed was a fantasy of storming the land's uncharted shore, covertly slicing through its dangerous jungle, and finding Connor imprisoned in an enemy camp. He imagined freeing Connor, and together they would annihilate the enemy and claim the land. For months Mercer's fantasy ended with praise from his once-doubtful superiors for finding such a plentiful land. He used to imagine they would attribute the salvation of the remaining world population to his tenacity. But now his fantasy segued into conquering that land, not for the good of his country but for the establishment of his new life.

Mercer tapped a screen to open his computer files and connected to the live image feed being relayed from the last functional satellites orbiting earth. After selecting the image options for the Southern Hemisphere, he touched a screen requesting coordinates and entered thirty-five degrees south, twenty-five degrees west. With both hands moving over multiple screens, Mercer zoomed in on the wide, blue swath of ocean and fixed his eyes where he anticipated making a home.

Thank you for reading my book. I'm so glad you went on this journey with me. More Uncharted stories await you! Are you ready for the adventure?

I know it's important for you to enjoy these wholesome, inspirational stories in your favorite format, so I've made sure all of my books are available in large print.

Below is a quick description of each story so you can determine which books to order next…

The Uncharted Series
A hidden land settled by peaceful people ~ The first outsider in 160 years

The Land Uncharted (#1)
Lydia's secluded society is at risk when an injured fighter pilot's parachute carries him to her hidden land.

Uncharted Redemption (#2)
When vivacious Mandy is forced to depend on strong, silent Levi, she must learn to accept tender love from the one man who truly knows her.

Uncharted Inheritance (#3)
Bethany and Everett belong together, but when a mysterious man arrives in the Land, everything changes.

Christmas with the Colburns (#4)
When Lydia faces a gloomy holiday in the Colburn house, an unexpected gift brightens her favorite season.

Uncharted Hope (#5)
While Sophia and Nicholas wrestle with love and faith, a stunning discovery outside the Land changes everything.

Uncharted Journey (#6)
When horse trainer Solo moves to Falls Creek, widow Eva gets a second chance at love. Meanwhile, Bailey's quest to reach the Land costs her everything.

Uncharted Destiny (#7)
The Uncharted story continues when Bailey and Revel face an impossible rescue mission in the Land's treacherous mountains.

Uncharted Promises (#8)

When Sybil and Isaac get snowed in, it takes more than warm meals and cozy fireplaces to help them find love at the Inn at Falls Creek.

Uncharted Freedom (#9)
When Naomi takes the housekeeping job at The Inn at Falls Creek so she can hide from one past, another finds her.

The Uncharted Beginnings Series
Embark on an unforgettable 1860s journey with the Founders as they discover the Land.

Aboard Providence (#1)
When Marian and Jonah's ship gets marooned on a mysterious uncharted island, they must build a settlement to survive. Love and adventure await!

Above Rubies (#2)
When schoolteacher Olivia needs the settlement elders' approval, she must hide her dyslexia from everyone, even charming carpenter Gabe.

All Things Beautiful (#3)
Henry is the last person Hannah wants reading her story… and the first person to awaken her heart.

Find out more on my website keelybrookekeith.com or feel free to email me at keely@keelykeith.com where I answer every message personally.

See you in the Land!
Keely

About Keely Brooke Keith

Keely Brooke Keith writes inspirational frontier-style fiction with a futuristic twist, including *The Land Uncharted* (Shelf Unbound Notable Romance 2015) and Aboard Providence (2017 INSPY Awards Longlist).

Born in St. Joseph, Missouri, Keely was a tree-climbing, baseball-loving 80s kid. She grew up in a family who moved often, which fueled her dreams of faraway lands. When she isn't writing, Keely enjoys teaching home school lessons and playing bass guitar. Keely, her husband, and their daughter live on a hilltop south of Nashville, Tennessee.